Say You Mean It

MEGAN REINKING

Editing by Jenn Lockwood

Proofreading by Sarah Ward

Cover Design by Lorissa Padilla

Say You Mean It is a contemporary romance story that includes on-page descriptions of feeling depressed and of having low self-esteem. Negative self-talk is prevalent, and the content within may be triggering for someone who struggles with any of these issues.

Your mental health and well-being is the most important thing to me, so please be mindful of this trigger warning and consider it before reading if you think you may be sensitive to it!

Other potential trigger warning: parent with Alzheimer's.

For anyone struggling to quiet a harsh inner voice.
I see you.

ONE
Blair

"Seat belts on!" the pilot shouts over his shoulder from the front of the plane. My stomach lurches and all but hurls out of my throat as the rickety floatplane dips, plunging steadily closer and closer to the lake water below. I force my eyes shut and take in a slow inhale, breathing the stuffy airplane air in through my nose and holding it for two beats before releasing it out through my mouth. The simple breathing exercise does nothing to quell the bubbling nervous energy that's been brewing in my gut ever since we departed from Baudette, Minnesota.

I was told our destination—a remote island in the middle of Lake of the Woods—was only a quick, twenty-minute flight away, but I'm beginning to question that. It feels like I've been trapped in this plane for much longer than that.

"You okay?" Isaac, a fellow lawyer, says, nudging my arm with his elbow.

"Uh-huh," I say with a shaky voice.

"Don't worry, it's very rare for turbulence to cause a plane crash." His voice is smooth, but I don't miss the way his own white knuckles grip the armrest.

I didn't think I would be a nervous flyer, but I'm finding it hard to not be affected by soaring through the sky in a way-smaller-than-average airplane—and one that lands on top of the water, no less. I can officially add this flight—and this entire company-wide retreat weekend, for that matter—to the list of sacrifices I've made for the sake of my law career. Right next to the countless sleepless nights spent studying, the massive student loans I'm still paying off, and the thousands of hours of tedious paralegal work under my belt.

Although, if I were to be completely honest with myself in this moment, I can't say that I really mind the minor anxiety that's ruminating.

At least I'm feeling something.

"Hold on tight," Paul, the managing partner at my firm, calls out from a seat two rows behind me. His voice is tinged with an exhilarating tone that proves he's on the opposite side of the spectrum and is somehow thoroughly enjoying every bit of this experience.

I peer across Isaac and out the small window to find us rapidly approaching the blue-green water of Lake of the Woods.

"Hmm." A strangled squeal involuntarily comes from the back of my throat as I squeeze the armrests, cringing as we hit the water with a thud that jolts all of us forward in unison.

A wave of relief washes over me at the simple fact that we're on top of the water and not submerged in it, and my hand flies to cover my heart, which is pounding wildly in my chest. I take a few more steadying breaths to slow it back to normal while the plane bobs up and down with the waves, moving slowly forward.

"There it is. Home sweet home for the next few days." Isaac points out the window. I follow his finger to where Takini Island is just coming into view. The rocky, charcoal-gray base of the island is submerged in the water, and there are towering lush, green pine trees that sprout up from nearly every possible inch of the surface. The trees are thick as they spread across the shoreline, only parting for the sporadic cabins that are tucked closely in between.

Some cabins look well-kept, with boats on the dock lifts and beach towels hung over the deck railings, serving as a clear sign of frequent visitors. Others appear barren, isolated, and forgotten, the rotting wooden boards of the structure seemingly falling apart at the seams.

They look so simple and quaint. I wonder who the owners of these cabins are and what their story is. What their life is like. Do some live here? Or do some just use theirs as a reprieve and escape from the real world? A quiet sanctuary to disappear for a few days. A twinge of something close to jealousy squeezes my chest.

I shift in my seat as the plane slowly follows the shoreline around the jutting corner of the island to where Ruby Lodge is nestled. A large dock system extends out into the water with three identical aluminum fishing boats tied to it. On the shore is a line of several quaint wooden log cabins that are spread out on both sides of a larger A-frame structure that I assume is the main lodge.

"Did you know that we're only three miles south of Canada?" Isaac asks, pushing his glasses up the bridge of his nose with his pointer finger. How is it that I've known him for years now but have only just today discovered his love of spewing random facts and sharing tidbits of random information? I'm not entirely annoyed, but I make a mental note to sit next to someone else on the flight back.

"I did know that," I say with a polite smile. "I read that on the website."

"And there are over fourteen thousand islands on this lake."

"Really?" That fact actually piques my interest. I guess my perusal of the lodge's website wasn't as extensive as I thought.

"Yup," he says smugly, relishing my response. "Stick with me this weekend, and I'll share plenty of other gems I learned when I was researching. There are some doozies, I'm telling you."

"Isaac, I promise you, nobody is interested in your fun facts," Stacy, another fellow lawyer, says dryly from the seat across the tiny aisle. "Except for maybe your mother and your dog."

"Hey, that's all the validation I need in this world," he retorts with a cheesy grin. The corner of my mouth twitches ever so slightly in amusement before my mood shifts back to its normal state of indifference.

"I've never been this far north," Stacy mutters, gazing out her window.

"Me neither." I don't feel the need to expand and tell her that other than one spring break trip to Okoboji in college with my best friend, Annie, I've never actually been outside of Chicago. I wish I could say I was feeling some sort of excitement about this change of scenery and what some might call a new adventure, but I just don't. Truthfully, I don't feel much of anything these days.

High-functioning depression is what my therapist jotted down at the top of my chart when I first went to see her five years ago. I've been living with it for as far back as I can remember. Regular therapy and antidepressants seem to help marginally, giving me brief pockets of time that are better than others, but it's not something that has ever completely gone away. I've come to accept that it's my way of life. My status quo. The gray undercurrent that the rest of my life sits on top of.

Twisting again in my seat, I busy myself with rearranging the backpack that's in between my feet before Isaac has a chance to ramble on about something else. The plane bobs a few more times before it slowly comes to a complete stop.

"Here we are," the pilot says, shifting levers and pushing buttons on the control panel in front of him. He unfastens his seat belt and walks through the cabin with hunched shoulders, not able to stand fully upright in the small cabin. He twists the latch on the door and swings it open for us. "Watch your step getting out."

I fall in line behind Stacy as everyone shuffles toward the open door. Stepping onto the dock, I blink at the harsh sunlight as I pull my backpack onto my shoulders. The very first thing I notice is the quiet. There's absolutely no sound in the air aside from a very quiet humming of what I can only guess is a mix of mosquitoes and flies. I can't decide if it sounds ominous or peaceful, but either way, it's a stark contrast to the city environment I'm used to.

My phone pings with a notification when it automatically connects to the resort's WiFi, so I pull it out to send Annie a quick text while I wait for Stacy to get situated.

Blair: Landed. Survived. Will call once I'm settled.

I slip the phone back into my pocket and shift my weekender bag to my left hand, following the others off the dock. The long, wooden dock creaks with each step we take, sounding about as old as it looks. A stretch of sandy beach takes up the other side of the bay, where Adirondack chairs are pushed into the sand in a haphazard kind of way, like they've been shifted and carelessly abandoned by beachgoers. A rack with canoes and kayaks is positioned on the far right side of the sand by the tree line.

A breeze whips through my long brunette hair, and I shake my head helplessly to knock a strand of hair loose from my

Chapstick-laden lips. The musty air smells like pine and just a trace of campfire smoke. No sign of car exhaust or cigarette smoke. When I glance behind my shoulder, there's only the lake water for as far as I can see, except maybe the faint outline of another island a few miles away.

"I wonder what made Paul choose this place for our retreat," Stacy says in front of me, also taking in our surroundings. "We're lawyers from Chicago, for Pete's sake. When have any of us had the time to learn how to fish, camp, or be one with nature?"

I huff in agreement with a shrug. "No kidding. With our luck, we'll be mosquito-bite-ridden, sunburnt, and covered in dirt by the time we leave."

My eyes catch on some movement from inside the main lodge. A few people are walking in front of the floor-to-ceiling window that looks out to the lake behind me—the rest of my coworkers who were on the earlier flight, no doubt. My gut feels especially hollow and uneasy at the thought of spending the entire weekend away from home with people that I consider friendly acquaintances at best.

You never want to go anywhere. I hope you plan on at least making an effort on the retreat. But who are we kidding? You won't fit in there either.

The words that my boyfriend, Barry, hurled at me this week, when he was annoyed that I once again didn't want to go to the bar with him for a nightcap, pops intrusively into my head.

Unaffected by hearing his voice in my head, I follow it with words of my own.

You don't fit in anywhere.

I step off the dock and onto the sand, following Stacy and the others up the grassy incline to where a tall, handsome, dark-haired man with a five o'clock shadow is standing next to a card table with rows of cups laid out.

"Welcome to Ruby Lodge," he says warmly with a smile, his friendly gaze scanning over our group. Something about his inherently warm voice and kind disposition seems to put me slightly at ease. When his sapphire-blue eyes connect with mine, I offer a small smile in return.

"Thank you for having us," Paul says eagerly.

"The first group is all settled and playing board games in the lodge. My name is Graham. Please let me know if I can be of any service to you during your stay. Our goal is to ensure that you feel like a part of our family while you're here." He points to a piece of paper on the edge of the table. "Your cabin assignments are here whenever you're ready. Help yourself to a glass of freshly squeezed lemonade while you journey to your cabin. We also have a jar of wild blueberries that we picked from the island this week. They go great with the lemonade, so feel free to scoop a spoonful into your cup."

"Wow, thank you, Graham," Paul replies before turning toward our group. "Alright, friends, I'll give those assignments to you now. I'm thinking we can all freshen up and then meet in the main lodge for the welcome dinner!"

I only half-listen as he rattles off cabin numbers, becoming distracted by a bald eagle that soars overhead as it cuts through the cloudless sky.

"Blair. You'll be in cabin four."

"Thanks," I say, grabbing a cup of lemonade and scooping a spoonful of blueberries into it. Then I follow the direction of his pointer finger toward the line of cabins on the right. There's a small grassy path that winds in front of and between the buildings. I pass by each cabin until I get to the one with a black number four nailed to the frame of the door. It's small and quaint, unassuming and simple with its wooden log structure.

I climb up the three steps of the porch, one of them creaking with my weight. A hanging wooden bench swing rests against the logs of the cabin, just under the window. I smirk, as there is hardly enough leg room between the bench and the wooden railing in front of it for it to be able to move anywhere close to what's considered an actual swing. But I appreciate the idea nonetheless. With a deep breath, I scan the front of the cabin, bracing myself for not only what lies inside, but for what this entire retreat weekend will entail. Then I twist the door handle and step inside.

TWO
Blair

I push the front door of the cabin open and find myself immediately standing in a small kitchen area. The inner cabin is blanketed in a deep-brown shade from the horizontal log columns of the walls, aside from the oak-colored kitchen cabinets that are adorned with old brassy hardware. Two tan, wicker stools are tucked underneath the countertop, and a tiny kitchen table sits in the left corner of the small main living space.

After setting my bags down on the floor by the door, I grab my phone to call Annie. I wander and inspect the rest of the kitchen while it rings. There's a white refrigerator on the left, next to a closet that, upon inspection, houses a few things I might need during my stay—a broom, a few cleaning supplies, and paper products.

"Hey, girl!" Annie's upbeat voice chirps in my ear.

"If I go missing, remember that I'm staying in cabin four," I say flatly in lieu of a greeting.

"Is it that terrible?" She laughs.

"Actually, it's not that bad," I admit. "It's just not my ideal location. I'm completely out of my element up here."

"It's only for a few days, right? You can do anything for a few days," she says encouragingly. "Remember when we spent five whole days practicing our hula-hooping skills?"

I smile at the memory. "I still think we were close to breaking the world record."

I roam past the closet and check out the small bathroom that's tucked in the back corner as my mind drifts back to hula-hooping in Annie's bedroom, the only place that truly ever felt like home.

Something tiny shifts in my chest as I walk back through the kitchen and up the small staircase. This always happens when I'm talking to Annie. I can actually feel a glimmer of my old self. The girl who, while she may not have had a present mother or father growing up, did have a best friend who valiantly filled those voids, whether she realized she did or not.

"Are there any hot guys there?" she asks, taking a bite of what sounds like a carrot.

"Annie," I say in exasperation, checking out the lofted area upstairs with a queen bed that has a blue-and-gray checkered quilt on top. A small bathroom is tucked in the corner of the room. "I'm here with work. And also, did you forget about Barry?"

"Barry's a jerk," she points out flatly.

I don't necessarily disagree with her there, but I don't feel up for going down the rabbit hole of defending my relationship yet again. That happens often enough.

"How's Eric?" I ask, stepping back down the stairs and out the front door to the too-small bench on my tiny front porch. My knees brush against the wooden posts of the railing when I sit.

"Great," she sighs happily. I can practically see her grin. Eric is her fiancé and fellow teacher at the elementary school where they both work in Ohio. "Our summer school class has a field trip to the zoo tomorrow, so we're spending tonight making paper plate animal masks for the kids to wear."

"That's cute." My gaze roams across the open view of the lake and the shoreline that runs just ten feet or so from my cabin. From deep in my chest, I can feel myself desperately trying to reach more of the person I was when I was eleven, playing *pick-up sticks* with Annie on her bedroom floor. The far-off place deep inside where a slightly happier version of myself lives, even though she's been lost and barely reachable for years.

Talking to Annie feels a lot like muscle memory in some ways, like I'm a different person when I'm talking to her without even trying to be. Like the layers of fraud and the inauthentic charade that I display every day gets peeled away a little bit at a time. It's in these conversations with her when I can feel sparks of color, albeit small ones, in the colorless sea that is my life.

"I've gotta run, lovie. These masks won't make themselves," she says regretfully in my ear. "Call me tomorrow?"

"Sure thing. Take it easy on those kiddos." When we disconnect, I set the phone next to me on the bench, building up the energy to get ready for the welcome dinner.

I watch as the floatplane we arrived in takes off across the lake, heading steadily for the horizon. As it disappears in the sky, the cloud slowly drifts back over my mind until there's nothing left but the familiar drum of melancholy. Using my arms, I reluctantly force myself off the bench and back inside.

"Argh," I grunt out as I hoist the straps of my bag onto my shoulder to haul it up the tiny stairs. At the top of the loft, I drop the luggage onto the floor next to the nightstand and climb onto the bed, falling face-first into the quilt. A faint lavender scent fills my nose as I push it against the cold fabric, allowing myself to pause there for a moment.

I don't think I've ever been this tired.

My depression is something that I've grown accustomed to living with. Hiding the emptiness in my soul from the outside world has become a necessary skill in my day-to-day life. I'm used to putting on the façade of a happy, put-together person—especially for my clients and coworkers—but some days, the mask feels a lot heavier to put on. Especially if that day has been a particularly long and exhausting one, like today's travel day has been.

Every single fiber of my being wants to stay curled up on this bed, preferably with that cozy knit blanket, hanging on the display ladder in the corner, draped over me.

I know the chances of me going anywhere but this bed dwindles with every passing second, but doing what is expected of me is something I take seriously. So I allow myself one full minute with my eyes closed before pushing myself off the bed.

Deciding on a white linen romper, I change into it, throwing a cream-colored chunky cardigan over the crook of my arm before heading back downstairs. I briefly debate whether or not I should bother calling Barry to check in with him.

Our relationship doesn't make a whole lot of sense to the outside world, and more often than not, it doesn't to me either. As a lawyer himself, we're both extremely busy, and admittedly, neither one of us puts a lot of effort into nurturing our relationship in our free time. It turns out that moving in together did not fix that problem like I thought it might last year, as it has only further highlighted our disconnect. I'm afraid we've become more of a relationship of convenience—simply coexisting, mostly detached from each other, but crossing paths every once in a while out of habit.

The only reason I haven't broken things off is because I'm too exhausted by the prospect of an argument, never mind the process of actually moving out and finding a new place to live. I can barely get through the bare minimum of daily life as it is.

You couldn't land anyone better than me anyway.

His cocky words make my eyes roll, and I slide my phone into my purse without so much as a text to him. I'm used to the fact that he doesn't have a filter and spews his honest thoughts—most often hurtful words—any chance he can get.

Or at least words that would be hurtful to someone who isn't as numb as I already am.

His words don't bother me.

Pulling the creaky door shut behind me, I set off toward the main lodge, wondering what exactly I'm in store for. A few birds sing in conversation above me in the trees, their lively chirping piercing the quiet, as if they're gossiping about the swarm of new guests occupying their territory. Again, I wonder how busy this little island gets and how frequently people are coming and going.

My strappy sandals prove to be the wrong choice as they shift on the uneven path, my feet nearly slipping out of them with each step. After the fourth near ankle roll, I yank them off in a huff. Now carrying them in my hand, I follow the dirt path as it runs along the shoreline, trying to ignore how dirty the soles of my feet are getting. Something tells me no one will mind—or perhaps even notice. The greenish-yellow leaves of the trees that surround me softly sway in the wind, and I watch their slow dance until some sort of bug flies directly into my eye.

Damn nature.

I blink rapidly, fishing the bug out with the tip of my finger. When I reach the lodge, I hastily brush the dirt off my feet and slip my sandals back on.

"Blair bear!" Cassidy, one of our office paralegals, bounds out of the lodge door before I even make it past the first step of the main staircase. I inwardly cringe at her nickname for me as she loops her arm around mine, leading me inside. She and I are about as opposite as two work colleagues can be. She's bubbly, friendly, and a bit aloof when it comes to social interactions. Unassuming and oblivious to corporate status, she befriends the entire office, regardless of whether anyone returns the same affection or not. Contrarily, to say that I'm an introvert would be an understatement.

"Hi, Cassidy," I say warmly, officially putting on my work smile like a shield of armor to prepare for the evening. The entryway inside the lodge is spacious with a large maroon-and-gray area rug covering the open space. A small, vacated, wooden desk is positioned along the right wall with a rectangular 'check-in' sign hanging on the front.

Past the desk looks to be a small library with brown leather furniture and two full-wall bookshelves. A hallway extends down both sides of the library, but before I get a good look down either side, Cassidy pulls me to the left where the dining area is.

"Isn't it gorgeous? I could totally live here." Cassidy breathes in awe before her face scrunches, seemingly remembering where exactly we are. "Well, maybe not live. For sure vacation, though."

Before I have a chance to respond, Paul comes out of the restroom on the other side of the dining hall, and Cassidy all but forgets me, dropping my arm and fluttering over to his side. With an amused half-smile, I wander over to a table where Stacy, Isaac, and several other associates are seated. The table is positioned next to one of the floor-to-ceiling windows that look out at the lake, offering an admittedly gorgeous view.

"Everyone all settled in?" I ask, sliding into an empty seat by the window.

"Yup." Stacy beams at me. "Aren't they the cutest little cabins?"

"I've got mine all set up for karaoke and charades if anyone is up for it later on tonight," Isaac says earnestly, earning a few nods of approval from the table.

"We'll see how the welcome dinner goes," I say, although I have no intentions of doing anything except going back to my cabin to sleep as soon as I possibly can.

As if on cue, Paul clears his throat and rubs his hands together in the center of the room, and I join the others in shifting my chair to angle it toward him.

"Staff of Gibson Law," he says, waving his outstretched arm in a circle around him. "I welcome you to the picturesque Ruby Lodge, here on beautiful Takini Island, in the middle of Lake of the Woods, Minnesota."

His chest puffs up in pride as he continues a slow rotation with his arms, showing off the lodge as if he personally takes credit for it. Then he walks to a nearby table where a stack of papers sits.

"Anita so graciously put together a retreat itinerary for the weekend, so we'll pass that out, and you can keep it to reference as needed throughout our stay." He hands the stack to the nearest table to pass along. "You'll find that we have plenty of activities planned to really maximize our time here and come away from it as an even stronger team than we are now."

I grab a sheet off the top of the pile and scan over the schedule that's laid out for the next four days. It seems that almost every hour is spoken for, with activities such as s'mores night, trivia games, and fishing excursions only a small part of the long list. I already feel exhausted just from reading it, and I wonder how I'll manage to muster enough energy to make it through the retreat.

"Everything with an asterisk is considered mandatory, and there is also a list of suggested activities to fill your free time if you need ideas. We'll plan to meet at nine a.m. to break up into teams, and then we'll go from there."

My eye catches on the group hike that's slated for Friday afternoon, and a twinge of dread hits my stomach at the mere idea of such a physical activity. My current and only form of exercise is the daily short walk to and from my office building.

"For tonight, we've got a chicken dinner buffet followed by a mingle hour. Everyone gets two drink tokens for the bar per day, so keep those handy for when you want to cash them in. And please enjoy yourselves! Take this as an opportunity to get to know your coworkers on a deeper level, as I look forward to doing with each of you. Now, please, help yourselves to dinner!"

The sound of shuffling chairs and low murmuring fills the air as a swarm of people start heading for the buffet table. Instead of following them, I stay seated, craving a less busy option. Across the room, I spot two bartenders moving behind the large bar on the far wall. One is a young Native American woman, who appears to be in her mid-twenties or so, happily taking a drink order. The other is Graham, who wears a smile on his face and a dish towel draped over his shoulder. Considering my options, I let those at my table pass by and then head across the room.

THREE
Graham

"What can I get you?" I throw a wad of paper towels in the trash bin under the bar top and turn to the pretty brunette woman I saw earlier that just slid onto a stool, feeling an exhilarating energy start to course through my veins. Now that all of the hard work we've done the past couple days to get ready for this retreat is finally over, I try to ignore the rest of my long to-do list so I can shift into my favorite part of the job—the hospitality aspect. Connecting with guests and serving them in any way I can during their stay is what keeps me trudging through the other parts that leave me stressed and overwhelmed.

"I'll have a vodka soda with a lime, please," she says, tucking a strand of soft brown hair behind her ear. Something about the heaviness in the way she exhales has me thinking she isn't exactly excited to be here. Not that I can blame her if that is the case. A forced getaway with work colleagues isn't exactly my idea of a good time either.

"Sure thing." I get to work filling a tumbler glass with ice from the ice bucket. "So you're a lawyer, huh?"

"What gave it away?" A friendly smile accompanies the heavy sarcasm.

"Well, it couldn't possibly be the law firm that you arrived with."

"Oh, you mean those people?" She jerks a thumb over her shoulder before raising her sky-blue eyes to meet mine. "Yeah, I guess I have to claim them. I'm Blair. Blair Williams."

"Graham Peterson." I place the drink in front of her on a cocktail napkin and grip the ledge on either side of me, leaning slightly in, intrigued by the subtle smile that plays on her lips. Women that look like her don't come around these parts too often—and definitely not without a significant other.

"Thanks for having us. Although, you might regret hosting a bunch of city folks. I'm not sure we fit in well here."

I scan the dining room that's bustling with people, noting the business suits, button-up collared shirts and perfectly done hair and makeup.

"Yeah, you do kind of look like fish out of water," I admit with a chuckle. "No offense."

"None taken." She shrugs, accepting my jab as she takes a sip of her drink. "This really is a beautiful place. How long have you worked here?"

"Pretty much my whole life. This is my family's place—I run it now."

"Oh, wow." She nods in approval. "So this is probably a dumb question, but do you live here, then? On the island? All the time?"

"I do. In a little apartment upstairs." I gesture at the ceiling, then brace for her reaction. This is the part where they always give me some incredulous look, wondering how I can survive out here on a remote island. The part where I'm inevitably left to defend myself and my lifestyle. But to my relief, the only thing that flashes across her face is appreciation.

"Cool."

"Graham, I need another roll of quarters and some pennies when you get a chance, please," Nita, one of my newer bartenders, calls over her shoulder from the other end of the bar where she's manually counting cash in the ancient register that I can't afford to upgrade. That's on the long list of things that need my attention, but as with most of the items on that list, I don't have the funds to do anything about it at the moment.

"Enjoy," I say to Blair before retreating into the back room where my safe is settled between my desk and a file cabinet. I unzip the money pouch from the bank in town and grab the coin rolls before securing the door back in place.

"Here ya go," I say while putting them in the register for Nita.

"Thank you."

I throw her a quick nod before going back to my side of the bar.

"Hey there, what can I get ya?" I ask, tossing a cocktail napkin down in front of a gentleman who just sat down.

I watch as he adjusts his glasses with the back of his knuckle and folds his hands together on top of the counter. "I read that there's a distillery in town. Any chance you stock any of their liquor?"

Impressed with his knowledge, a wide grin lifts one side of my face. "I do. I source my bourbon, vodka, and gin from them. Right over here."

I point to the wall of shelves behind me where the bottles are stacked in front of a tall mirror backdrop.

"I'll try a bourbon on the rocks, please."

"You got it." I grab a tumbler glass and the bottle of liquor from the shelf.

"I also heard that Lake of the Woods is nicknamed the Walleye Capital of the World," he says. I'm not sure if he means it as a question or a statement, but he looks at me expectantly.

"That's right. You'll probably catch a whole bunch on your fishing excursion. Do you like to fish?" I hand him the full glass.

He shrugs. "Not really, but I'm looking forward to trying it out. I did some research on the best spots. Anyway, thanks." He lifts the glass and saunters back toward his table.

"He really knows his stuff," I say to Blair, who I notice is biting back a smile.

"I wouldn't ask him too many questions. He's hard to shake once he gets attached."

"Noted." I snicker, leaning a hip against the ledge.

"So, do you host retreats like this often?" she asks, looking at me expectantly. I'm beginning to wonder if she's avoiding her coworkers.

"Not really. Once or twice a year, I suppose. I'd say most of our clientele are anglers who come on fishing trips, but we get people from all over, really. Lots of people looking to escape the real world and experience an up-north getaway."

"You can't escape much farther than coming to an island," she agrees with a small laugh.

"It's certainly not everyone's idea of a fun getaway, but for plenty of people, it is."

"Do you stay pretty busy?" A tinge of pink sweeps across her cheeks just then. "Sorry for all the questions."

"Don't be sorry at all. We stay busy enough. Some days we're fully booked and other days we don't have any guests at all. The restaurant side of things is typically busier since the residents who have cabins on Takini come here often for meals. We also get the occasional boat full of fishermen who stop for a bite to eat as they pass by on the lake."

Her eyes glaze over, lost in thought as she takes the last sip of her drink.

"I know that look. Let me guess: you're trying to process what life is truly like out here? Hatching a plan to fly home early? Run far away?" I have enough self-awareness to know that this little island that means so much to me isn't most people's cup of tea, especially ones who are used to city life.

"No, I wasn't. I swear!"

"Uh-huh. It's okay. You won't hurt my feelings," I tease.

"I promise I'm absolutely giddy to be here. Over the moon. Can hardly contain my excitement."

"You know if you said that with a little more enthusiasm, I just might believe you."

"Seriously, though, how much wildlife do I need to be concerned about here?" she asks with a crease in her brow.

"A fair amount of concern, I would say. Lots of dangerous wildlife lurking in these woods."

"Really?" Her eyes widen.

"No," I chuckle. "I mean, we've got bears, wolves, and moose, but they're all more afraid of you. Stay away from them and you'll be just fine."

"Are you sure? 'Cause I brought bear spray."

"Eh, you won't need to use that. We only have black bears, not grizzlies."

She deepens the furrow of her brows. "Why does that not make me feel any better?"

"Just keep your eyes peeled, and you'll be fine. If you come across a bear, holler at it real loud." I wink at her for full effect, secretly loving when I can make city dwellers shake in their boots. "It'll keep you on your toes. It's good to live a little, right?"

"Sure," she says slowly and hesitantly. "Well, on that lovely note, I guess I should get back." She tosses a glance over her shoulder at her colleagues. I don't miss how her chest takes a little bit longer to inflate than her other breaths have, as if she's steeling herself for something.

Little quirks and shifts in body language are things that I've gotten good at picking up on after all these years of interacting with different people. I feel a sudden urge to know what her story is. What kind of wall she just put up.

"Nice to meet you, Blair," I say, picking up her empty glass.

"Likewise, Graham." With a purse of her lips, she slides off the stool and walks off toward where a group of people are mingling by the window.

I wipe down the bar top and busy myself with dishes before turning to the next person who approaches. In addition to the hospitality aspect, I also love being able to connect with so many people. The fact that I get to have a unique interaction with each new guest keeps things interesting around here. There's a new personality waiting for me with a turn of my head.

Being around the resort's guests this way makes living on Takini Island a little less lonely, especially since I'm basically the only one in the family around to run this place. I accept the responsibility—I do. But in the late-evening moments, when the grounds are quiet, when I'm all by myself, sitting on the balcony of my suite upstairs, the tug of loneliness can start to feel pretty heavy.

"Graham, we're running low on beer in this one," Nita says, taking the second-to-last bottle of Coors Light out of one of the beverage refrigerators underneath the countertop.

"On it." I survey the bar, making note of anything else I might need before running to grab more inventory and restock the fridges.

The rest of the night passes in a blur, with the lawyers proving to be a lively bunch until well after dark. I officially lost count of how many half-drunk conversations about wild animals and the basics of living on an island were had.

A sigh escapes me as I finally make my way up the stairs to my apartment just before midnight, looking forward to what the rest of the weekend will bring, especially if it'll mean more opportunities to chat with a specific dark-haired lawyer.

FOUR
Blair

The soft chime of my alarm brings me slowly out of a sleepy haze. My fingers curl around the soft sheets and the quilted comforter that I have tucked up to my chin. Unsurprisingly, I find myself in the same exact position I was in when I climbed in last night; the sign of a deep sleep. Sleeping isn't usually a problem for me—I can fall asleep at any point in the day—but the waking-up part tends to get rough.

No. No. No. Go back to sleep.

Not one single cell in my body wants to move away from the strangely comforting place of my empty dreams, but I manage to force one eye open. Then the other. My arms feel like dead weights in quicksand, but I manage to slide one slowly out of the covers to reach for my phone on the nightstand. After fumbling to turn the alarm off, I roll onto my side, stretching my legs out in an attempt to wake up the rest of my extremities. Then I capitalize on the momentum to finally push myself completely out of the bed.

My still-packed suitcase sits on the chair next to the night-stand, and I rifle through it to pull out an oversized gray sweatshirt. My feet shuffle on the cold, hardwood floor in the general direction of the loft stairs while I pull it on. Once in the small kitchen, I power on the mini Keurig that sits on the counter and reach for a large sage-green coffee mug the size of a cereal bowl. I watch mindlessly as the coffee drips, filling it almost all the way to the top. Not bothering to look for creamer or milk, I take the black coffee outside, where the crisp morning air catches in my chest, stinging the inside of my throat all the way down to my stomach with my first full breath in.

An eagle soaring through the sky across the lake catches my eye as I walk a few steps to the grassy shoreline and sit on the ground, crossing my legs, not bothered by the fact that I'm sitting in a mixture of dirt and sand. I'm tucked close in between two trees whose branches tower over me, and I look out to where the sun is sitting low over the water, just starting its climb for the day.

I mindlessly drink my coffee while I watch the lake rippling just inches from my feet, trying to will myself to feel any sort of wonderment or appreciation for the obvious beauty all around me. For any spark of life inside. But without needing to put on an act for anyone else, all I feel is the dull lifelessness that exists at my very core. There's a heaviness that constantly pushes against my chest and seeps all throughout my body, pressing on my brain and all the way down to my toes. Somehow, every single part of me feels heavy and utterly empty at the same time.

The logical part of my brain knows that the way I feel isn't normal, but if I'm honest with myself, I really don't know what normal feels like anymore. It's hard to fight for something that feels so out of reach, especially when I'm not entirely sure I've ever known it.

Pulling out my phone, I blink my heavy eyes and scan through work emails that have come through since last night. As a personal injury lawyer, my inbox is filled with a wide array of motor vehicle accident reports and litigation paperwork that my paralegal, Jamie, has forwarded on to me. Once I flag a few emails to circle back to later today, I drain the rest of my coffee and trudge back inside, swatting at a mosquito on the way up the cabin steps, wishing that caffeine did more for me than just send the slightest of buzzes through my veins.

Wishing that anything did.

After a quick shower, I rifle through my bag, assessing my clothing options for the day. I could go basic and stick with jeans and a T-shirt, or I have a black jumpsuit that I could pair with a headband—that could be cute if I curl my hair into loose waves.

What's the point? Nobody's looking at you anyway.

Barry's words from yesterday morning only accelerate the direction of where my own thoughts were heading, and I ultimately choose the least amount of effort, settling for jeans and a white tee. I pull my hair back into a loose, low bun at the base of my neck, then apply concealer and a bit of mascara to my eyes to make me look a little more alive.

Once it's clear that it's as good as it's going to get, I head out of the cabin, trying to summon enough energy from somewhere deep within to get me through the day. I'm just pulling the door shut when I hear Stacy from behind me.

"Hey, Blair. Looks like we're cabin neighbors."

"Morning, Stacy. How was your evening?" I ask as she falls into step beside me. I mentally pull up the facade of being a well-rested, carefree, jovial person, trying desperately to emulate what I would look like if I were, in fact, feeling all those things. I feel like a complete and transparent fraud, but I do my best anyway. What else can I do?

"Did you end up in Isaac's cabin for charades and karaoke?"

"God, no," she laughs. "I did stay at the lodge a little bit too late, though. I'm regretting that third glass of wine."

"Oh, shoot." I give her a sympathetic smile. "Maybe they'll go easy on us today."

"Doubtful. You know how Paul is. So, a scavenger hunt," she muses at the team-building activity on the schedule for this morning as we walk. "I haven't done one of those since I was a kid."

"I'm more nervous about the 'untangle a human knot' portion of the day," I say with a cringe.

"I don't even know what that is, nor do I particularly want to."

I stumble on a golf-ball-sized rock in the middle of the path and then kick it off to the side with my foot. The large, peaked roof of the lodge comes into view as we round the last cabin.

Cassidy spots us and waves from the top of the deck stairs. She holds the door open for us as we pass by.

"Thanks, Cassidy," I say, stepping inside and then grabbing the door to hold it open for a coworker coming in behind me. I let a few people pass by and then turn forward, running straight into the sharp corner of a cardboard box.

"Oh my gosh, I'm so sorry." Frazzled, I glance up to see Graham behind the box.

"Blair. No, that was my bad. I wasn't paying attention. Are you okay?" he asks, searching my face intently, scanning for signs of injury.

"Totally fine. Don't worry about it." I wave him off with a reassuring smile. He shifts the box under one arm, revealing his lodge uniform of a light-blue polo shirt and khaki shorts. He runs his free hand through his thick hair, looking slightly disheveled, and I wonder if anyone else can tell how stressed he looks. Who takes care of him while he takes care of running this place?

"The mornings can get a little busy around here," he says sheepishly before gesturing toward the dining area. "My amazing cook, Shirley, made a brunch buffet for you guys. It's all set up inside. Help yourselves."

"Great, thank you," I say. My legs move to follow the girls, but my body is still half-twisted to look back at him.

"You have to try a muffin. She makes them from scratch every morning." His dark-blue eyes hold mine, and once again, I can't help but notice how friendly and inviting they appear, just as they did last night from behind the bar, when I was more drawn to talking to him than anyone else.

"Will do. Thanks." I wave and watch as he disappears down the hallway, then catch up to Stacy and Cassidy. I follow them, weaving in between the dining tables, crossing to the other side of the room where the buffet table is set up.

"This smells amazing," Cassidy gushes, passing me a plate. I walk past the scrambled eggs, breakfast potatoes, and pancakes. Instead, I spoon some fruit onto my plate and grab a cinnamon-streusel muffin.

"Morning, everyone!" Paul says, standing up in the middle of the room just as we find a table to sit at. "I hope you're all feeling well rested and ready for a day of fun! It's time to break you off into teams for the scavenger hunt."

I bite into the muffin—which notably lives up to Graham's hype—while Paul starts calling names from the list in his hand. "On team one, we've got Steve, Cassidy, Blair, and Isaac."

Cassidy claps her hands giddily next to me, elbowing me with an enthusiastic wink. I give her a forced smile while further mentally preparing myself for how draining this day is about to be. I eat the rest of the muffin, only half-listening as Paul reads off the rest of the team names, then I join the rest of my team that's gathering by the window.

"Ready to kick some butt?" Isaac raises his hand up in front of each of us for a high-five.

"Born ready," Cassidy replies enthusiastically, a spirited hunger in her eyes.

"I didn't know you were so competitive, Cassidy," I say, not even close to matching her energy.

"Oh, just wait. You'll be glad you're on my team, let's just say that." She rubs her palms together. Paul passes out a nicely designed scavenger hunt detail page to each team.

"The first team to collect and bring back every item on this list wins. These will be your same teammates for the duration of the retreat, so go ahead and get used to working together. You have the resort grounds to explore, so please watch out for wildlife. I'll blow my whistle when a team has successfully completed the challenge to signal your return to the lodge. Have fun!"

"Let's do this!" Isaac leads our team out of the lodge, and we gather off to the right in front of the deck.

"Alright, what do we have?" Steve asks, scanning the checklist. "We need to find a pinecone, a feather, a bug, a flower, something purple, something rough, and something smooth."

"Should we just go down from the top of the list? Does that sound like a good strategy?" Cassidy asks.

"Sure," I offer, looking to move things along and get this started. The sooner we start, the sooner we finish.

"Pinecone it is," Isaac says.

We fan out as we start exploring the property in front of the cabins that are on the opposite side of the lodge from mine. The trees are thicker on this side, with a few more bushes and vegetation filling the area between the cabins. We pass the last cabin and venture farther into the woods.

"Oh! A feather!" Cassidy calls out, holding up a grayish feather the size of her forearm.

"That's probably filled with some sort of lice or bugs," Isaac warns in his matter-of-fact way, cringing in disgust at the feather.

"Well, we need a bug too—so two for one!" She's completely unaffected as she slips it into our team bag.

"There's no way that'll pass, so don't mark 'bug' as complete," Isaac tells me as I cross off 'feather' with a check mark. Then I scan the ground for a pinecone, using my foot to lazily shift leaves and sticks out of the way. I wish I was a more enthusiastic team member, but alas, I can't seem to summon anything more.

"A grasshopper!" Cassidy shrieks, causing Isaac to nearly stumble over an exposed tree trunk in his quest to get to her side as fast as possible. Steve and I stand, watching in amusement as they both bend over to examine it. The grasshopper jumps, causing them to bump heads when they sharply follow its direction.

"Does a grasshopper count as a bug?" Cassidy asks, absentmindedly rubbing the spot on her head while intently following it.

"Grasshoppers are insects," Isaac replies, slowly trailing after her. "Technically speaking, all bugs are insects, but not all insects are bugs."

"Close enough for me," Cassidy replies, lunging for it with cupped hands. Steve stifles a laugh behind his fist as the grasshopper jumps between them, both of them trying desperately to catch it.

"Come on!" Cassidy yells, flinging her hands up in the air in frustration. "I don't understand how this is supposed to help us bond."

"Do you think we should help them?" I murmur to Steve, who has his arms folded across his chest, leaning against a tree trunk.

"Nah, this is way more entertaining," he replies with a grin.

After what seems like a very long time, Isaac finally manages to capture the grasshopper with an impressive lunge. I cringe, holding the open bag out to him, hoping it won't hop out of his hand and onto me. When he slides it into the bag, I clasp the opening of the bag shut as tightly as I can, wondering how I got stuck being the one to carry it, and follow the group as we set off to find a flower.

FIVE
Blair

"Hit us with another fact, Isaac," Cassidy says, moving her blue *Sorry* game piece two spots to the right on the game board.

"Besides Alaska, Minnesota has more wolves than any other state," Isaac says immediately, making me wonder how many facts are sitting on the tip of his tongue. They've seemed to be readily available whenever somebody—namely Cassidy—asks for one.

We've had a full day of retreat activities. First, our team failed miserably at the scavenger hunt, having only collected three items by the time the whistle blew. Then we performed decently at untying the human knot, which is a memory that's best left forgotten, and now, here we are, fulfilling the rest of our daily obligation by playing board games for the past two hours.

"That's a very unsettling fact, actually," I say, moving my red game piece four spaces.

"I'm getting hungry," Cassidy blurts out. "Paul said we could be done whenever we want to and order something to eat from the bar, right?"

"He did," Steve answers. "I'm pretty hungry too. Should we attempt a *Sorry* rematch another day?"

"Works for me," I say, immediately helping to clean up the board. I have some work I need to sift through for a deposition before I'll be able to go to sleep tonight, and I'm already exhausted, so I fling the pieces into the box as fast as I can.

"Good job today, Gavel Gang," Isaac says, referencing the cringe-worthy team name he and Cassidy came up with earlier.

"I can't wait until tomorrow." Cassidy beams.

With a wave, we all disperse in separate directions across the dining room, and I take the game back to the shelf. Through the window, I can see that the front deck is relatively empty, so I head outside the main door and find a lounge chair that looks out at the lake. I pull out my phone and call Annie, who answers after the second ring.

"I take it you haven't been eaten alive by mosquitos yet?"

"No, but I'd say I'm getting close," I say, absentmindedly scratching at a new bite that just appeared on my forearm.

"How are you?" she asks, growing serious. Annie knows everything about me, the good and the bad, including my long struggle with mental health.

"I'm alright." Which is about as honest as I can be at the moment. "It's been a long day."

"Tell me about it," she gently pries, her typical way of getting me to talk about my day.

I recount the last several hours, explaining in particular detail the mouthwatering cheeseburgers they served us for lunch, which happens to be my favorite part of the day so far. My stomach grumbles just thinking about it.

"Now I'm just sitting on a lounge chair, watching some of my coworkers play yard games." The sun paints the sky a dark pinkish orange as it gets closer to the horizon, descending for the day. I press my back against the chair, settling into the comfort of talking to her. "I actually think you would love it here, Annie. You know, since you like nature and all that stuff."

"Hey, just because I'm willingly going on a hiking trip with Eric doesn't mean I like nature any more than you do." She laughs.

"How is the trip planning going?"

She fills me in on their upcoming end-of-summer backpacking trip to Glacier National Park and the work they're both doing to get their classrooms ready for the school year. Once again, I feel the tiniest reprieve from the heaviness that sits on my chest just from listening to her voice.

We say goodbye, promising to talk tomorrow. Before I put my phone away, I pull up Barry's number and send him a quick text.

Blair: How are you?

I don't even expect a response, as most of our texts to each other get ignored or forgotten about, but I send it anyway. At least, that's what a girlfriend would typically do.

The lure of my quiet cabin is tempting, and I briefly debate skipping dinner altogether, but my stomach grumbles again, forcing me to head back inside the lodge and wander over to the bar.

"Hey." Graham stops what he's doing when he spots me approaching.

"Hi, Graham." I slide onto the same stool I sat on yesterday and try to mimic the grin on his face, but I know I end up coming miserably short.

"Long day?" he asks, placing a cocktail napkin in front of me.

"You could say that. I think all of this fresh air is tiring me out."

"You sure it isn't because you were paired with Isaac all day?"

I smirk at his comment, appreciating that he's not afraid to poke harmless fun at his guests. "I'm definitely up to par on my state-of-Minnesota facts—that much I can say with certainty."

"Useful information, I'm sure." He chuckles. "Are you hungry?"

"Starving, actually. What do you recommend?"

"Well, the specialty tonight is Shirley's lasagna, homemade garlic bread, and a Caesar salad, which I highly recommend. But you can also order anything à la carte off our regular menu."

"Oh here, dear." A woman, who I'm assuming is Shirley, comes bustling out of the back with a food container in hand.

"Perfect timing. I was just bringing Graham his lasagna, but he'll happily give you a taste to help you decide."

"I couldn't possibly," I object, but my words are ignored as she flips the lid off the top and uses a fork and knife to cut off a corner.

"Here you are. Be careful, it's hot." She hands me the fork and watches intently, waiting for me to take a bite of the steaming-hot lasagna. Unsure of what I should do, I flick my eyes to Graham, who gives me an unbothered nod, which tells me that this might be a common occurrence for him.

Slowly, I take a bite, letting the warm, flavorful mixture melt into my mouth as I savor every last bit.

"Wow." Somehow the aftertaste it leaves in my mouth is just as enjoyable as the actual food. It tastes warm and oddly comforting in a way, the kind of food that feeds not only your stomach but a part of your soul. I can't remember the last time I had a home-cooked meal. Barry and I live off of takeout, which is most often eaten at our separate desks.

"She'll be disappointed if you don't say that it's the best lasagna you've ever had," Graham says out of the corner of his mouth.

"It actually *is* the best I've ever had." And I mean every word too.

"Well, now you're just saying that," Shirley says humbly, waving her kitchen towel in the air as she turns on her heels and disappears back into the kitchen.

"Thanks for sharing your meal." I huff a small laugh.

"Eh, I'm used to it. It happens all the time. Should I give you a minute to decide?"

"No, I'll definitely have the lasagna, please. But is there any way I could take it to go?"

"You don't want to stay?" I don't miss the flash of surprise on his face as his eyes dart to the full dining room that's bustling with my coworkers.

"I have some files to go through for work, so I figured I'd bring some food back and kill two birds with one stone," I explain.

"Sure thing." His pen starts scribbling across the ordering pad.

"So, did you always want to be a lawyer?"

"More or less," I say, inclined to leave it at that. Maybe it's the lingering effect of having just talked to Annie, or maybe it's the way he's looking at me, but for whatever reason, talking to him seems to take less effort than it does with others, so I act on the urge to expand. "My mom and dad are both lawyers, so that's the world I grew up in. I guess I always wanted to follow in their footsteps."

What I don't say out loud is that going to law school was my way of desperately seeking their attention and approval. I was naive enough to think that maybe they would actually give me more than a second glance if I followed in their footsteps. It turned out that wasn't enough to override the fact that they never wanted me in the first place. That I was unplanned and an inconvenient result of a careless anniversary celebration. Nothing has ever been enough.

"What about you? Did you always know that you'd live here? Run the resort?"

He shrugs, scratching the dark scruff that lines his jaw. "I always knew I'd have a hand in it, but no, I didn't expect to be running it."

"I feel like there's a story there," I say gently, not wanting to pry, but I'm curious about his backstory.

"My grandparents built it back when they were just starting out as newlyweds. They built the main lodge first and rented out two rooms while they lived in the third. As time went on, they expanded with more and more cabins. Later on, when I was a kid, my parents and aunt and uncle shared the responsibility of running it. We lived in Baudette, where my sister and I went to school, and we would either fly or boat over here every weekend to bring supplies and help out as much as we could."

"Was Ruby your grandma's name, then?"

"Yup." His face softens at the mention of her.

I nod slowly, my interest piqued at this small-town existence way up here in northern Minnesota—a place not even close to being on my radar before this weekend. What a childhood he must have had—and what a stark contrast to mine.

"After high school, I went to school with plans of becoming a conservation officer with the Department of Natural Resources," he continues. "But long story short, my aunt and uncle moved away for a job offer in Nebraska at the same time my sister left for college, and none of them ever moved back."

"And your parents?" I ask, hoping I'm not overstepping. I watch as his expression hardens.

"My mom developed Alzheimer's a while back and has been slowly declining for the last few years. My dad helps as much as he can, but he spends most of his time with my mom at the nursing home." He lifts his shoulders in a shrug. "There was nobody left, so I moved in two years ago and have been here ever since."

"I'm sorry about your mom," I say quietly. His gaze skirts over my face, and a part of me wonders why he decided to share all of that with me in such detail.

He's just being nice. I bet he talks to all of his guests this way. Don't kid yourself—you're nothing special.

"Thank you," he says genuinely before looking around the dining room. "Anyway, this is home now. And I really do love it. It's just a lot of responsibility that I didn't exactly bargain for."

"At least you have a stunning view from your office," I say, pointing out the window.

"It could be worse." He smirks, tapping the order pad on the counter. "Although, tell me that again in the winter."

I force a smile as he backs away into the kitchen, dropping off my order ticket before tending to other guests from behind the bar. While I wait for my food, I seem to hit a wall and unintentionally zone out, hyperfocusing on the noise surrounding me. Two fellow attorneys are chatting loudly a few barstools over. Cassidy is squeal-laughing at something Paul said at the table behind me. The roll of dice is loud against a table where four people have yet to give up on their Yahtzee game. It's in moments like this when I wish I could will myself to be as invisible as I feel. I'm emotionally exhausted, completely drained from the activities of the day and the interactions with so many people.

"Here you go." Graham's warm voice breaks me out of my thoughts as he sets a bag on top of the counter. "Enjoy."

"Thank you." I use the last of my strength to force another smile and push myself off the stool. I make my way in what's left of the lingering daylight to my tiny little cabin by the lake.

SIX
Graham

"What can I help you with?" Dad asks as he places a mug of coffee in front of me before sliding into a chair across the table. His eyes dart around the dining room, assessing the state of the lodge, and I immediately take note of the slight shaking of his hand that loosely grips his mug. His nerves are almost palpable as I take the mug from him.

"I'm good, Dad. Really," I insist, once again attempting to convince him that he has nothing to worry about here. Ever since Mom got sick, he's had a one-track brain, focusing entirely on her, which is amazing—I'm glad Mom is in good hands—but the downfall is that he tends to get agitated and stressed when it comes to anything outside of the nursing home bubble that he lives in. Everything beyond the routine care of Mom is very clearly an overwhelming topic for him. Each time he comes out here, he brings a cloud of anxiety along with him. More often than not, his energy tends to rub off on me, and sometimes, I can't tell if him being here is more of a burden or a help.

"I know I haven't been around much, but—" he starts.

"I've got everything covered." I reassuringly place a steady hand over his shaky one. "Shirley even has enough wild blueberries leftover to make her famous jam, so we're thriving at the moment. You know how excited she gets about a fresh batch of jam."

I force a smile behind my mug as I take a sip of coffee. The growing list of repairs this place needs and the rapidly dwindling funds available to cover them remains left unsaid. I don't like to add to his worry, especially when it comes to things that he wouldn't be able to fix anyway.

He eyes me warily, not completely convinced. I know he feels guilty for not helping run Ruby Lodge as much as he'd planned, and I also know that he feels guilty every second he's out here and away from Mom too. The last thing I want to do is add to the burden that he already feels by unloading all of my concerns onto him. I can handle the stress and responsibility if it means keeping it off his shoulders.

"Should we go through the books while I'm here?" he offers.

"No need." If I answered too quickly, he doesn't show any sign that he noticed.

"I just went through them yesterday." The lie rolls off my tongue easily.

"Alright. How about that broken deadbolt on cabin twelve? Is anyone staying in there currently?"

"No, that one's empty. Actually, it would be a huge help if you wouldn't mind fixing that for me." I know he won't stop asking until he finds something to do, so that small job would actually be ideal to make him feel useful.

"Perfect. I'll do that." He sounds pleased, but the line between his brows is still plenty deep with tension.

"How's Mom?" I ask, redirecting the conversation. He pushes his lips together, stalling, unsure of how to answer.

"About the same as last week when you came to see her," he finally says. "Not much has changed. She has her lucid moments, but they're short-lived as usual."

My chest tightens with emotion, and a heaviness ruminates at the very top of my stomach. "You still singing to her?"

"Oh, yeah." His smile grows nostalgic. When the doctor first told us to try and do things that might jog her memory, Dad started singing some of her favorite songs to her. He can't carry a tune to save his life, but Mom loves music, having played several instruments throughout her life, and he'd do just about anything for her. I force a sad smile back, making a mental note to look for her old music sheets to bring with me next time I visit.

"You talk to Syd recently?" he asks, his knee starting to bounce at the mention of my sister.

"A few days ago." I nod my head and purse my lips together, already knowing what he's going to ask next.

"She planning to come home anytime soon?" I don't know why he bothers to ask. We both already know the answer to that.

"I don't think so. She didn't mention anything anyway," I reply. He doesn't say anything else about it. He knows it's not worth pushing.

Out of the corner of my eye, I can see one of the Lund Alaskan fishing boats slowing as it comes into the bay. A second boat out of the three that went out this morning trails not too far behind that one. I hope the fishing excursion went well and without incident for the guests.

"So, a bunch of lawyers, huh?" Dad asks, following my line of sight.

"Yeah. Nice folks. It's been a good few days. They head home tomorrow." I take a sip of my coffee and watch as everyone starts climbing out of the boats. I'm well aware that I'm scanning them in search of a glimpse of Blair, though I'd never in a million years admit that out loud.

A smile tugs at my mouth when a brunette topknot comes into view among the crowd of people. I'm not delusional enough to want to pursue a romantic relationship with an out-of-town resort guest—and I'm honestly not even sure if she's single or not—but I can't deny that there's something that draws me to her.

She's wearing an olive-green raincoat and black rain boots. Judging by her frown, I'm assuming that fishing is not her favorite activity. The corner of my mouth tugs up at the mental image of her reeling in a walleye or baiting her own hook with a leech.

I watch intently as she suddenly spins to help a woman, who I've learned is named Cassidy, when the woman's foot gets caught on the rim of the boat and she literally falls forehead-first into Isaac's back.

"City folk," Dad says with an amused sigh, and I chuckle, watching the scene unfold with bated breath. Blair helps pull Cassidy to stand while Isaac shuffles a few steps to regain his own balance. I breathe a sigh of relief after ensuring that no one is about to fall into the lake, and then I notice Paul, who is headed off the dock.

"I'm gonna go check in, Dad. I'll be right back." I stand, sliding my chair back in.

"Sure. I've got Sam coming to pick me up in about an hour, so I'll go fix that lock and then give Shirley a hand until then."

"Thanks, Dad." I give him a pat on the shoulder and head outside. To my disappointment, Blair and the rest of her team have already dispersed to their cabins, leaving Paul and a few others still hanging around on the grass.

"Any keepers?" I call to Paul as he turns to greet me.

"We got a whole slew of walleye, a few crappie, and some perch too!" He displays a full-mouth grin that's full of pride. "And that's just on our boat."

"Aha! I knew we'd turn you into a fisherman." I shake his outstretched hand firmly, offering him the praise he's so clearly seeking. "Your guides will filet them in the hut over there. After that, if you take the fish meat inside, Shirley will fry them up for you—there's nothing better than fresh fish."

"I'll go do that right now," he says earnestly. "Thanks again for all the hospitality you've shown us, Graham. We've had a great time the last few days."

"It's been our pleasure, truly," I say, meaning every word. "Make sure you remind your employees to let us know if they need any extra amenities in their cabins."

"Will do. Speaking of, I better get that fish to Shirley so I can shower and get this smell off me before the hike this afternoon." He extends his hand out to me again, which I gladly shake in return.

"Have fun. We'll see you later on," I call out as he walks to the hut.

With a final wave, he walks away, and I take the opportunity to scan the beach area. I pick up a few stray sticks laying in the sand and straighten the Adirondack chairs as I pass by. After tossing the sticks into the woods, I grab the rake that's leaning against one of the trees and start clearing the weeds that have washed onto shore since yesterday. Just one of the never-ending chores that needs to be done to keep this place looking presentable.

We used to have a groundskeeper on the payroll, but the budget for that diminished about a year ago, leaving the mainte-nance mostly to me now—and occasionally Dad when he's here. I actually don't mind the physical labor. Mowing the grass and trimming the shrubs is the kind of mindless work that allows me to zone out, which I find kind of peaceful in a way. I like being outside and getting my hands dirty. The only problem is that there are usually a million other things that I also need to be doing at the same time.

In an attempt to push that to-do list out of my mind and to de-stress a little bit, I let my mind go and lean into the work. I run the rake along the shoreline, feeling the sun beating down on my neck. It warms me from the inside out as I soak in the sunshine and continue the chores.

SEVEN
Blair

Even though I just showered for an entire thirty minutes, the faint, putrid smell of fish seems to be following me around. I wonder if it's possible for it to actually be seeping out of my pores. I internally recoil, plugging my nose in an attempt to thwart the disgusting smell as I walk down the loft stairs inside my cabin.

"How is everything at home?" I ask Barry through the speaker on my phone, still not over the surprise that he actually picked up my call this time.

"Normal," he says. I can practically see his shrug of indifference. I wonder if he can even tell the difference without me there. "Barely been home, actually. I've been in court all week. The Larson case has been dragging."

I pull out the Gibson Law water bottle from the retreat swag bag that Paul passed out yesterday and wash it quickly in the sink while Barry rambles on about his case.

"We should be able to wrap things up in the next few days, though, if everything goes as planned." He mumbles quietly, as if he's talking to himself. He's clearly distracted by something more important than this conversation.

"That's good," I reply, admittedly just as distracted with filling my water bottle.

"Anyway, what are you doing there?" he asks.

"I'm about to head over to the lodge. We're going hiking this afternoon."

"Pfftt," he scoffs. "You? Hiking? I can't picture it."

"It's mandatory," I reply flatly, dismissing his stinging comment.

"Have fun, I guess? Is that what I'm supposed to say?" He mumbles, and the shuffling of papers is loud in the background, still only giving me his partial attention.

"You don't have to say anything. In fact, I'll call you later," I say, ready to be done with this pointless conversation.

"Bye." No argument comes from him. No 'I love you' or 'I miss you' is said from either of us, and the click of the phone hangs heavy in the air.

Attempting to brush off the frustrating effects of talking to Barry, I slide my phone into my cross-body pouch that hangs over my black workout tank and eggplant-colored leggings and turn the faucet on. Once the bottle is filled to the top with water, I slide a pair of sunglasses on and head outside.

Let's get this over with.

I find my teammates at the bottom of the lodge stairs. Cassidy is pulling her ankle back in a quad stretch, and Isaac is bent all the way over, touching the tips of his shoes with his fingers. Steve is sitting on the bottom step, occupied with his phone.

"Oh, good, you're here!" Cassidy says to me, pulling her high pony tight. "Do you need to stretch at all, or can we get going?"

"We can go." I shrug, not seeing the point of warming up. No amount of stretching will be able to help my weak muscles. I fully expect to be sore at the end of this hike.

"Great, let's head out." Isaac curls his arm, and the rest of us fall in line behind him.

After passing the entire row of cabins, we veer onto the dirt path that gets narrower and takes us farther into the woods with each step. My legs already begin to ache in protest—a silent plea to turn around before it gets even worse. Ignoring the protest from my muscles, I continue trudging along behind the group. After a few minutes, we come across a stick in the ground with red tape tied to the top.

"Paul told us to wait here for Graham to take us up to the trail with his ATV," Isaac says confidently, clearly taking great pleasure in his role as our self-imposed leader.

"You mean this doesn't count as the trail? We haven't started yet?" Cassidy asks, her chest heaving already just like mine.

"Nope. I got all the details last night. The path up to the trail is on an incline, and it's pretty rough, so Graham is running each of us up to where the groomed hiking trail is in one of his fancy vehicle things."

"Oh. Great." Her overly enthusiastic tone is disingenuous and full of sarcasm.

As if on cue, the roar of a loud engine can be heard from somewhere in the thick trees up ahead. The snapping of twigs and rustling of brush announces his arrival before Graham comes into view, maneuvering the red four-wheeler expertly through the trees. We huddle together on the edge of the trail to leave space for him to come to a stop.

"Who's ready?" he asks with a smile, his gaze landing on me. As the unlucky one who happens to be standing closest to the vehicle—and without anyone else jumping in—I blow out a steadying breath and step forward. Taking his outstretched hand, I step on the footrest behind his foot and swing my leg around to sit behind him. There's enough space between us that it doesn't feel awkward, but my nerves still kick in. I've never ridden on one of these things before, and I'm not exactly the most agile of people.

"You can slide your fingers through those holes by your sides and hang on tight," he calls over his shoulder. "I promise I'll go slow, okay? You ready?"

"I guess." I nod, gripping the handles tightly. With a jolt, he shifts out of park, and I squeeze the seat firmly with my thighs. I'm determined to stay on and not embarrass myself by losing my grip and toppling off. Graham carefully guides us around large mud piles and boulders that jut out of the ground, holding tree branches out so they don't swing in my face. Eventually, we make it to a clearing near the top of a hill where Paul is standing.

There's a walkie-talkie hanging from his neck and a clipboard in one hand. I slowly let a deep breath out as I take Graham's outstretched hand and climb off the ATV.

"Good luck," he says with an unsettling smirk, which tells me he thinks I'll need it. "Watch out for snakes."

"Snakes?" My stomach drops.

"They like to hide in the mud." He smiles innocently, then winks and takes off to get the next person. I walk on my jelly legs to where Paul is standing.

"Beautiful day, huh?" He beams.

"Uh-huh," I agree with a forced smile, thankful that I have a few minutes to compose myself before continuing on. I rest against a large rock, the uneasiness in my gut starting to dissipate as I close my eyes and feel the sun beaming onto my face.

Graham arrives quickly with Cassidy, who joins me on the rock while we wait for the last of our team.

"Alright, team!" Paul beckons for us to follow as he moves to the start of the trail. "The trail is clearly marked, and it's a relatively easy two-mile path, so you shouldn't have any difficulties. Isaac has a whistle to be used in emergencies only. Please watch out for poison ivy, mud pockets, and any wildlife you might come across. This path will lead you right back to the resort where you can freshen up for our closing dinner this evening."

"Thanks, Paul," Cassidy chirps, twirling the end of her ponytail with her finger. I marvel at how fast she was able to find a second wind, while I'm over here still not able to take an easy breath in.

"Enjoy your time in nature," he says exuberantly, stepping off to the side with an outstretched arm pointing at the trailhead.

Isaac motions for Steve to take the lead and then trails closely behind him. I take a deep breath, mustering any internal strength I have left, and take up the rear behind Cassidy.

"We could absolutely come across bears in these woods," Isaac bellows over his shoulder. "So keep your eyes peeled."

"Oh, great," I mutter.

He suddenly lifts his arms to regain balance when his shoe lands funny on a rock, throwing him off center.

"You okay?" Cassidy calls.

"Yup. Watch your step, though."

My ankle aches, and my legs start throbbing with each step I take. I curve widely around the mud puddles that are sprinkled along the trail. Barry's right; I'm definitely not cut out for this. I haven't worked out or done anything this physical in years.

"You coming, Blair-Bear?" Cassidy twists her body to look back at me, her hair flipping in the air.

"I'm coming," I huff. Blood pumps through my veins, and my lungs burn inside my chest as we round a corner, our feet kicking up dirt from the dusty path. I feel slightly lightheaded, and sweat starts forming across my forehead when Barry's voice gets loud in my head.

You're absolutely pathetic. Can't even make it half a mile.

I don't fight the words as they echo repeatedly in my mind, making me feel weak and worthless. In front of me, Isaac lets out a gargled yelp as he slips on another pile of loose rocks, narrowly correcting himself.

"Oh my gosh, Isaac," Cassidy says, stretching her arms out to help steady him from behind. "How in the world are you this uncoordinated?"

"You're one to talk," he replies sharply. "You fell while climbing *out* of a boat this morning."

A smile tugs at the corner of my mouth at the memory from earlier. Before she can hurl a comeback, she slips on the same pile of rocks and falls directly onto his back, sending both of them barreling to the ground. They land in a huff, a jumbled pile on the side of the trail.

I'm not sure if it's watching them fall for the umpteenth time today, or if it's the fact that I'm teetering on the edge of consciousness and dripping with sweat, but something breaks deep inside of me, and I let out a tiny bark of a laugh. It comes from a place deep inside my gut. It's rough and timid at first, but it's quickly followed by another louder cackle.

All of a sudden, I'm hunched over my knees, laughter pouring out of me as if a dam has burst, and it can't possibly be held inside. Unbridled emotion flows out of me. Whether it's a positive or negative kind is indecipherable, as I seem to have absolutely no control over it. I have to steady myself against a rock as the deep release consumes me, rushing out without restraint or a care in the world.

"I'm glad you find this entertaining, Blair," Isaac says flatly as Steve helps pull him to his feet. I'm able to gather myself enough to reach for Cassidy's elbow with one hand, but I still cover my mouth with the other, unable to stop the fit of laughter.

"I'm sorry." I hiccup another laugh as tears start forming at the corners of my eyes. I wipe at them with the bottom of my tank top. My mind feels like I'm floating in a wind tunnel, disheveled and not entirely sure which way is up or down, caught up in a sea of this strange feeling I'm not familiar with.

"You guys need training wheels for walking or something?" Steve comments to Isaac and Cassidy.

My giggles slowly dissipate as we all dust ourselves off and continue on the path. Whatever release I just experienced ever so slowly slips out of my reach, leading me back to feeling exhausted and out of breath. I trail a bit farther behind Cassidy this time, not wanting to get caught up in her path if she falls again.

We continue on without any more incidents, and although we're all sufficiently drenched in sweat and looking battered and bruised, a small sense of pride hits me once we make it to the resort trail.

"We made it!" Cassidy squeals, her voice slightly shaky.

"Barely," Steve grumbles.

We trudge, notably slower than our pace at the beginning of the hike, and we wave goodbye one by one to each team member as we pass by their cabin. Eventually, it's just me left, and I walk back to cabin four to take my second shower of the day. I'm smelly, exhausted, and achy, but I can't help but feel a fraction lighter than I usually do.

EIGHT
Graham

Ignoring the nervous pit in my stomach, I click open the email from Scott, my buddy from high school who works for the HVAC company in Baudette. Inside, I find an estimate for the labor and units needed to replace the heating system for Ruby Lodge.

We're looking at roughly nineteen thousand dollars.

A ball of dread swirls deep in my stomach as I read each line of the email twice. The quote factors in a new furnace for the main lodge and the baseboard heaters needed for each of the fifteen cabins. That's nineteen grand that I absolutely do not have and cannot foresee coming up with in the next month or so.

What other options do I have? We can't survive without heat in the winter, that's a given. And the current system won't hold out for another winter season—we barely made it through last year. How am I supposed to handle this? Maybe the best route would be to only fix a few of the cabins and not all of them.

I can maybe get a loan for the money, but closing that many cabins will drastically cut our winter bookings.

I swallow down the rising nausea and power my computer off. This'll have to be dealt with another day. Right now, I need to put my host hat back on and focus on the closing dinner for Gibson Law. This problem will still be here tomorrow.

"And the team who accumulated the most points is...drumroll please..." Paul's voice booms from the corner of the dining room when I come back into the bar.

"Nathan, Julie, and Scott! Congratulations!" He leads a round of lackluster applause, and I bite back a smile. As a whole, I'm not sure if many of his employees have matched his enthusiasm this whole retreat—aside from a few of the people on Blair's team, of course.

"Moving on, the reward for Best Team Spirit goes to...Cassidy!"

The responding squeal pierces the air, and I watch in amusement as Cassidy jumps up and down, clapping her hands while she runs up to retrieve her certificate.

"That concludes my portion of the evening," Paul says once he frees himself from her hug. "Please enjoy the rest of the night and our remaining time together. The floatplanes will arrive in the morning to start our commute back home."

The room relaxes as hushed conversations pick up and people start moving about. I tend to the first few people that approach the bar, mixing drinks and making small talk about the day.

Eventually, I turn my attention to Blair, pretending that I haven't had the corner of my eye on her the whole night.

"So you survived the hike, huh?" I ask, setting my forearms against the bar top to lean in and give her my full attention. I hold her gaze intently as she slides onto a stool.

Her mouth curves up into a flat smile, and she tilts her head to the side. "You should ask Cassidy, here, how the hike went."

Cassidy sits on the stool next to her and offers a sheepish smirk along with an eye roll. "I may or may not have fallen a few times."

"Ah, don't sweat it. Most hikes end up with a casualty or two." I chuckle, half wishing I would have been able to see their team on the hike.

"It was quite comical, actually," Blair says.

"Blair couldn't stop laughing, which was extremely rude if you ask me," Cassidy says pointedly.

My gaze shifts to Blair, and I get caught on a mental image of her laughing hysterically. It's such a contrast to her generally serious facade that I can hardly picture it. I wonder how often she lets loose like that, and what else it would take to be able to see it.

"I've just never met two more uncoordinated people in my life than you and Isaac," she says.

"Well, I fully blame Paul for giving us such rigorous activities. I didn't know I would be climbing a freaking mountain while we were here." She loops her arm around Blair's elbow. "But other than some questionable activities, I really have had an amazing time on this retreat. I feel like we've bonded, don't you?"

I bite back a grin at the expression on both of their faces. One is hopeful and excited, while the other is nothing more than tolerant and clearly unimpressed. To her credit, Blair forces a smile and pats Cassidy's arm gently.

"Me too," she says, although not at all convincingly.

"That makes me happy, Blair. Okay, I'm off to mingle! Don't worry, I'll catch up with you later!" Cassidy slides off the stool and saunters away.

"Don't give me that look," Blair chides when her eyes slide to mine, waving a finger in my direction.

"What look? I didn't say anything," I reply innocently, stifling a smile.

"The one that says you pity me...although, you're not wrong to."

"Oh, come on," I chide. "She seems harmless. This retreat couldn't have been all that bad, was it?"

"I'm now officially a member of The Gavel Gang, Graham," she says, pinning me with a pointed stare. "The Gavel Gang. And I get the feeling that it's a lifelong membership. It can't get much worse than that."

I can't contain the laugh that bursts out of me. "Point made. I think you need a drink. What can I get you?"

"How about a dirty martini?"

"You got it." I get working on making her cocktail behind the bar. The urge to continue a conversation and inquire about her relationship status sits at the tip of my tongue, but I bite it back down. I'm dying to know, but I remind myself that it doesn't matter. It's not like it would make a difference either way. She'll be gone tomorrow.

"So, do you go up into Canada often?" she asks as I set the martini in front of her.

"Yeah, all the time. Lake of the Woods borders both Minnesota and Ontario, so we end up fishing in Canadian water pretty often. Sometimes my buddies and I will go up into Kenora for a change of scenery or when we're looking for someplace new to stop and eat while we fish. There are limited options up here, you know?"

"Do you get to fish often? You seem pretty busy."

"It doesn't happen much anymore," I admit. "But every so often, my buddies get sick of hearing my excuses and will come drag me out."

She nods, taking a sip.

"What do you do for fun at home?" I ask, grateful that no one else has come up to the bar yet so we can continue our conversation. She looks contemplative for a moment, staring almost blankly down at her hand that's holding the glass.

"Certainly not hiking, I'll tell you that much." She offers a smile. It's not lost on me how she seems to redirect a lot of the questions that I ask about herself and her life in Chicago. I don't know much about her beyond the basics, but my desire to know more feels like a relentless tug from somewhere inside.

Out of the corner of my eye, I notice another person approaching a few seats down from her.

"I should go mingle," Blair says, noticing the new guest as well. "Thanks for the drink."

With an internal sigh, I bury my disappointment and turn to greet him.

"What can I get you?" I place a cocktail napkin in front of him and fulfill his drink order.

The rest of the evening passes in a whirlwind. Shirley and I conduct our well-practiced dance that we perform frequently, moving around each other with ease as we serve and provide for our guests.

At the end of the night, when my end-of-the-day checklist is complete and the lodge is empty, I say goodnight to Shirley and wave her off to her own cabin. I flick off the bar lights, lock my office, and head down the back hallway to the stairwell that leads up to my apartment. Each step feels increasingly more difficult to pass as my legs and back are screaming from standing all day. Once I lock the door behind me, I toss my keys in the glass bowl on the entryway shelf that's positioned against the wall and inhale a relaxing breath.

My studio-style apartment is simple—just how I like it. Open space and minimal furniture with just the bare essentials. The surrounding walls are made of long planks of light-colored knotty alder that covers every inch of the space except for the kitchen that runs the span of the wall on the left.

Gram's small, old, wooden kitchen table is filled with scattered tools and outdoor gear in the corner—things I've been meaning to put away for some time now. A thin, woven, red-and-cream rug sits in the middle of the wood floor—my attempt to break up all the brown—and my rustic-framed bed is settled on the right where the structure looks like it was carved out specifically for just the bed and the two nightstands on either side of it.

I'm tempted to fall directly into my bed, but my nightly routine calls to me in a quiet, soothing way. So I cross all the way to the sliding door that opens onto my balcony. I flick the light switch on to illuminate the string lights that give off just enough light to see my way to the futon, but not enough to attract a sea of bugs to the screen.

The guitar sits on the stand next to the couch. My fingers twitch at the sight of it, offering a reprieve from the busy day, just as it does every night. I pick it up and settle onto the cushions, lazily strumming at the strings while the mosquitos and fireflies offer a buzzing serenade in return.

NINE
Blair

I push the white 'I heart Ruby Lodge' coffee mug into the gravelly sand next to me before wrapping my arms over my bent knees. I sink into the urge to watch the waves for as long as I can. Having my morning coffee on the ground by the shore these last few days is something that I've come to look forward to. Not exactly in a 'this view is breathtaking; I'm really enjoying this' kind of way, but in a 'I guess I'd rather look at this than the taupe-painted wall of the kitchen' kind of way. It's the slightly better of the two options. One that's at least somewhat calming.

Regardless, I think this morning ritual has been the best part about this retreat—aside from Shirley's home-cooking—and I might actually miss it come tomorrow morning when I wake up in my Chicago apartment.

"Morning, Blair!" Stacy calls from behind me.

"Hi, Stacy." I twist and shield my eyes from the glare of the morning sun to look back at where she stands on the porch of her cabin.

"Ready for another floatplane adventure today?" she asks with a smirk.

"I don't think I'll ever be fully ready for that. I am ready to head home, though." The comfort of my own bed and the quiet life I lead in our apartment is majorly enticing and was the sole motivating factor for getting all the way out of bed this morning.

"Me too. I'm ready for fewer bugs." She swats at a fly that landed on her calf. "I'll see you over there."

She grabs her luggage and heads along the trail as I make my way back inside my cabin. I wash the mug quickly before returning it to the cabinet where I found it.

Making one last sweeping gaze over the entirety of the cabin, I step outside and pull the front door shut behind me. While grabbing my luggage from the porch, I pause when my eyes catch on the number four on the door frame. I run my fingertips over the black metal number—my way of bidding the cabin farewell, I suppose.

I breathe in the pine-scented air and make my way down the steps and onto the trail. The crunching of my tennis shoes on the gravel echoes into the trees as I walk along the leaf-riddled path. Up ahead, just past the cabins, my coworkers are scattered about. Some are already on the dock by the floatplane, and some are lingering on the lodge's deck.

Paul stands right in the middle of the grassy hill next to Graham and Shirley, who are both holding trays of what looks like an assortment of food. As they seem to have been the past couple days, Graham and Shirley are a welcome sight.

"Good morning, Blair. You'll be in this next shuttle, which will be taking off in about twenty minutes," Paul says with a grin and the unmistakable cheesy look of a proud father who just successfully planned and executed a forced family vacation.

"Great, thanks." I look up to find Graham's blue eyes watching me. The calmness behind them lures me in, and I hold his gaze.

"Morning," he says quietly with a dip of his head.

"Good morning," I say back. His smile further puts me at ease, and I suddenly feel grateful for finding an unexpected friendship with him here. Maybe I will miss more than just a couple things about this place. Perhaps I should come back with Annie someday to visit Graham and Shirley.

But really, why? What's the point?

"Shirley made donuts and croissants from scratch this morning. Take one for the road if you want." He holds out his tray.

"I tried to make a variety of donuts," Shirley pipes in. "There's maple, sprinkled, coconut crusted, cinnamon twist, and chocolate frosted."

"Wow, these look amazing, Shirley. How can I possibly choose?"

"I won't tell if you take more than one," she says with a wink.

"You might want to eat them now if you get queasy in small planes," Graham suggests.

"Noted." I decide on a coconut-crusted one, and out of the corner of my eye, I see Stacy and others starting to board. "It was really nice meeting you both."

Shirley smiles with a nod. I lock eyes with Graham, holding his gaze for a heartbeat. He opens his mouth and then shuts it, as if there's something more sitting on the tip of his tongue, but he can't quite decide what to say. Finally, he settles for a simple, "Likewise."

The walk across the creaky dock feels like it takes much less time than when I first arrived here, and before I know it, I'm popping the last sugary bite of the donut into my mouth before handing my luggage off and ducking into the plane. Squeezing into a window seat, I get situated and put my earbuds in, the view of the lodge holding my gaze as the plane starts to slowly move across the water.

"I'm home!" I call out as I push open the door of my apartment. Silence and the faint drum of the bathroom fan down the hall is all that echoes back. I can't remember it ever being this sterile and cold, but that's exactly how the apartment feels at this moment. Its stainless-steel fixtures and metallic accents now seem harsh against the slate-gray walls, which feel like they're ever so slightly closing in. I've always been indifferent when it came to this place I call home, but now it's like I'm looking at it through a different lens, immediately picking up on these small perceptions of things that feel off about it.

Fatigue weighs heavy on my bones from the long travel day, and I pinch the bridge of my nose where a dull headache has pressed behind my eyes for the last few hours.

I've barely taken two steps past the foyer when Barry comes barreling out of our bedroom, yanking on the tie around his neck. For a brief millisecond, I wonder if maybe things with him will feel different through this new lens too. If maybe absence made either of our hearts grow fonder and yearn for a deeper connection.

"Hey," he says breathily. "I've gotta head back to the office." His impatient tone is almost jarring and brings me right back to reality—the notion squashed before it ever even manifested as a real hope.

"Right now?"

"Yup." He plants a kiss on my temple as he passes by, grabbing his briefcase off the floor by the door.

"For how long?"

"Not sure. Don't wait up." The rough slam of the door causes me to flinch. I wait for the feeling of disappointment to hit, but it doesn't come; just the familiar emptiness that ruminates inside me—and throughout every corner of these walls.

So stupid to think it would be different. This is the kind of love you deserve. It's the only kind you've ever known.

I haul my heavy luggage down the hallway and drop it all in a pile just inside our closet. Everything inside the closet is neat and tidy, with not even a sock out of place. My bags look big and clunky from where they lay against the wall, but I'm too exhausted to unpack right now.

Leaving everything where it is, I drag myself to the bathroom, where I turn on the shower head. When the steam starts billowing out above the glass door, I undress and slide in. Although rinsing off the germs and grime from my travel day was my initial intention of this shower, I don't immediately reach for the soap. Instead, I stand under the sharp stream of water and just be, letting it batter against almost every surface of my body.

I often come in here and zone out under the water, finding comfort in the simple act of feeling something—anything—touching my skin. Each pelt of water pathetically serves as a reminder that I'm alive and not just a hollow vessel. Occasionally, it helps to wake up my body from its tired, robotic state—tonight, it doesn't.

Stay here. Drown under the water.

After several long minutes, I force myself back out into the cold bathroom and get dressed into an oversized sweatshirt and a pair of leggings before shuffling back down the hallway. I pass by a large gray print of the Chicago skyline that hangs on the wall and the small bookshelf filled with both of our law books, again noting how they look different somehow. They feel different.

Once in the kitchen, I fill up and turn on the electric kettle that sits in the corner. I pull a chamomile tea bag out from the tea drawer and make myself a cup, adding a squeeze of honey at the very end for some added sweetness.

The pile of mail stacked neatly next to the fridge catches my attention, and I thumb through it, but the bills and junk mail don't hold my attention. Instead, I take my tea and wander to the large picture window that looks out over the noisy city, hyper-focusing on the cyclical flashes of the streetlights below.

I sip my tea, watching the cars as they pass, listening to the faint noise of the air conditioning kicking on and off. I'm in a robotic, trance-like state until finally I can't fight the exhaustion anymore and shuffle back down the hallway to my room where a dreamless sleep is calling.

TEN
Blair

"How many days do you think I can survive off of granola bars and apples?" Annie asks through my phone as it sits on my bathroom vanity. I have it propped up next to the sink so I can talk to her while I get ready for the day.

"Definitely longer than I could, that's for sure." I tilt my head to the side, leaning toward the mirror to find where to slide an earring in. "I barely survived a two-mile hike in Lake of the Woods."

"Hey, you put in a valiant effort," she says before sighing. "Ugh. I'm only two sweatshirts into packing, and I'm already regretting this backpacking trip, Blair. Why am I even doing this?"

"The things we do for love, huh?" I tease my roots with my fingers and stand back to assess myself in the mirror, still not satisfied with how I look. I feel like a fraud underneath the freshly tailored pants, silk blouse, and flawlessly curled hair—a perfectly polished pretense to the outside world that hides the desolate shell of a person underneath.

Why do you even try? You look ridiculous. Everyone can see right through you.

I force myself to move out of the bathroom and away from my intruding thoughts, spritzing myself with perfume on the way.

Barry left before sunrise, so the apartment is quiet. Each click of my heels echoes against the tile floor of the hallway. In the kitchen, I head immediately for my espresso maker, keeping the connection with Annie open, even though we've both gone silent. I find comfort in the simple fact that she's breathing on the other line, and although I'm starkly aware of how little I bring to the table of relationships, I at least hope that I offer the same sort of comfort to her.

"What does your day look like?" she eventually asks, just as I'm pouring steamed milk into my latte.

"The usual. I have a busy day at the office and then probably just a low-key evening at home. I have a bunch of files to go through that I probably won't finish at work."

"Sounds fascinating."

"Always is." My tone is thick with sarcasm as I grab my business tote bag and step out into the hallway, locking the apartment door behind me. I blow out a steadying breath, closing my eyes and pressing my forehead against the door.

Ten long hours until you can come home.

Letting the truth of that statement sink in, I repeat it several times before pushing myself away from the door and down the hallway.

"Hey, let me know what evenings work for you after I get back from my trip. I'll plan to come into the city for a girls' night. I think we're about due for a taco-and-margarita night, don't you think?" she asks.

"Absolutely." I try to ignore the gnawing pit in my stomach when I think of how I'm going to possibly manage not being in touch with her while she's gone. Our daily phone calls are sometimes the only thing that keeps me going. "But no karaoke bar this time. You know that stuff is pure torture for me."

She barks a laugh. "I'm not sure I can make a promise like that."

"Annie," I warn.

"Listen, I've gotta run," she says just as I push the down arrow on the elevator. "Eric's taking me on a day hike to train. Call me later?"

"Will do. Good luck. Try not to sprain anything." I slide my phone into my purse and watch the arrow on the dial above the elevator door as it gradually rises past each number, getting closer and closer to my floor.

Without the distraction of talking to Annie, the stale air inside the elevator suddenly feels too thick, and my heart starts pounding a touch faster than it has all morning. The entire ride down, the only thought that goes through my head is how small this elevator truly is. A shiver runs down the back of my neck, making me feel claustrophobic and cramped, as if the wall is physically breathing hot air against my skin.

By the time the elevator door opens, my chest feels heavy, and each step feels like walking through mud. It feels like an eternity and a massive amount of effort to get to the entrance doors of my building.

The breeze that hits my face the moment I open the door and step out onto the sidewalk helps to quell some of the built-up pressure. However, instead of fresh air greeting me, it's cigarette smoke that fills my lungs. I stifle a cough and pick up my pace, falling into place with a sea of people walking briskly toward their morning destinations. I curve to the outside of the sidewalk, managing to avoid the smoker.

After a quick five-minute walk across a handful of busy intersections and past several skyscrapers, I hook a left into my office building. The lobby is quiet and sterile, without a single person in sight. I take the elevator up to the ninth floor that houses Gibson Law. As the elevator door dings and slides open, I dig deep and summon a happy guise, painting a smile on my face as I step out.

"Morning, Blair!" Mandy, our receptionist, says cheerfully when I approach her desk. Faint music plays in the background, barely heard over the distant sound of several phones simultaneously ringing from their respective offices down the hall.

"Good morning, Mandy," I reply with a polite smile, taking the message slips from her outstretched hand and turning right down the hallway. My office is dark and quiet, and the fluorescent lights feel jarring when I flip them on. I've barely just set my latte down when Jamie, my paralegal, knocks on the open door.

"Knock, knock. How was the retreat?" she asks, sliding into one of my black leather chairs.

"It was great," I say flatly. Our relationship has always been mostly surface level, so I don't feel the need to divulge details, and as expected, she doesn't ask for any more.

"What do you need from me today?" She leans forward in the chair with her notepad and pen poised, ready for anything I'll throw at her.

We spend the next twenty minutes going over case files, and after giving her a list of tasks I need her help with, she slips back out, leaving me in the quiet of my office. I power on my computer for the day and zone out at the black screen while it boots up, listening to the buzzing sound as it comes to life.

I have mixed feelings about working here at Gibson Law. I like practicing law—at least, I think I do. And I like my colleagues well enough. But as with most things, my work life isn't exactly fulfilling, serving primarily as a means to an end to get through the days. I've considered going to another firm, but I don't even know if I'm capable of feeling fulfilled in general, so without that guarantee, I just don't have the motivation to make a career change. I wouldn't even know where to start. And the thought of making those kinds of decisions causes a deep-rooted, anxious reaction. That particular mountain of finding a rewarding job seems just as insurmountable as ending my relationship with Barry. So, I'll stay, complacent and indifferent, just like in every other area of my life.

I flip through my messages that have built up since I was last in the office. I organize them in order of importance and then set them next to the phone before signing into my email inbox. I have over fifty unread emails—actually not terrible for being away the last portion of last week. I was expecting to have a lot more. There are a jumble of client emails, notices from fellow lawyers, and a few junk emails scattered in. The very first one at the top of my inbox, sent at five-thirty this morning, catches my eye. An email from Isaac with the subject line that reads *The Gavel Gang.*

With a smirk, I click it open and skim the group email that he sent to all four of us. Inside, he explains in detail how we must heed the purpose of the retreat and keep the close connection that we forged while there. Our bond must remain strong. Apparently, he's committing to sending a weekly email to stay in touch, given all of our busy schedules. The very last line at the bottom of the email reads, *Fun Fact: Water skiing was invented in Minnesota in 1922.*

Mildly amused by his antics, I shake my head and huff a small laugh. I guess I was right about being a member of The Gavel Gang indefinitely. I flag it as unread, planning to respond to it later, and then get started on answering the rest of them.

ELEVEN
Graham

My phone buzzes through the back pocket of my jeans, sending a loud vibrating noise through the otherwise quiet air. I softly curse the fact that I didn't silence it before starting on this shrub project, but I guess now is as good a time as any to take a break. I still need to eat the lunch that Shirley shoved in my hands when I left the lodge an hour ago. If I come back without having eaten it, she won't stop following me until she sees me eat with her very own eyes. I won't make that mistake again.

Peeling off my work gloves, I take a seat on the top porch step of cabin one and grab the paper sack sitting by the front door. I take a long swig from my water bottle and allow myself two bites of the ham-and-mustard sandwich in peace before calling Sydney back.

"Graham!" My sister picks up in the middle of the first ring.

"Sydney," I reply in greeting.

"You didn't answer when I called earlier, so my guess is that you're either buried deep in paperwork, or you're up to your arms in mud, doing some sort of manual labor—my guess is that you're muddy?"

I glance down at the dirt smudges that cover my jeans and the gardening tools that are spread out on the grassy ground in front of me.

"You know me well." I finish off the last bite of the sandwich and unwrap a chocolate chip cookie from the wax wrapper. The heat of the day has kept the cookie warm, and I lick a dab of chocolate that's melted onto my thumb. I suppose there are worse things than Shirley doting on me.

"How are you?"

The question makes me pause. Sydney calls to check in at least twice a week, which I really do appreciate, but I never know how to respond. Aside from the financial state of the lodge that I have no intention of sharing with her, nothing is ever new. The answer is always the same.

"Same old—working and sleeping. On repeat."

"That sounds incredibly boring, actually," she teases. "I don't know how you're going to find me a sister-in-law if you don't venture into town every once in a while. You gotta dust off those dancing shoes at some point."

"I don't have time for that, and you know it." I huff. The only reason I ever leave the island is to sit by Mom's bedside for a night or two. I hardly have enough time for my friends these days, let alone finding someone to date. My last relationship ended shortly before I moved out here. It's hard to form any sort of connection with someone when the only people visiting this place are our temporary guests and the part-time cabin owners that are spread out around the island.

"Seriously, though, do you need help? Should I come up there?" Worry seeps into her tone—partly for me and the lodge's well-being—but I know her well enough to know that a part of that worry is that I'll actually ask her to come.

"It's all good here, Syd. Promise," I say, convincing yet another member of my family that things are going well, even though it's a flat-out lie.

Sydney moved down to the Twin Cities after high school for college and found a job pretty quickly after graduation at an architecture firm where she's been ever since. She used to visit pretty often, but she hasn't come home once since Mom started forgetting who she is. She says it's because she's too busy, but I know what she really means—it's too hard.

"How are things with you? Have you checked your engine oil recently?" I ask.

"I think I'm at twenty-six percent."

"Promise me you won't get all the way down to zero before going in for an oil change." She's the most stubborn, independent woman I know and can clearly take care of herself just fine, but that doesn't stop me from being her big brother and taking that role seriously.

"Pinky promise." The line goes quiet for a beat. "How's Mom?"

"You should come up and see for yourself," I suggest gently, as I do in every single conversation we have.

A heavy sigh responds. "You know I can't."

Can't or won't? I don't ask the question out loud, but it hangs heavy in the air nonetheless.

"She's about the same," I finally say. "Doesn't know who I am. It's hit or miss whether she recognizes Dad or not."

She sighs again in my ear as I try to swallow down a ball of emotion at the mention of Mom and her condition. As hard as it can be to do, I much prefer to keep my head down, pushing forward with my responsibilities and not getting too caught up in the grief of watching Mom disappear before my eyes, but every once in a while, it catches up to me, especially when I'm talking to Syd.

"Anyway," I say, clearing my throat. "You're staying out of trouble? Any guys I need to have a brotherly chat with? Rough 'em up a little bit?"

"No." She huffs a laugh before redirecting the conversation, completely disregarding my inquiry. "What are you working on anyway? I didn't ask."

"We needed new shrubs around one of the cabins. The other ones were dead. I'm trying to get them planted before our next set of guests come tomorrow, but it's proving to be a pain-in-the-ass job."

"Why don't you have Jimmy come help you out? Does he still work for you?"

"Not really. I can handle it." I also can't afford to pay him or anyone else other than the skeleton staff I have now, but I don't want her knowing that. Thankfully, she doesn't press on it.

"Who are your guests that are coming in? Are they locals?"

"No, it's a group of businessmen from North Carolina coming for a fishing weekend."

She hums in response. "Well, as fascinating as it is to hear about your life up there, I've gotta go. I just wanted to check in. Please call if you need me, okay?"

"Will do, Syd. Love you."

"Love you back."

After collecting my lunch garbage, I finish planting the last of the shrubs. Then I take the wheelbarrow that's filled with a mixture of the old plants and dirt and push it behind the lodge to where the shed is. Once I discard everything out of the wheelbarrow, I tuck it back where it belongs inside and reach for a ladder that hangs on the wall above it.

I tie the ladder to the back of the ATV using bungee ropes and then drive down the trail to cabin seven, where I spend the next two hours replacing a few shingles on the roof that came loose after the thunderstorm that ripped through here two nights ago. All the while, I wonder if it's even worth it to keep maintaining all fifteen cabins if I'll be forced to shut some of them down soon anyway. There are plenty of other tasks that I could be doing, so the thought that I might be wasting my time sickens me.

It might be a waste of effort on my part, but I truly don't know any other way. Until I make a final decision one way or the other, I'll keep doing what needs to be done to keep the whole place running. I'm almost positive it's what Dad would do if he were in my shoes.

After finishing the roof and getting the shed put back together, I head back to the lodge. My shoulders ache, feeling the stress of both the physical labor and the weight of my worries pressing down on them.

"There you are," Shirley says from the deck when I round the corner.

"Hey," I call out, wiping sweat and dirt from my forehead as I climb the stairs.

"No offense, but you look about as good as you smell." She crinkles her nose and takes a step back.

"None taken." I force a weak smile. "Thanks again for the lunch. It was delicious."

Her gaze scans every inch of me, and if I was less exhausted, I might be uncomfortable with her scrutiny. But if anyone gets a glimpse of me when my walls are down, when I'm stressed and exhausted, it's Shirley. She sees too much of what goes on around here for me to be able to lie to her about anything.

"What are you still doing on the island anyway? I thought I told you to go back home for the night?" I ask.

"Oh, I wanted to get a head start on some baking." She shrugs. I can see right through the lie, but I do appreciate that she stuck around. She doesn't like to leave me here when I'm by myself, and I admit that it's nice to have someone to talk to.

"Some baking, huh?" I eye her suspiciously.

"Yes. It's none of your business."

I chuckle as she gestures toward the lodge.

"How about you go take a shower, and I'll whip you up something to eat?"

"That sounds amazing, actually. I'm starving." I hold the door open for her and then follow her inside to get cleaned up.

TWELVE
Blair

"So, then I asked my neighbor, Conrad, if he could please check on Sprinkles, my Pomeranian, for me, and you know what he said?" Cassidy asks, taking a bite of her salad from where she sits on the other side of my desk. She's looking at me expectantly with eager eyes. Apparently, she agrees with Isaac's assumption that we should be lifelong best friends, because she's invited herself to have lunch in my office nearly every day since we've been back from Minnesota. And by 'have lunch,' I mean me nodding robotically while she rambles on about the latest happenings in her life.

"What did he say?" I have absolutely zero interest in how he responded, but I ask anyway. Regardless of my mood, I'm more than capable of being cordial and kind, especially when she's making an effort to be friendly toward me.

"No." She throws her hands up in the air incredulously. "Can you believe that? He said no. I don't mean this in a braggy kind of way, but not a lot of people in my life say no to me."

She lifts her shoulders in a tentative shrug. "I mean, granted, I was only gone for twenty minutes at that point—and I admit that I may over-ask him for favors at times—but honestly, the nerve..."

"The nerve," I agree flatly, leaning back in my chair, having already finished my own salad. I wonder if, in another life, I could have been the kind of person who matches her energy. If I could have been someone who was as carefree and happy-go-lucky as Cassidy is, because I am definitely not that person in this lifetime. I'm afraid a quiet listener is the most that she'll get out of me today.

"Anyway, we have volleyball practice tonight, and I'll probably take her with me in her carrier this time instead of leaving her in my apartment."

"That's probably a good idea."

Not even her chipper storytelling can squeeze a smile out of me today. Being stuck in my office building this week has been putting me in a funk, even more so than usual. I've been glued to my desk, spending long days and late nights working on a new workers' comp litigation. Every single second I spend here has me feeling more and more certain that there's not nearly enough oxygen in this building, and the walls are, without a doubt, closing in. My chest is chronically tight, and there's a ruminating sense of melancholy that sits just under my skin, reaching every nook and cranny of my body, never ceasing.

It doesn't help that Barry has been gone from the apartment just as much as I have. Aside from a brief conversation yesterday morning, I've hardly seen him at all. To make matters even worse, Annie just left for her backpacking trip this week, so I haven't had a chance to connect with her at all.

You're completely alone. No one around you cares.

I wouldn't be surprised if Cassidy can notice the sullenness behind my eyes, and I feel a twinge of guilt at the thought alone. The last thing I want is for her to think that I'm being rude or that I'm not interested. But I just can't summon the extra energy today, as much as I'd really like to for her. As if she can read my thoughts, she closes her salad lid shut with a click and jumps out of the chair.

"Anyway, I've gotta get back. No rest for this paralegal." She blows a kiss in my direction and practically bounces to the door.

"Good luck with Sprinkles," I manage to call out right before she disappears out of my office.

After vowing to check in with Cassidy tomorrow about the Sprinkles saga, I focus back on my computer and get back to work. The next hour is spent typing away, getting lost in the mundane world of personal injury law, working on my new case, and preparing a final closing statement for a case that didn't end up going all the way to trial.

At half past two o'clock, my office phone rings. I answer as if on auto-pilot, picking it up immediately.

"Blair Williams," I mumble, continuing to type away at the document on my screen.

"Hey, Blair." My whole body freezes at the voice. It takes me a millisecond to place it, but once I do, my brows furrow with confusion.

"Graham?"

"Yeah, uh…sorry to bother you. I Googled your law firm to find your number. I hope that's okay. I didn't really know who else to call." His voice is thick with tension, making my stomach uneasy.

"What's up?" I ask warily.

"I was hoping you could give me some legal advice, actually."

"Words I never want to hear from a friend," I say, leaning back in my chair, curious what he could possibly need from me.

"Yeah," he snickers nervously. "So there was an incident out on the docks this week."

"Tell me more." I instinctively reach for a notepad and pen.

"We had a group of guests here this past week, and one of them slipped and fell when walking out to the fishing boats. Broke his wrist, from what I understand."

"Let me guess, he's threatening to sue?"

"I think he already has. I just opened the mail, and I got a summons of some sort. Apparently, it's my fault that he's a clumsy idiot. From what I can gather, he's blaming his fall on the fact that it was raining and the dock was slippery. He's suing Ruby Lodge for medical expenses and emotional distress."

"You're kidding me." I've come across some ridiculous lawsuits over the course of my career, but every once in a while, I can't help but judge the character and greediness of others.

"Wish I was. It was barely drizzling out, I swear. I don't know what to do here, Blair. We can't afford to go through a lawsuit. The lodge is barely holding on as it is."

I pick up on the rising panic in his voice.

"Hey, it's okay. No need to worry yet. We can figure this out. Let's gather some information. Can we do that?"

"Sure." His voice is slightly muffled, and I can practically envision him running a hand over his jaw.

"Let's see, when was the last time the dock was repaired? Can you prove that it was in good shape at the time of the incident?"

"I mean, possibly. I'd have to dig through my paperwork. But most of the repairs around here are made by me. I don't necessarily have documentation."

"I don't suppose you have surveillance or video feed around the lodge?"

That earns me a laugh. "Blair, I can barely afford to keep my bartender on staff let alone install a camera system."

"Okay." I smirk at his self-deprecating tone while scribbling notes on the notepad.

"You know what? Actually, we do have some trail cams set up around the property to document the wildlife. There's a chance one might have captured some images of the fall."

"That's a good start. Can you look through those?"

"Sure. Ugh, this is the last thing I need right now," he mumbles quietly, and I'm not entirely sure if he's talking to me or himself. "I'll have to ask Dad if he can come help run the lodge for a few days so I can deal with this."

Guilt tugs at my chest at the mere thought of his dad being pulled away from his mom, given what I know about their situation.

"Listen, I have to be in court tomorrow, but after that my caseload frees up a bit, and I would be able to work remotely for a little while... Why don't I come up there and see if I can help sort this out?"

"Oh, no. I couldn't ask you to do that," he starts. But the thought of flying up there and traveling to Takini Island again...while it does sound physically exhausting to get there, it's also definitely my most appealing option at the moment. The lure of the quiet island feels strong.

Yes, do it. Go disappear up there.

"Honestly, Graham. I wouldn't mind at all. In fact, I miss the fresh air. I, um...I kinda need some right about now."

He's quiet on the other line, and for a second I wonder if we got disconnected.

"Are you sure?" he asks quietly.

"Yes," I insist immediately.

"I don't know how I'll be able to pay you, Blair," he admits.

"Don't even worry about that right now. I'll see you in a couple of days. In the meantime, why don't you fax me a copy of the summons and then start collecting trail-cam images to see if you can get a visual of what happened."

"I can do that," he says. "And Blair?"

"Yeah?"

"Thank you." He says the words slowly and vehemently.

"You're welcome. Graham?"

"Yeah?"

"Is cabin four available?"

THIRTEEN
Blair

The sport-craft ferry boat pulls away from the dock in Baudette, and I clutch my backpack to my chest, tightening my core to hold myself steady with the movement from the waves.

This is pathetic.

Why are you putting this much of an effort in? Going there is a little extreme, isn't it?

I blink a few times, attempting to bury Barry's irritating words. Then I push my feet against the floor of the boat to further steady myself, gripping the seat cushion with one hand. The vinyl seat feels cold on the backs of my legs, even through the thin material of my leggings.

"Which island are you heading to?" the woman sitting next to me asks, yelling over the almost deafening sound of the motor and the whistling wind that blows through my hair.

"Takini!" I shout, cupping my hand over the outside of my mouth to thwart the wind. "How about you?"

"We have a cabin home on Oak Island!" she yells back. "We'll be there for a week. It's our annual end-of-the-summer family trip." She gestures at the man sitting next to her and the two teenage girls beyond him, each of them clutching their own backpacks and holding weekender bags between their feet. There's a plastic bin settled off to the side of the boat that contains boxes of crackers, cereal, and a few loaves of bread. The girls both have earbuds in and matching scowls. My guess is this is a forced family trip.

"That's amazing. How fun to get to come here every year," I reply kindly with a smile.

"Oh, we have the best memories," she says before gesturing at the water. "We're lucky the lake is calm today. There have been days when this boat ride has taken us hours to get across because the waves were so big. You just never know what this lake will be like."

"Yikes." I cringe. "I was hoping this would be a better, calmer option than the floatplane, so I'm glad to hear that."

She nods in agreement just as the captain shifts into gear, ramping up our speed to go even faster. I make a futile attempt to hold my hair back from whipping in the wind, but I quickly realize it's a lost cause and let it free.

For the next half hour, the boat takes us across the open water while the captain points out the names of the other islands that we pass along the way. Some islands are large, with lodges and cabins tucked between the sea of trees that grow tall and wide. Some are small and uninhabited, nothing but a mixture of boulders, trees, and foliage sticking up from the middle of the water.

The outline of Takini Island comes into view long before we reach it. It starts out as a tiny shadow of trees on the horizon, and each dip of the boat brings us closer to it. Eventually, the captain slows to an idle as we approach the docks of the lodge. Graham, dressed casually in jeans, a gray T-shirt, and a backward baseball hat, comes bounding out of the lodge to meet us as we approach. He smiles broadly, the line of his scruffy face spreading wide, accenting a dimple ridge on his cheek that I haven't noticed before. I admit, it feels good to see his friendly face.

"Hey!" He waves, and I smile as he grabs the side of the boat to help it line up with the dock.

"Here you go, ma'am. Enjoy your stay!" the captain says while Graham offers a hand to help me climb out.

"Thank you so much. And nice to meet you guys. Enjoy your vacation!" I say before the ferry boat pulls away and heads off toward the next island. I turn to Graham, and our gazes connect. He gives me an awkward, hesitant hug—probably unsure about our level of friendship at this point. I loosely pat between his shoulders with my free hand with the same uncertainty, getting a waft of his woodsy, spiced scent. I don't remember him smelling this good when I was here last. But then again, I was never exactly this close to him.

"I can't thank you enough for coming up here," he says against my ear before pulling back.

"It's my pleasure...truly." I nod. "It's good to be back."

He takes my bag from my hand and I fall into step beside him, a light breeze kissing my face as we walk off the docks. I take a deep breath of smoky air, wondering how it's possible to have missed the way an island smells.

"How was your flight?"

"Uneventful. I took a nap, so I'd say it was a win."

"I can never sleep on planes. Can't turn my brain off that easily." His low voice snickers.

"That's one of my talents." I mean it as a sarcasm, but I silently acknowledge the deeper reality of not having much to turn off.

It's always off.

"We've got an empty lodge currently. New guests will be arriving tomorrow, but it's pretty quiet around here today."

"So, is it just you here, then?" I ask, looking around at the vacant grounds.

"And Shirley. She's inside somewhere. She lives in Angle Inlet and travels back and forth, sometimes daily, but lately she's been staying more often. I think it's one of her life's missions to make sure I'm well fed."

"I can see that. I'm actually looking more forward to seeing her than you." I hope he doesn't mind my teasing.

He gives an amused shrug. "I actually get that a lot. She's definitely the heart of this place."

I smile, nodding in agreement.

"But it's perfect timing. We should be able to go over the case without too many distractions before they all get here tomorrow. I don't want to take up too much of your time."

We step off the dock, and Graham turns to me, pulling a key from his pocket. "Cabin four is all ready for you. I figured you might want to get settled first?"

"That would be great, actually. I'd love to drop all of my stuff off. I can meet you in the lodge in a half hour?"

"I'll make us some coffee." He dips his baseball hat-clad head and walks off. I take the familiar path past the quaint log cottages, the wind lightly rustling at the leaves of the trees above.

Cabin four looks just as I left it—a quiet dwelling, standing firm with its strong wooden frame, yet still simple and meek in appearance surrounded by towering trees. The wooden bench gently taps the exterior of the house as it sways with the wind, and the same step makes a creak when I climb the stairs. Inside, I set my bags on the kitchen table and breathe in a full breath, attempting to ease the weight that's now found permanent residence on my chest. I take a small amount of comfort in the fact that everything looks untouched and just as I left it.

Leaving my bags where they are on the table, I head back outside and have a seat on the bench, gently stilling its movement. Without any guests moving around the resort grounds, it's almost eerily quiet. The only noise that fills the air is the chirping of birds as they flutter in the trees above and the sound of my own breath as I let out a sigh.

The lake looks infinitely vast, with a pair of seagulls flying above the rolling waves out in the distance. It looks beautiful and poetic all at once. It's a picturesque scenery with no one else around to see it. The beginnings of tears form at the corners of my eyes, emotion tugging at my throat for no apparent reason other than it's easily accessible.

The emptiness in my soul and the sadness that surrounds it comes all the way to the surface, threatening to spill over. Maybe I should just disappear up here in the middle of nowhere. Stay on this island and forget the rest of the world. Lead a quiet, insignificant life among the trees.

Nobody would even notice.

Maybe I could somehow convince Graham to let me stay in cabin four forever and only come out when my body eventually screams that it needs nourishment. I could wander around the property when my muscles ache from lying in bed too much. No unnecessary human interaction aside from the strangers that come and go. That's a life I could live up here.

Acutely aware of how my brain works and how easily I can spiral, I clear my throat and shake my head, refusing to sink deeper into my own self-pity party when there's work to do. So I allow myself one more moment of quiet sadness, and then I fight like hell to push myself off the bench and head toward the main cabin to meet Graham.

FOURTEEN
Graham

"Alright, what have you figured out in the last few days?" Blair asks, taking the mug that I offer to her. She leans over the coffee table in the library, where I have the paperwork spread out, and I take a seat on the couch opposite her. The dark circles under her eyes look more prominent than they did the last time I saw her, and another wave of guilt hits me that she traveled all this way just for me.

"Well, there's one trail cam that has a partial view of the docks, but unfortunately, it's not on the section where he fell." I scoot to the edge of the couch to be able to reach the papers.

"Did it capture anything at the time of the incident?"

"I printed out a few images." I fan out some of the paperwork and pull out a few pictures from the bottom of the stack. "But they're only pictures of him and his friends walking toward the dock before he fell."

"Okay," she says, looking them over. "And what did we figure out about the proof of the dock's condition?"

"Well, that's where I'm stumped. I replaced a broken board myself a few months back, but before that, it hadn't needed any repairs for a few years. I honestly don't remember the last time we had anything new installed."

"Do you have the receipt for your purchase of the board or the tools you needed for it?"

"I used my own tools, but I'm pretty sure I have the receipt for the board. I save all my receipts in a file cabinet in my office."

"Good. We'll want to find that." She nods, taking a sip of the coffee. "Has the lodge ever been sued previously?"

That one I have to pause and think about. "I don't think so, but I can ask my dad if anything ever happened when my grandparents owned it. I'm sure I would have heard about it, but it wouldn't hurt to ask."

"That would be great. If anything like this has happened before, that could hurt our case."

"I'll talk to him tonight."

"Show me what else you have here," she says.

We spend the next hour going through the mess of paperwork and talking strategy, barely lifting our heads until Shirley's shadow eclipses the doorway.

"You two plan to stop and eat dinner anytime soon?" She leans against the doorframe.

"Hi, Shirley." Blair smiles at her warmly.

"Nice to see you back, sweetie. How about I whip you two up a couple roast beef hoagies?"

"That would be great. Thank you," I say. When she backs out of the library, Blair nods her head in the direction of the front entrance.

"Do you mind taking me to the dock and walking me through exactly what happened? Allegedly, of course."

"Sure thing." I lead her out of the empty lodge, across the grass to the docks.

"And you didn't actually witness what happened, right?" she asks as we step onto the first wooden board.

"Right. I was inside, but one of my guides was in the boat and watched the whole thing."

"Okay. I might want to talk to him. No rush on that, though."

"Anything you need." I nod before pointing at a specific dock section. "So, the group of guys were walking this way toward the boat that was tied up in that slip. Somewhere along the way—from what I gathered, it should be about here—he tripped over his own two feet and fell. I'm assuming he put his hands out to catch his fall, hence the broken wrist."

"Okay." She scans every last inch of the dock. "So, as I mentioned earlier, the first big step is to answer the interrogatory questions that they sent, and then we'll compile questions of our own to send to them."

"What kinds of questions would we need to ask?"

"Anything and everything that pertains to the case. Medical records and diagnoses from wherever he went to be treated. We'll also need a lot of random information, such as the exact shoes he had on—questions that might seem insignificant but will help to build our case. We don't want to leave any stone unturned."

My slow processing of the information must be visible on my face, as she smiles.

"Don't worry, I can do this in my sleep," she says reassuringly.

"So, I'm in good hands, then?"

"The best," she says sarcastically, but it falls a bit flat.

"Dinner's ready!" Shirley calls, setting two plates on a table in the middle of the front patio before disappearing back inside.

"After you." I gesture with my outstretched hand for her to go first and then follow behind all the way up the stairs.

"This looks amazing," she says breathily as I settle into the wooden chair across from her.

"Shirley knows how to spoil me."

Something flashes across her face that looks a lot like longing or maybe even envy. She takes a bite, and I watch her, my gaze slowly studying her features, from the wisps of chocolate-brown hair that hang out of her ponytail to frame her face, to the small scar above her left brow. As put together as she looks, she also looks weary in every sense of the word. Again, guilt creeps into my chest. This is probably the last place she wants to be right now.

"I'm sorry again for dragging you away from home," I say quietly.

She flicks her tired eyes up to meet mine. "Like I said before, it's no problem at all."

I nod slowly, accepting her words. Just the right blend of curiosity and bravery inside me rises to the surface. "Do you have a significant other back at home?"

Her brows lift in surprise, and her lower lip drops open slightly, clearly taken aback by my question. I suddenly feel stupid for blurting it out in the first place.

"That's none of my business. You don't have to answer that." I bite into my sandwich to keep from further embarrassing myself.

"No, it's okay." She insists before clearing her throat. "I do. His name is Barry."

I try to ignore the sudden knot that forms deep in my stomach. Disappointment swirls there, even though the logical part of my brain knows I have no right or claim to her. I never did.

"He a lawyer too?" I slide a sweet potato fry in my mouth.

"He is. But we work for different firms. He's a corporate lawyer." The way she talks about him coldly—as if he's a distant relative—piques my interest, but I don't want to pry. We finish our meals in a comfortable silence, and then Blair turns in her chair toward the lake.

"I still can't get over this view."

I follow her gaze out at the bay where the lake looks like glass, not a soul or boat in sight except the ones that are tied to my dock. The sun is starting to set off to the left, almost completely eclipsing the tiny shadow of O'Dell Island off in the distance. Grasshoppers have started their quiet nightly buzzing from somewhere in the woods, and the warm evening air has a few wasps flying around the potted flowers on the patio. I scan the property in front of me, and although I agree it is beautiful, all I can see is the amount of work and projects I need to get done.

"Do you do this every night?" she asks, not moving her head from the direction of the water.

"What? Have dinner with my friend-turned-lawyer who is only here because I'm a helpless commoner who knows nothing about law?"

"No." She smiles. "I mean sit out here and watch the sun go down?"

"More or less. Depends on how many guests we have and when I can close down for the night. Most nights, I end up on my balcony with my guitar, serenading the flies."

"You play guitar? Do you sing too?"

"God, no. The few chords I can strum are the extent of my musical abilities."

She nods, leaning her head back on the chair with a lazy smile. I act on the sudden urge to share more.

"My mom gave me the guitar as a birthday present when I turned eighteen. Taught myself how to play a few chords at the time, and then life got too busy to learn any more. I picked it back up a few years ago when Mom got sick. Makes me feel closer to her in a way, I guess."

Her head rolls to the side until she meets my waiting stare. I feel bare at my vulnerability, but she puts me at ease with the way that she tips her mouth up into a soft smile. My admission hangs in the air, but further words don't feel necessary.

We sit quietly, listening to the soft roll of the waves onto the shore, as the sky rapidly darkens. Eventually, it's pitch black, with the soft light from the lodge illuminating our backs.

"I think I'm going to turn in," she says, slowly coming to stand.

"I'll walk you." The lingering guilt that won't go away has me wanting to do everything I possibly can for her while she's here, including walking her to her cabin.

"That's not necessary," she insists.

"Did you finally realize your fear of bears is unwarranted?" I tease, unabashedly using fear to coerce her.

Her eyes widen slightly. "Good point. That would be great. Thank you."

We walk side by side down the gravel path that's lit from the soft glow of string lights draped between the trees. Without guests, the other cabins are dark and lifeless with no lights on, making it an even dimmer than usual walk along the trail. When we reach cabin four, I pause and wait for her to climb the steps. She turns back, her hand resting on the door handle, and my gaze zeroes in on her eyes in the dark.

"Goodnight, Graham."

"Goodnight, Blair."

FIFTEEN
Blair

The door swings shut behind me as I walk into the entryway of the lodge, which is bustling with activity. This is the busiest I've seen this place. I watched at least three boat loads of new guests arrive while I finished my coffee by the shore a few minutes ago.

"Excuse me." I squeeze in between two people who are standing in the long line in front of the vacant welcome desk. Graham is behind the bar in the dining room, rushing back and forth along the span of the counter, his arms stretched in opposite directions. To say he looks frazzled would be an understatement. The tension that holds his shoulders a bit too high is obvious, and his expression is locked with worried concentration.

"Hey!" I lean against the counter. "I wanted to discuss the case, but you look pretty busy. I can come back."

"Ah." He barely glances up, only briefly flicking his gaze my way. "I'm so sorry. I'm swamped. Nita called in sick today, and my other bartender is on his way, but he won't be here for at least an hour. It shouldn't take me too long to get a handle on this, and then I should be able to take a quick breather. Is that okay?"

"No problem at all. Take your time. Can I help with anything?"

"Oh no, I got this under control." He forces a tense smile.

"Okay," I hesitate and linger until he turns his back to me, retreating to help the two gentlemen at the far corner.

I wander the halls and stumble upon the library—the perfect spot to wait. The dim, cozy lighting pulls me in like a moth to a flame until I'm sauntering slowly around the perimeter of the room, brushing my fingertips along the book spines. Every so often, I pause to pull one out to read the back cover. I'm impressed by the options available in this library—everything from thrillers and historical romance to self-help books and autobiographies. I've never been much of a reader, but I like the vibe of this little room. It's warm, snug, and inviting in its own way.

The ding of my phone pulls my attention away from the bizarre synopsis of a psychological thriller, and I unlock my phone to find an email from Isaac. I skim through it, oddly eager to see what his fun fact will be. I find it there at the bottom of the check-in email.

Fun fact: Minnesota has more coastline than the combined states of California, Florida, and Hawaii.

I'm just sliding the phone back into my pocket when movement from the entryway catches my eye. The line of people waiting to be signed in has grown exponentially, now completely out the door. Most of the people are displaying annoyed, impatient expressions. It only takes a millisecond for me to move, and I squeeze my way through guests again to approach a frazzled Graham.

"Hey, what do I need to know about checking people in?" I demand gently.

His gaze darts anxiously toward the long line and then back to me. A line of hesitation runs down the middle of his forehead, and then I watch the exact moment he must realize that he's out of options.

"Inside the second drawer is the booking calendar. Find the guest's name and cabin number. Keys are hanging inside the bottom cabinet door. I can confirm payment info later."

"You got it."

"Thank you," he calls to my back, but I'm already halfway across the room, a new purpose in my step.

"Hi, thank you so much for waiting," I say to the couple behind the desk while I reach for the calendar. "Last name?"

"Ferguson," the woman replies with just the faintest hint of impatience.

"Welcome to Ruby Lodge. Have you been here before?" I run the tip of my pencil down the register to find their name.

"Thank you," she says, her tone only slightly warming up. "Yes, my husband and I come every August on our anniversary weekend. Nothing says 'I love you' like him going fishing while I lounge around on the beach, right?"

"Hey, you promised to come fishing with me this year," her husband chimes in.

"We'll see about that." She smirks.

"Either way, it's sure to be a great getaway." I hand her a key. "You'll be in cabin ten, which is down the trail on the right. Please let us know if you need anything."

"Thank you." They both wave and move aside, allowing the next group to come forward.

"Hi, welcome to Ruby Lodge," I say to the two gentlemen. "Last name?"

"Nelson. Busy place, huh?" the older man replies.

"Must be a good weekend for a getaway, I guess." I find their name and cabin key, then send them on their way.

When the last of the guests are checked in and the line is no more, I walk back into the kitchen, completely uninvited, and tell Shirley to put me to work. I stay there for the next several hours, helping assemble sandwiches to send with the fisherman tomorrow morning and then making food for the dinner buffet. I'm just setting the last tray of food onto the buffet for the guests' dinner when Graham approaches.

"I'm so sorry you got dragged into helping today," he says, his features tight and somber. "That was not my intention when I asked for your help with the case."

I wave him off. "It was my pleasure. It felt good to be useful."

He nods, but I don't think he realizes how my own words echo in my head.

It DID feel good to be useful today.

He looks past my shoulder, out the window behind me, before pinning his gaze on me. "I'm about due for a break. Any chance you'd want to sit by the bonfire out there while you ask your questions?"

As exhausted as I am from all of the interactions and busyness today, there's also a small glimmer of energy ruminating in my core. Maybe it's from feeling productive, doing something other than work, or maybe today has just been a nice distraction from my looping negative thoughts. Either way, it's a feeling that I welcome.

"I'd like that." The very corner of my mouth pulls up into a soft smile.

With a slight dip of his head, he holds his hand out. "After you."

He grabs two wine glasses from behind the bar and hands one to me before grabbing a bottle of wine. The bonfire pit is settled down on the beach, nothing more than a circle made of rocks with wood stacked inside and Adirondack chairs surrounding it. I lower into one that faces the lake and settle back against the hard wood.

I watch patiently as he fills the pit with more sticks and another log of wood. Then he lights it, expertly building a roaring fire in no time.

"Thank you," I say when he fills my glass with Pinot Grigio. He hands it to me before pouring one of his own and claiming the chair next to me.

The sigh that escapes him sounds heavy as he slouches down in the chair. "Alright, what did you want to talk about?"

"I just wanted to touch base about where we're at." I take a sip from my glass and stare into the crackling fire. "I should be able to wrap up our interrogatory question paperwork tomorrow morning. The other party has thirty days to answer their questions, so we'll just have to wait for that. At that time, we'll have more information on when the deposition will be."

"Okay. So you'll have everything you'll need after tomorrow? For now, anyway?"

"Yes. I'll get out of your hair and stop asking all these questions," I joke, but my stomach feels nauseated and emotion stings the bridge of my nose at the thought of going back home. To that suffocatingly quiet apartment. The stuffy, windowless office building. There's absolutely no part of me that wants to leave.

You won't survive if you go home.

"You know, I don't mind the company," he says, his tone relaxing.

"You have a whole resort full of people now," I point out.

"That's true. But nobody ever stays." He smiles, but I wonder if there's truth in that statement and how much it affects him.

"Except Shirley," I say softly. He must get lonely up here. He has to. I wonder why he doesn't have more help, given how busy he always seems to be.

"Except Shirley," he confirms, taking a sip of his wine. The sky is dark now, illuminating his features in the soft-yellow glow from the fire. I notice how with each breath, his shoulders seem to drop a little bit more. The tension oozes out of him slowly.

My own body feels sore from the day on my feet and a bit sleepy from the wine. I curl my legs up and onto the chair, then tip my head back against the backrest to look up.

"It's so beautiful." Tears threaten the corners of my eyes at the sight of the million tiny stars that fill the entirety of the sky. I suddenly feel every bit as small as I am—insignificant and worthless down here on this island in the middle of nowhere.

"More wine?" Graham's soft voice pulls me out of my spiral. I blink a few times, staring at him in the darkness of the night, until words eventually come.

"No. Thank you. I'm pretty tired. I think I'll call it a night." I stand, pouring out the last tiny sip of wine left into the grass.

With a nod, he pushes himself out of his chair and throws a bucket of water on the fire. I'm too tired to protest when he silently falls into place beside me and walks me to my cabin.

SIXTEEN
Graham

"Cinnamon streusel or chocolate chip?" I extend both muffins toward Blair, who's sitting on the edge of the couch in the library, leaning over an open book in her hands. She looks up expectantly, curling her finger in the pages to hold her place.

"You brought me muffins?" Her brows push together in curiosity.

This isn't the first time she's seemed surprised when I do something nice for her. Although, I hardly consider bringing her a muffin to be anything out of the ordinary. A sharp twist of disgust hits my gut at the thought of the bare minimum that her boyfriend must do for her if this is impressive.

"I mean, it's not a bouquet of flowers or anything." I shrug, pettily pointing out another no-brainer when it comes to how a man should treat his woman. "But it's the least I can do as a thank-you for helping me out. I remember you saying you liked the cinnamon."

"Thank you." Her gaze holds mine, the expression on her face unreadable, if not a little bit sullen. I find myself, again, wondering what's going on in that head of hers.

She slowly reaches for the muffin as I sit across from her. I unwrap the chocolate chip one as she sinks against the back of the couch, looking at ease and comfortable here.

"I think I saw you in here yesterday too, right?" I ask, noting the pile of books stacked next to her on the couch.

A soft smile pulls at her lips as she pans the room. Her eyes spark with a look that doesn't quite reach wonder, but I'd say it's close.

"I like it here," she admits softly. "It's cozy."

I nod in response, that statement making me happier than it should.

"What are you reading?" I point to the book in her hands.

"It's a mystery about a woman who goes missing while on vacation. It's getting kind of creepy, but I can't seem to put it down."

"Sounds like fun," I chide. "I've never understood why crime shows and horror stories are entertaining to people. How is scaring yourself a good time?"

"Hey, don't knock it 'til you try it. These books have a way of pulling you right in. You should try one. I've binged two of them since yesterday."

"Yeah? Which one do you recommend for me?" I have no interest, or frankly, the time to read, but I do like listening to her talk.

"Hmm. Probably not this one." She raises the one in her hand. "You might scare too easily."

I chuckle and roll my lips, biting back a smile at her jab.

"The one I read yesterday would be good to ease your way in." She points to one at the bottom of her stack.

"Maybe I'll give it a go, then." I enjoy the way she looks down with a smug smile.

"Anyway, most of my guests left this morning," I tell her after I swallow another bite of muffin. "I need to run over to a friend of mine's cabin to check on some things, but I wanted to see what your travel plans are before I leave to go do that. Do you need me to arrange a floatplane or anything for you?"

"No, no. But thank you." She dismisses my offer with a wave.

"Alright."

"What do you have to check on?"

"It's my buddy Cole's cabin. He lives down in Longville and hasn't been able to make it up for several weeks, so I offered to go check on his property for him."

"To make sure it hasn't been mauled by bears?"

"Exactly." I huff a laugh. "Nah, pretty much just making sure everything is still in one piece. No trees down. I usually clean up his beach a little bit while I'm there. Sometimes I mow the grass—maintenance stuff like that."

"That's awfully nice of you to do."

I shrug. "We take care of each other up here. He'd do the same for me."

When she doesn't say anything, I push my hands against my knees and stand. "Well, I should get going. I know I've said it a million times already, but I really do appreciate you coming all the way up here."

"And I've said it's no problem every single time." She smiles softly.

"Let me know if I can do anything else before you leave. I'm assuming you'll call me when you hear back about the deposition thing, right?"

She hesitates, her mouth parting slightly as her brows furrow. I know enough to know that it's the look of a woman with a million thoughts running through her head, but again, I have no idea exactly what. And it's not exactly my place to pry.

"Actually...can I come with you?" Her eyes meet mine, a hint of desperation in them.

"Right now? To the cabin?" I stare back at her, bewildered by her question. Surely that can't be what she meant.

"Yeah," she says simply, nodding slowly as if she hasn't quite convinced herself yet either. "I haven't made travel plans to go home yet. I was going to, but...I...I don't really want to leave."

A spot right in the middle of my chest warms, and my lips threaten to lift up. Hearing in her own words that she likes it here does something to me that I'm not proud to admit. She has a boyfriend after all—I'm well aware of that. But I'm sure as hell not going to turn her down if she wants to stay.

I blink at her for what seems like a long time, further contemplating her motive for wanting to be here, wondering what's going on in her mind, and then chastising myself for thinking I have a right to know any of it.

"Of course you can come," I finally say. A flash of relief crosses her face.

Why doesn't she want to go home? Is she running from something? Is she in a bad situation back in Chicago? There are so many questions swirling in my head, but again, I know it's not my place to pry, so I gesture toward the front of the lodge.

"Let's go, then. The ATV is around back."

"Okay." She hops up, a renewed spring in her step. She places the books in her stack back where they belong on the shelf.

"You realize I'm not doing anything exciting, right?" I ask, leading her out of the lodge.

"Yup," is all she replies with.

"Alright. As long as we're on the same page." I shrug.

The ATV is already parked in front of the shed from when I pulled it out earlier.

"Hop on," I say, pointing to the rear of the seat. I wait for her to get situated before carefully climbing in front of her.

We head off, taking the lodge trail that leads east. Unlike the first time I gave her a ride, I'm now acutely aware of the small space between us and the way her knees inadvertently touch my outer thighs when we jostle side to side on the trail.

It's suddenly hard to think of anything other than how close she is, but I push the thought out of my mind as best I can to focus on the trail ahead. At the intersection, I take the path that runs along the shoreline, skirting around trees and empty stretches of bare, sandy beach. Eventually, I take the path that brings us inland through a thicker stretch of woods. We pass small wooden signs hammered onto trees that point to which direction Ruby Lodge is. The name Fredrickson on another sign points to the direction of his cabin.

"You alright?" I call over my shoulder after narrowly dodging a haphazard branch that hangs low.

"I'm good!" she shouts back.

Up ahead on the left, I take a final dirt path that leads straight up to the cabin.

"Wow, this is such a cute little spot," she says into my ear as I park the four-wheeler by the utility shed. I offer a hand to help her down, noting how soft her hand feels in mine.

"It's one of my favorite cabins on the whole island," I agree. "It has one of the best views."

It's a small studio cabin sheltered snugly between towering spruce trees. It sits on top of a slight incline and faces a stunning view of the lake.

"Shoot. Looks like the storm knocked quite a few branches down." Sticks and twigs are haphazardly spread across his front porch, blocking the stairwell enough to make it impassable. I grab a few and toss them onto the grass where Blair picks them up and carries them to the trees surrounding the property.

"It must have hit this side of the island hard," I mutter, grabbing the last stick from the porch. When I turn around to figure out what area to clear next, I notice that Blair is already wandering down to the beach.

"I'll check down here," she calls over her shoulder.

SEVENTEEN
Blair

I should just go home. He's probably so annoyed with me trailing after him like a child.

The words echo loudly in my head as I bend to pick up a twig that's half-buried in the sand. I haven't been able to pinpoint exactly why I keep dragging my feet about booking a flight home. One would think that the simple act of making an airline reservation wouldn't require a lot of emotional strength, yet here I am, unable to do so.

Taking a boat or floatplane to the mainland even sounds like too much of a feat, let alone traveling all the way home. I don't have the energy to make that move just yet. The only thing I want to do is stay here, nice and numb, on this quiet little island a little while longer.

Aside from my reluctance to travel home, I've also become acutely aware of what an ass Barry really is. Being with Graham the last few days has reminded me that putting an effort in really can be simple and easy. It shouldn't be as hard as Barry makes it out to be. I know, logically, that I deserve more than the bare minimum he gives me—even if I don't always believe that I do. The thought of going back home to him isn't appealing enough to bring me out of this funk to actually go home.

I spot a larger branch a few feet away and add it to the growing pile in my arms, trying to ignore the voice in my head that keeps asking when I'll be brave enough to break up with him.

"Bet you're regretting tagging along now, huh?" Graham passes behind me with a rake, interrupting my thoughts. "Now that I have you doing manual labor."

"I don't mind," I say, picking up another stick. "It's better than being in my office building for twelve hours a day."

"That sounds like prison to me. No offense."

Sometimes it feels like that to me too.

I track his movement as he runs the rake along the sand, collecting weeds in the prongs, making a pile of it off to the side. He lets out a low whistle, the start of a slow melody that he croons while he works. I'm captivated at the sight of his ease and calmness. Even his neutral expression has a subtle hint of joy to it, and a pang of jealousy hits me in my gut. How can it be so easy for others to just be happy, even at their resting state? Without even trying. How is that their status quo? And why can't it be that way for me?

"You look happy," I blurt out, not exactly meaning to say the words aloud.

He cocks an eyebrow, and his mouth tips up in a lopsided smile as he stares back at me.

"Do I?"

My head dips in a nod, forcing a small smile in return. "You do. You're in your element here."

A slight patch of red paints his cheeks as he looks back down, making a half-pass with the rake before pausing to rest his arm along the top of it. He studies me for a minute, a probing curiosity in his eyes as they search mine.

"And what makes you happy, Blair?" he asks quietly.

Heat flushes the entire length of my body, and my face tingles at the attention. At the weight of the question. I consider throwing out a lighthearted reply about Shirley's food, but I pause at the sincerity on his face.

"Actually, not a whole lot," I tell him, surprising myself at my honesty. Yet, at the same time, I feel a tiny bit of weight lift off my chest. I reach for another stick to distract myself from the tears that threaten to surface. He doesn't say anything in return, and I purposefully avoid his stare. When I assume he's moved on and gone back to raking, I dare another sideways glance.

He's standing in the same position, his gaze still pinned on me in a quiet, patient way. There's a gentleness in his stare that somehow puts me at ease. My breath catches in my throat, and I contemplate how much I want to open up to him. How good it might feel.

Before I can decide how far I'm willing to go, he drops his rake and walks a few steps to lower himself down into the sand. Taking a seat, he bends one leg at the knee and raises the other, his elbow finding a new resting spot there. He stays quiet, looking out at the lake in a contemplative way. He doesn't mutter a single word, but the invitation is clear.

With a heavy sigh, I set my pile of sticks on the sand and lower myself to sit next to him, feeling drawn to him and his calm, soothing energy.

"You want to talk about it?" he asks quietly, his head still facing forward.

I swallow hard, not entirely sure how to put into words what I feel, but I manage to push out in an almost-whisper, "That's what I've been trying to figure out...what makes me happy."

He simply nods, shifting his gaze down toward his fingers that are thumbing a twig.

"I feel a little bit stuck right now, honestly," I admit, finding a bird in the sky to focus on as I force the words out. "I'm not sure what I want out of life. What I want to do. Where I fit."

"That sounds like a tough spot to be in," he says gruffly, finally shifting his gaze to mine. Nothing but compassion sits behind his eyes. My impulse is to deflect, uncomfortable at the conversation, but something about his quiet stare reminds me of what my therapist, Rachel, often tells me. That opening up to people I can trust and speaking my feelings out loud to them can be validating. Freeing, even.

I'm not sure how much I believe her, and I've only ever been completely honest with her and Annie, but here on this secluded island, with no one else around, I feel like I can trust

Graham. Or maybe I just desperately want to have someone else to trust.

"I haven't been in the best headspace lately." The quiet words hang heavy in the air, my chest tightening and pulse racing.

"Are you okay?" Concern coats his words.

"Yeah," I reply, quick to reassure him. "I just...I dunno...struggle to feel motivated or get excited about much of anything. There's not a whole lot of joy happening for me. To be honest, a lot of my life is just empty. But it's silly. It's nothing, really."

"No, it is. It is something," he insists firmly.

"It's nothing worth you worrying over. I'll be just fine, I promise." I start to feel foolish and embarrassed for saying anything in the first place. I don't want the attention or fuss.

"Blair." The way he says my name hits me square in the middle of my chest, stopping my attempts to brush over this conversation. I drop my head toward the sand before tilting it to slowly bring my eyes to his.

"If it feels real to you, then it matters," he says gingerly before rolling his lips together. I give him a timid nod.

"And I'm honored that you would share any part of yourself with me. I don't know what kind of help I can be, but I'm here in any way that you need."

A blush heats my cheeks. Maybe it's the way he's looking at me like he truly can see the deeper parts of me, or maybe it's just the fact that I acknowledged it out loud at all, but my next breath does feel easier to take than the one just moments before.

We sit quietly for a moment, letting the words we both spoke ruminate.

"For what it's worth," he says, pushing himself up to stand and then offering a hand to help me up. "It's okay if you don't want to go home yet. If you want to stay. You're safe here—safe to figure out whatever it is you need to."

I clutch his hand as I stand, ending up mere inches away from his body. Emotion prickles the inside of my nose at the kindness in his words. I smile, push my lips together, and meet his gaze.

"Thank you." The words come from deep inside, holding the weight of the burden I've been carrying with me for so long.

With a curt nod, he picks up his rake and goes back to work on the weeds. I blow a steadying breath out, then busy myself with the rest of the sticks. When I've compiled them all, I throw the pile into the woods and help Graham finish a few other minor projects around the property before climbing on the back of the four-wheeler to ride back to the lodge.

On the ride back, gripping the handles of the ATV tight, I feel a closeness with Graham that has nothing to do with our proximity. I guess my therapist was right about opening up. I'm glad that Graham has become someone that I trust enough to be vulnerable with.

Later that night, as I sit on the porch swing of cabin four, watching the sun disappear on the horizon, I make the decision to stay on the island—not indefinitely, of course, but at least for a little while. There's a strong urge hidden deep inside that wants to fight to feel better. It's a small, dust-covered part of me, but I'm desperate to reach it. I don't know how exactly to do that, but I do know without a doubt that I sure as hell won't figure it out in Chicago.

Barry will think it's ridiculous.

Annoyed at the thought the moment it pops into my head, I blink a few times, take some calming breaths, and think of Graham's words instead.

You're safe here.

He's right. I knew it from the moment I set foot on this island for the retreat—this place is different from any other place I've been before. Maybe a change of scenery is the missing piece to shift my life back into focus and pull myself out of this. To prioritize myself for once and create a newer, healthier version of myself.

The sun vanishes, and I stare out at the dark sky. The rolling waves that crash onto the shore are barely visible under the soft twinkle lights in the trees.

I'm safe here.

EIGHTEEN
Graham

"What happened?" I demand into my phone from where it sits on my nightstand. The frustrated grumble my dad lets out does nothing to lessen the apprehension that's rising in my stomach. I listen with bated breath as my fingers swiftly button my work slacks.

"It's your mother. She had a bad fall yesterday." There's a weariness in his already anxious voice.

"Is she okay?" Panic stops me in my tracks, my sock dangling from my hand mid-air.

"The doctor says she should be alright, but she did break her hip and a couple of ribs. They're monitoring her for a few other things, but the prognosis looks good."

"Shit." I drop down onto the edge of my bed and pinch the bridge of my nose. "I need to come over there."

My to-do list flashes through my mind, and I start mentally running through options for who might be able to come over and take my place for the day. I have about two minutes before

I'm supposed to be downstairs to have my weekly food meeting with Shirley, then I need to finish prepping the rest of the cabins for the new guests that are checking in this afternoon. My heart is pulling me toward dropping everything and being with Mom, but I can't exactly leave the cabins unfinished.

"There's no rush, Graham. She's going to be fine. I know you have your hands full out there," Dad offers.

"I can't just not see her," I spit out, my frustration targeting him.

"It's your call, of course, but...they have her pretty drugged up. I can let you know as soon as I hear anything new from the doctors," his patient voice says. But I hear what he doesn't say out loud.

That there's no point. She won't even know I'm there anyway.

I exhale slowly, grazing my fingers through my hair and down the stubble of my jaw. "Alright. I'll work on finding someone to fill in. I'll plan to come out sometime in the next few days."

"Sounds good. I'll keep you updated. Also, Graham? This means I have to push back my plans to be out there this weekend. Are you going to be okay without me?"

"I'll handle it," I say curtly.

"I'm sorry, son." His apology feels all-encompassing. I know he's silently referencing more than just this incident.

Blowing out a frustrated breath, I quickly pull my work polo on and rush down the staircase. In the dining area, I find Blair sitting at a high-top, inhaling Shirley's lemon ricotta pancakes.

"Morning." She glances up, bringing a napkin to her mouth.

"Morning," I reply, attempting to force-smooth the tension building between my eyes as I lean an elbow against the bar.

"What's wrong?" she asks immediately.

I contemplate keeping it to myself, but I don't see the point of lying to her, especially after she was so vulnerable with me yesterday. I figure I can return the favor and let her see a glimpse of this less-than-perfect part of my own life.

"My mom's in the hospital. I guess she fell and got pretty beat up."

"Oh, I'm so sorry, Graham." Her brows crease, and her eyes probe mine.

"Thanks," I mumble. I've never been good at this part when it comes to Mom's situation. The pity. The stares. The uncomfortable silence. I don't know what to do with all of it.

"Do you need to go see her? Can I do anything to help?"

I shake my head. "I'm needed here. We've got guests coming in this afternoon, and I need to turn over several cabins before then. Not to mention go over the menu with Shirley. There's too much to do."

"Let me help," she says firmly, pushing her empty plate to the side.

The last thing I want to do is burden her, especially given everything she mentioned yesterday. It's gut-wrenching enough to know that she's struggling right now. I don't want to add anything else to her plate.

"No. You've helped so much already." I push off the counter and round the bar, running a rag over the counter in an attempt to clean.

"Graham," she says firmly.

I shake my head, avoiding eye contact. I already know what she's about to say, and I don't know if I can trust my willpower to stay strong if I look at the pity in her eyes.

"Graham," she repeats softly, and this time I look up.

She rolls her lips, tilting her head as if to further drive her words home. "I wish more than anything in this world that I had a family. Please go be with yours if that's where you want to be right now."

"Blair—"

"I promise I want to help. It's good for me to be busy." She looks down at her hands. "It helps."

Conflicting emotions pull me in different directions. I told her I would be there and support her in any way that she needs, but I'm pretty sure that shouldn't include me dumping my burdens on her. But if she says it helps, who am I to say no?

"You're not going to break me," she says earnestly. "I'm not broken...I can handle this."

"Handle what?" Shirley says from behind me.

"You and I are running this place today. Graham is needed in town," Blair says with confidence before I can open my mouth.

"Everything alright?" Shirley asks, eyeing me.

"Mom fell overnight. She's in the hospital, but she'll be alright," I assure her. As a longtime friend of my parents, I know she worries about my mom too.

"Goodness, yes. What are you still standing here for? Go see her."

"But—"

"But nothing. I know what you're going to say, and I don't want to hear it. Everything is just fine, especially if Blair is willing to chip in."

"Come on, show me what I need to do." Blair stands.

"Go on." Shirley urges, shooing me out of the bar area.

"Alright." I'm still not completely convinced this is the right move, but I give in and gesture for Blair to follow me down the hallway, past the library, and into the laundry room. Dirty bed sheets are piled high, overflowing out of the laundry bin, and cleaning supplies are spread messily across the countertop.

"Don't mind the mess," I say sheepishly. "If I go now, I should be back by the time the first guest arrives. All the cabins are ready to go except for three through seven. The bathrooms need to be cleaned, trash taken out, and bedsheets replaced. Those are over here." I point to a floor-to-ceiling cabinet that houses linens and towels before crossing the room to the pantry shelves.

"Each cabin needs to be stocked with bottles of water and coffee pods. Let's see, what else?"

Blair is standing next to me, taking it all in with a steady nod, and a pang of guilt hits me.

"This is ridiculous. The last thing you want to be doing is scrubbing toilets."

"I love to clean," she says flatly.

"No, you don't."

"I really don't," she admits with a smirk. "But I can handle it. What else have
you got for me?"

"There are two large garbage bins behind the building—one for recycling, one for garbage. You can throw all the trash in there, please."

"Got it. Now please leave."

"I feel like I'm being kicked out of my own house."

"You are," she says, turning away from me to gather supplies.

"Alright, then. Well, thank you. I promise I won't be long."

"No rush. Please take your time." With a wave of her hand, she lifts the bucket and scurries out of the room.

I follow behind, then run upstairs to grab a few things before pulling on my rain jacket. Then I grab the brown paper bag of food Shirley left on the counter and head to the docks.

"We'll keep her for a while to make sure her pain is under control and monitor her so no potential complications, such as pneumonia, develop," the doctor says from the other side of Mom's hospital bed. "Do you have any questions for me?"

Dad looks at me, his knee bouncing nervously. I'm pretty sure my blood pressure has risen significantly just from being in this room with him. The cloud of anxiety that follows him around is palpable on a good day, but when Mom is in distress, it's ten times worse. My stomach twists with a pang of guilt when I think of what will happen when he finds out that the lodge is going under.

I shake my head. "None from me. Thanks, Doc."

"Let my nurses know if any questions arise. Otherwise, I'll see you on my next rotation."

Dad and I both shake his hand before he walks out of the room.

"Have you called Syd?" I ask, reaching for Mom's hand as she lies sleeping on the bed.

"Of course," he answers. "She's been texting me every twenty minutes, asking for updates."

"Did she say anything about coming home? To see her?" It's a futile question, but I ask anyway.

"Nope." He shakes his head. One of these days, I'll figure out a way to convince her to come home, but I'm at a loss for what it'll take if this doesn't do it.

"Who did you get to cover for you at the lodge?" he asks.

"Shirley and Blair," I say automatically.

"Blair?"

"She's a new friend. She was here with the group of lawyers and liked it so much she came back." I omit the part about her helping me with the lawsuit. Our legal trouble is definitely not what I want to be bringing up right now.

"And she's doing work around the lodge?" he asks, eyeing me warily.

"We can trust her, Dad. Don't worry." I push back the too-small folding chair to stand. "But I should get going if I want to be back before this afternoon."

I kiss Mom's cheek and round the hospital bed to give Dad a reassuring hug.

"Call me with any changes, okay? Or if you need any help with anything."

"I will," he says quietly, the same look of apprehension on his face that never lets up.

"Oh, I almost forgot." I halt in my tracks and dig into my pockets for the items I brought with me.

I pull out an old picture of the four of us when I was about ten on our annual trip to Duluth to watch the freighters coming into the harbor on Lake Superior. Then I take out a perfectly smooth skipping rock to remind her of the many hours we spent as a family perfecting the skill. She was always the best one out of all of us at rock skipping.

I place the items on her nightstand, knowing Dad will eventually take them back to the nursing home to put with the collection of other things I've brought her.

I squeeze Mom's foot as I pass by and head for the door. Before I pull it open, I pause and look back at Dad.

"Sing her one of my favorite songs, will you?"

NINETEEN
Blair

"And then Steve went on a rampage, confronting everyone in the office about who ate his soup that he left in the fridge," Cassidy says in my ear.

"That doesn't sound like Steve." I take a sip of coffee while using the tip of my toe to push against the porch floor, rocking the bench back and forth. There's a thick fog that's lingering above the lake water this morning, casting a melancholy ambiance that isn't exactly helping my mood.

"I know, right? I'm telling you, the office is weird right now. Steve is all moody, Isaac won't stop talking about Minnesota, and you're not even here, for Pete's sake. When are you coming back?"

"Soon." It's not a flat-out lie. It's not like I plan to stay here forever, but I'm also not exactly rushing back. I'm comfortable here.

I'm safe here.

I've been helping Graham and Shirley as much as I can during the day, which has been a welcome distraction from my mood and the negative thoughts that are ever-lurking. And the quietness of the evenings here have been comforting in a way that the city has never been.

"I hope so. Paul said you've put a pause on any new cases. Is that, like, a leave of absence? That's not a long-term thing, is it?"

"No, it's not long-term. I'll be back soon, Cassidy."

"Okay, great. 'Cause I don't think I can handle much more of these weird vibes. I need my Blair-Bear back. Oh, there goes Nancy. I've gotta run. Talk later!" The phone disconnects before I can even mutter a word. With an amused shake of my head, I down the last sip of my coffee.

Just as I'm about to get up, Annie's name lights up my screen. The sight of her name alone makes me smile. I've missed talking to her. She must be home from her trip.

"Hi, Annie," I say.

"Blair, are you okay?" her voice is rushed and panicked. "What's going on? Where are you? I wasn't expecting you to make life-altering decisions while I was off-the-grid. I just turned my phone back on—literally thirty seconds ago—and I'm trying to make sense of these messages. I need answers immediately. You're back up in Lake of the Woods? What was with the picture of you cleaning a bathroom? Are you trapped there? Do I need to arrange a sting operation to rescue you?"

"Annie," I laugh, interrupting her rambling. "I'm fine, I promise."

"I'm not convinced," she says warily.

"I'll send you a picture of my view right now and let you decide." I take a snapshot, making sure to get a good angle that includes the arching trees, the grassy shore, and the lake that now has just a thin cloud of haze atop it. I angle my coffee mug in the frame for good measure.

"There." I send the image to her, no editing or photo-shopping needed.

"That is beautiful..." she admits before sighing. "You sure you're okay? Tell me what's going on? How long are you planning to be there?"

"I'm helping Graham with a legal case and came up here to help gather some information. I meant to come home after a couple days, but Annie, I just couldn't...I've been in a major funk. More so than normal. And the thought of going back home was just too much."

"Oh, Blair." Annie knows everything about my life, including my deepest, darkest secrets. As my closest—and only—confidante, I've never been anything but an open book when it comes to talking to her about my depression, and I've always been grateful for the way she supports me. Before I came here, she was the only one that did.

"I'm okay, I promise. I think being here is actually starting to help a little bit." It's not that I thought a simple change in location would drastically change things for me, but the weight on my chest hasn't felt quite as crushing, and I did notice that it was slightly easier to climb out of bed this morning.

"Really?"

"Yeah. I'm not sure if it's the fresh air, the slower pace of life, or being distracted at the lodge, but yeah..."

"Well, alright, then. Forget the rescue operation. Now I'm demanding you stay there."

"I have a virtual therapy appointment this afternoon too, so that'll be good to check in with her," I say. I know she'll be happy to hear that. "I'm way past due for that."

"Good. I've been trying to get you to do that for months now," she gently reminds me.

"I know, but I guess I just wasn't making it a priority. Work got in the way, and I didn't care enough, honestly. I will now, though. It might help. I'm sick of feeling this way, Annie."

"I know you are. What does Barry think of you being up there?"

"It seems like he couldn't actually care less." My tone is thick with annoyance. "He hasn't answered many of my phone calls, and if he does, it's usually with a one-or-two word text back."

"Well, that's rude. And typical. Since you seem to be on a path of making healthy decisions for yourself, what are the chances that you'll make one regarding him?"

"Annie," I warn quietly.

"I know, I know. I promised not to bring your relationship up anymore. Wishful thinking, I guess. But you know I think you deserve more than what he gives."

"We'll see what happens." I know it's irrational, but I almost feel like I'll jinx it in some way if I say what I've been thinking out loud. The truth is, breaking up with him has been at the forefront of my thoughts. I can't help but think that's another big piece of the puzzle of fighting for a better life for myself—cutting the dead weight, so to speak.

"Have you told your parents where you are?" she asks cautiously.

"No," I say curtly. What's the point? They don't care anyway. They lost the right to know where I am a long time ago.

"Okay," she says simply. She's always been respectful of my decisions when it comes to them, so she doesn't push.

"Enough about me. Tell me about your trip."

"Oh, Blair, let me tell you. It was intense. A little too much physical exertion, though, if I'm honest. Next time, I'm pushing for a spa retreat."

"Spa always trumps adventure in my book," I chuckle, glancing down at my watch. "Listen, Annie, I have to go. I'm sorry I can't hear more. I promised Shirley I would help her whip up a large brunch buffet in time for the fishermen to come back in from the morning fish."

"Alright, Cinderella. Talk to you tomorrow?"

"You got it." I hang up and give myself an extra minute on the bench, soaking in the comforting feeling of talking to my best friend before leaving the mug on the railing for later and heading off toward the lodge.

"I'm glad you have a plan set in place in regards to your relationship," my therapist, Rachel, says later that afternoon as we finish up our virtual session. My laptop is perched on top of the kitchen table with a view of the rolling lake behind it. "Let me know how it goes. And Blair? Don't wait so long next time, please."

"I know," I say sheepishly. "I need to make this a priority again. I'm determined to."

"Why don't we get something on the books right now? Now that it seems like your schedule has freed up a little bit."

"Yes, let's do that," I agree, and we set up another virtual visit for two weeks, with the promise that if I'm back home by then, I'll come in person.

When we disconnect, I decide to roll with the momentum and do what needs to be done before I lose the courage to do it.

Grabbing my phone off the table, I scroll to find Barry's name and put it on speaker, setting it on top of the closed laptop.

"Hey." To my surprise, he answers after the third ring. I was expecting to have to leave a voicemail—I can't decide which one would have been better.

"Hi," I say back, suddenly feeling nervous and unsure of how to rip the Band-Aid off, even though I just spent the last hour crafting a perfectly direct and to-the-point conversation with Rachel.

"What's up?" His disinterested tone is clear, but it's his choice of words that amuses me. He doesn't ask how I am or even when I'm coming home. But then again, I don't know why I expected him to in the first place.

"We need to talk," I blurt out. There's silence for a few beats, and I wonder if he actually heard me or if he's focusing on something else.

"Shoot." His lazy response gives me fuel to surge forward.

"This isn't working, Barry. It hasn't worked for a while, and I think we both know that." I wait for any sort of interjection from him, but all I get is silence. "I want more from a relationship...I need more."

"Okay."

The fact that he doesn't ask what I need or offer any sort of protest only serves as validation.

"I think we should break up."

"Okay," he repeats, still aloof and cold.

It turns out, I was nervous and avoiding this conversation for no reason, because it seems as if I'm having this conversation with myself. Clearly he's not going to fight for me at all.

"That's it? That's all you have to say?" Anger buzzes under the surface of my skin.

"What do you want me to say, Blair?"

"Oh, I don't know. Maybe that you're sad to see this end? That you don't agree? I don't know..."

His silence is the only response I need.

"Well, thank you for making this easy, at least. I'll figure out how to get my stuff out of the apartment soon."

Again, nothing in return.

"Bye, Barry." I hang up, not exactly sure of what it is I'm feeling. Indifference, but also a bit of anger that he didn't fight for us—even though I'm well aware that I didn't either.

The chair leg screeches against the linoleum floor as I push out of it and meander outside toward the lakeshore. Having a seat on my favorite spot on the ground, I gaze out at the horizon, shielding my eyes with my hand from the glare of the late-afternoon sun. A heavy tug in my chest threatens to pull me down into darkness, where I would be free to wallow in the stark loneliness and truth that I'm now even more alone than ever.

Instead, I take a deep breath, mentally pushing away the negativity with my exhale, and think of Annie's words from earlier instead.

I deserve more.

I might not believe the words, but I cling to them like a mantra anyway.

I deserve more.

Maybe the more I say it, the more I'll actually believe it. I sit in the quiet stillness, with the water lapping onto the shore and the birds intermittently chirping above my head.

I'm safe here.

The corner of my mouth pulls up into a sad smile, and I bring my legs up to hug my knees.

I deserve more.

I'm safe here.

TWENTY
Blair

"Hey, Blair," Graham calls to me from the docks as I'm passing by the next morning on my way to the main lodge. He pulls on the collar of his shirt and wipes some moisture away from his hairline with the back of his arm while a toolbox hangs from the other hand.

"Hey." The smile that emerges on my face takes a little less effort than it did yesterday.

"How are you?" he asks as he walks toward me. Even though I specifically told him the other day to not worry about me, the look of concern on his face is sharp every single time he asks me how I'm doing. I've only been here for a short time, but he's already asked me that question more often than anyone—other than Annie—has ever asked me in my life. My own parents certainly couldn't be bothered to.

"Pretty good." It's always been my standard response, but this time, it doesn't feel as much like a lie as it has in the past. "How's your mom doing today?"

"She's doing better. Healing nicely. They're keeping her for a few more days, and then she'll be released back to the nursing home."

"That's great, Graham. Really."

"Thanks again for pushing me to go. That really meant a lot to me." He gives me a crooked smile, roughly scratching at the back of his neck.

"I broke up with Barry," I blurt out. I'm not entirely sure why I feel the need to share this information with him, and why it needed to be said at this very moment, but it comes out nonetheless.

His whole body seems to still, as if my news was an actual force that stopped him in his tracks. He blinks for a few beats, his gaze pinning me with an unreadable expression.

"You did, huh?" The shock slowly wears off of his face, and it now settles with a look of bewilderment.

"Mm-hm." I nod, feeling silly as he intently roams over every inch of my face. "Not that you'd care or anything, but—"

"I do care," he insists quickly. His voice is gruff and scratchy.

I bite my lip, unsure of why it all of a sudden felt so significant to tell him. And why his approval feels so comforting.

"Are you okay?" The same concern flashes between his eyes again.

"Yeah, I am." I nod, feeling my answer deep inside. I know the breakup was the right move—a necessary move—and I find myself even a little bit eager about what the future might hold without Barry. There are a lot of things left to figure out still, but this feels a little bit like I've reached the top of the endless mountain I've been climbing. Maybe everything else won't be such an uphill battle anymore.

"I'm happy for you?" He shrugs, a boyish grin pulling his face wide. "I don't know, is that the appropriate thing to say in this situation?"

A laugh bursts out of me. "You don't have to say anything. Just wanted you to know, I guess."

He studies me, his grin relaxing into a contemplative stare.

"And I'd like to stay for a bit longer, if that's still alright with you? While I figure things out?"

"Of course." He nods as if it's a no-brainer. As if I'm not an imposition.

"You don't need cabin four for anything? I can move around if needed."

"It's all yours," he says with a shake of his head.

"Thank you. Anyway, I'm going to go check in with Shirley, so I'll see you later?" I start backing away.

"You got it." His eyes stay on mine before I turn and head off the docks. I'm just about to reach the grass when I hear, "Hey, Blair?"

I turn halfway, looking behind my shoulder at Graham, who still hasn't moved from the same spot.

"How does it feel?"

"How does what feel?" My forehead tightens in confusion.

"To choose yourself?"

I bite the corner of a smile that threatens to explode. The way he stares at me with a slow smile spreading on his face makes me feel exposed—in a good kind of way. Like he sees an inner part of me without even needing to try.

"Really good," I say quietly before continuing off the dock.

I choose myself.

The words repeat in my head until I reach the door. Inside the lodge, a few guests are scattered around, playing card games, and a couple more are leaning against the bar. I skirt behind the bar opening, smile at Nita, and head back to the kitchen.

"It smells amazing back here." I glance into a large mixing bowl that has shredded barbecue chicken piled up to the top.

"Barbecue chicken sliders for lunch," Shirley says with a smile, pulling a tray of toasted buns out of the oven.

"What can I do?"

"How about helping pull together the fruit salad? All you have to do is dice up the fruit, and then I can walk you through how to make the dressing."

"My pleasure." I grab the stack of fruit containers from the fridge, pull out a cutting board, and get to work dicing strawberries.

"So it seems that you've taken a liking to this island, huh?" Shirley snickers warmly while slicing the buns. "Most people don't end up staying this long, you know."

"What's not to like?" I skirt around the question, knowing that she's fishing for the real reason why I haven't gone home.

"I know it's absolutely none of my business, but..." She pauses. "Does our handsome caretaker out there have anything to do with why you're still here?"

"Absolutely not," I reply resolutely, guffawing at the ridiculous notion.

"Alright, alright." She tries to hide a knowing smile by dipping her head. "I'm just saying...there's a certain twinkle in his eye when he talks about you. I've known him a long time, and I don't recall ever seeing that look, my dear."

My cheeks heat with a blush. Is that true? Does Graham look at me that way? I've been so preoccupied with my own pitiful relationship and focusing on feeling better. Has he been sending me signals that I've somehow missed? I will admit there seems to be an ease between us, and I've caught myself lingering on his handsome features a few times, but I'm not convinced that he would actually be interested in me.

"He's been a good friend," I manage to force out, completely flustered by the topic.

"He's good at being a friend...among other things." She scoops some chicken mixture onto a fork and places it directly in front of my mouth. "Here."

"Oh, wow." I chew the bite, savoring the flavorful kick of the barbecue sauce, feeling it warm me from the inside out. "That's amazing, Shirley. I don't know how you do it."

"Many years of practice." She winks.

"How long have you been the chef here?" I ask as I dice some mangoes.

"Coming up on eight years now," she says. "For years, I worked in the kitchen of the church in Angle Inlet, but after my Ernie passed away, I needed a change of scenery and of my daily routine. So Graham's parents took me on as head chef, and I've been here ever since."

"And you stay here quite a bit, right? On the island?"

"I do." I catch the faintest of smiles as she assembles sandwiches. "Every so often, I need to go home to catch up on things there, but there's something about this place...I don't often feel the urge to leave."

Her words resonate with me. I understand the lure of the island for her because I'm starting to feel something similar.

"Plus, that man out there would work himself silly without an ounce of food if I wasn't around."

I snort in agreement as I finish dicing the last of the mango slices. Then I follow Shirley's instructions meticulously to make a honey-lime dressing to toss in.

"That's all I need you for, sweetie. But I sure wouldn't turn down your help before the dinner rush."

"I'll be back by three," I promise, washing my hands in the sink and drying them on the nearby towel. Before I can even take a step toward the door, she places a plate with a sandwich and a big heaping pile of fruit salad in my hands, all of which she must have assembled quickly in the time it took me to clean up.

"Thank you," I say, feeling grateful for the way she takes care of those around her. I'm not used to being taken care of, but

I think that might be part of the lure of Takini Island for me. I'm taken care of here, seen and acknowledged in a way that feels foreign but is so desperately needed at the same time.

The dining area is quiet now, not yet full of people seeking lunch, so I head toward the library. I've been naturally gravitating here when I have the spare time, enjoying the reprieve that reading seems to give my brain. Escaping the emptiness of my own life to be carried away into a fictional universe for a while has become a welcome distraction.

I place the plate of food onto the table and hurry over to the far right corner of the bookshelf, searching for the book I was reading yesterday. I find and pull it out, holding it to my chest until I settle into the corner chair. With a bite of my sandwich, I open the book and quickly delve right back into where I left off.

And that's how I spend my afternoon, tucked away in the corner of the quiet lodge, taking bites of deliciously nourishing food and allowing myself to get lost in a story.

TWENTY-ONE
Graham

"Have a safe flight," I say, tapping the metal frame of the floatplane. "We'll see you next time."

"Later." Sam lifts his hand in a salute before pulling the door shut from the inside.

I back away slowly, watching as the propeller starts up and the plane makes its way out of the harbor. The satisfaction from a successful booking warms my chest as the plane takes off into the air. When I turn around, I'm surprised to find Blair sitting in an Adirondack chair on the beach, a book in one hand and a coffee mug resting on the arm of the chair. She must have settled there while I was helping load the plane.

"Good morning." I nod, and a dull ache squeezes my gut at the sight of her, with her chestnut hair loosely braided off to one side and looking extremely cozy in a caramel-colored, loose jogger outfit. The effects of spending the past week in the sun has tinted her skin, making her look more awake than I think I've ever seen her.

She looks good.

Really good.

Am I allowed to admit that now? Now that she's officially out of her relationship? Not that I would pursue anything, of course—she's going through enough as it is. But I do allow myself to enjoy the way my chest tightens as I step closer to her.

"Morning." She smiles, resting the book in her lap. "Were those the last of the guests?"

"Yup. The next round is set to check in tomorrow afternoon." I step off the dock, my shoes sliding through the sand before easing into the chair next to her.

"How many cabins do we need to clean today then?" she asks.

Her question doesn't sit right with me. I don't like that she automatically expects to be put to work. I haven't outright expected anything out of her since she's been here, but she willingly steps in at each turn, offering help in any way that's needed. I appreciate her lending a hand, but the more that I think about it, we could both use a break. Shirley is always telling me to slow down, so maybe it's time I take her advice.

"Actually, what do you have planned for the next twenty-four hours?" A buzzing energy starts to skate along the surface of my skin as an idea takes shape in my mind.

She looks at me quizzically. "Um, I don't exactly have a full calendar right now," she chuckles. "I still have work paused, and I've yet to hear back about your deposition. So I guess you're looking at it?"

"Can I show you something?" I scratch at the back of my neck, hoping she'll say yes to my idea. "It may or may not involve a tent."

"Like...sleeping in one?" Her brows lift as she stares at me, wary of my proposition.

"Yeah. And a little bit of hiking...but I promise it'll be worth it."

She blinks a few times as she considers my offer. "Are you going to give me another one of those 'it's good to live a little' speeches that you love?"

"If I need to." I laugh.

"Can I bring a book?"

"Bring as many as you want."

"Alright." She smiles, slowly nodding. "Where are we going?"

"It's a surprise." I push up to stand, excited to get going. "Go pack an overnight backpack—not too much. You'll want it light. Meet me back here in twenty?"

"Will I need my pepper spray?"

"No." I shake my head, swallowing a laugh.

"I won't need to defend myself against bears?" The tiniest of smirks plays on her face.

"Not if you stick with me."

At that, she heads off down the trail toward her cabin, and I walk up to the lodge, where I find Shirley sitting at a dining table, hunched over a notebook.

"Hey, Shirley. Blair and I are going camping for the night, so feel free to head home if you'd like. There'll be no one here to cook for if you stay."

"Oh, that sounds like a fun time for you two." Her brows lift in amusement.

"We'll be back first thing in the morning to get everything ready for the new arrivals. Please go home if you want to, Shirley. You deserve a break too."

I ignore the knowing smile on her face as she taps her pencil against the paper, and I make my way to the back hallway.

"Have fun!" she calls just as I'm climbing the stairs to my room. I quickly gather supplies of my own and change out of my work clothes, then head around to the back of the lodge to the storage shed to find the tent and a few other necessities. I'm able to tie the tent and other supplies securely onto the back of the ATV.

When everything's ready to go, I ride it up front just in time to meet Blair, who's waiting on the front step, her backpack settled next to her on the ground. She's changed into a pair of black leggings and a loose white tank top, and her hiking boots are tied tightly.

I hop down as she eyes the materials that are strapped to the ATV. "I'm going to regret this, aren't I?"

"Possibly," I say as I pass by her, taking the steps two at a time. "I'll be right back."

I jog back upstairs to my balcony and gently place my guitar in its case before carrying it back down.

"Ready?" I secure the guitar and her bag with the bungee cord and then swing my leg over the seat, patting the spot behind me. "Hop on."

She places a hand on my shoulder to use as leverage, swinging her leg over the seat, then grabs hold of the handles on either side of her hips.

"Remember, I'm a city girl, so go easy on me," she says, leaning in close to be heard over the engine. Her breath causes a wave of goosebumps to run over the back of my neck.

"Where's the fun in that?" I yell back, shifting out of park. I take us in the opposite direction of the cabin we visited the other day. Passing through the wide trail, the ride is smooth and easy as we make our way deeper into the woods. Not too far ahead, I come to a stop on the side of the trail and shift into park. I stretch a hand out to the side to help her off before following.

"This is the hiking part of our adventure?" she asks, nervously scanning the thick woods that surround us.

"Unless you know of another way." I wink. "The only way up is through. It's a little less than a mile. Do you think you can handle it?"

"I survived the company hike. I think I can handle this." She sounds about as unsure as she looks, with a cringe that spreads the entirety of her face.

"That's the spirit." I unhook the cords and unload the ATV, strapping everything onto our shoulders except for the guitar, which I carry in my hands.

"Let's do this." I grin at her. She follows behind as we start walking through the barely-there trail. It's overgrown and unkempt since other projects have taken priority over me maintaining this particular trail. I pause every so often to hold tree branches and wayward shrubs out of the way so she can pass by without being scratched. The echoing of birds chirping and the twigs that break under our feet fill the air as we trudge through the rough dirt.

"You good?" I glance over my shoulder.

"Yeah," she huffs, the shimmer of sweat on her forehead visible. To her credit, she hasn't complained once. I add her perseverance to the growing list of things that I admire about her.

"Did you know that a large percentage of murders occur in remote woods?" she asks, out of breath.

"I was not aware of that fact."

"You're not going to murder me, are you? Strangle me and bury me deep in these woods for no one to ever find me?"

"Okay, it's definitely time to ease up on those creepy books you're reading." I huff a laugh. "What's wrong with a good old autobiography?"

"You actually have a few of those in your library," she points out. "But they're about the life of a private investigator and an inmate on death row, so I don't think you'd like those any better."

I shake my head and mutter, "Remind me to give the library a once-over when I have the time."

After a little while longer, we approach an open clearing at the very top of the hill. Outstretched before us is a tree-lined grassy field and a fire pit off to the side that's overgrown and hasn't been used in many weeks. Beyond that is a clear view of the open lake down below, and a small, uninhabited island sits just a couple of yards out. From this high up, you can see the outline of several larger islands spread out in the distance.

"Wow," Blair breathes, moving past me to the edge of the cliff.

"Decent view, right?" I carefully set the guitar case down and toss the tent bag and my backpack on the grass nearby.

"Is this still part of your property?"

"Yup. This is pretty much the end of it on this side. There was talk of expanding Ruby Lodge at one point, but that would require a lot of excavating and restructuring of the land—that's off the table at this point. Too expensive."

"Okay, I have a dumb question." She sets her backpack next to mine. "How do you get big machinery over here? If you were to tackle a project or renovation like that?"

"We fly it over in a really big plane."

"Really?"

"No." I chuckle, feeling a little bad about teasing her. "Most of the time, they drive the equipment over the ice in the winter and store it on the island until the project starts in the spring."

"Impressive." She nods in approval.

"You learn something new every day, right?" I rub my hands together. "Alright. Want to learn how to set up a tent?"

TWENTY-TWO
Blair

"There's nothing better than a fish fry. This is as fresh of fish as you're ever gonna get," Graham says, flipping a piece of battered fish in the oil.

"It looks...delicious?" I try to sound enthusiastic about the meal he's cooking for us over the open fire, but I'm afraid I'm not exactly convincing. I've been doing my best to keep an open mind ever since he pulled the fish out of the small cooler, but I'm not sure I'm prepared for this level of outdoorsy living.

"But they probably won't be as good as the frog legs I almost brought," he says nonchalantly. The fabric of his flannel button-up is taut against his brawny frame as he kneels over the fire pit, poking at the fish with a spatula.

"Stop." I let out a laugh that naturally settles into a lingering smile. It hits me that doing so doesn't take quite as much effort as it used to. It was a genuine laugh—one that I actually felt instead of forcing for show.

"You want to grab a plate?" He points to the small stack of paper plates sticking out of the bag.

"Sure."

He slides a piece of fried fish onto my plate and then spoons me a big scoop of baked beans from the pot that sits next to the fish on top of the fire grate.

"Bon appétit," he says before grabbing a plate of his own.

I sit back into the tiny portable chair and mix a piece of fish with some beans and take a bite. It's crispy and buttery, with the sweet, tangy flavor of the beans offering a nice contrast. It has a warm, smokey flavor to it from the fire.

"Okay, that's not bad," I admit.

"I told you," he says smugly, settling back into his chair.

"Do you come up to this spot a lot? To camp?" I ask, taking another bite.

He takes a large bite of fish and beans and nods slowly. "Yeah, but I haven't been in a while. I came more often before I took over running the lodge." The corner of his mouth tips up, and his eyes shine when he says, "In high school, I used to bring girls from town up here for roasted hot dogs and a night under the stars."

"How romantic." I smirk sarcastically. A tiny twinge of jealousy squeezes my stomach, and I instantly don't like the feeling. My conversation with Shirley about Graham has clearly been messing with my head. I haven't let myself read too much into it, but the few times I have, the more and more I'm convinced it can't be true. Why would he want to be with someone like me anyway? I'm the opposite of a fun-loving, adventurous woman. There's no way I'm even remotely close to his type.

I'm not good enough for him.

"Hey, you have to get creative when it comes to dating up here." He shrugs.

"How's your mom doing?" I ask, veering the subject away from his past love life, having no interest in hearing more about it.

"She's better. Back to her regular routine at the nursing home."

"How often do you visit her?"

"I try to make it over a couple times a week, but it's been hard to sneak away from the lodge lately."

"Can I ask you a question?" I ask, not wanting to overstep but curious to see if maybe he'll answer.

"Shoot." His gaze connects with mine over the fire.

"How come you don't hire extra help? I may be way out of line here, and I apologize if I am, but it seems like you could use an extra employee or two to take some of the work off your shoulders."

He blows out a breath as he tosses his empty plate into the fire. "I can't afford to hire anyone else right now. The lodge isn't doing so great. We're kind of struggling at the moment."

"Oh," I say, surprised by the admission. I've definitely gotten the impression that they were tight on money, given his reaction to the lawsuit, but I didn't know it was that bad.

"It's not worth talking about, though. I'll figure something out." He shrugs and offers me a gentle smile. I wonder how much stress and worry is hidden behind it. But I pick up on the subtle hint that he doesn't want to talk about it.

The sky starts to darken, and the next breeze that rushes past has a slight chill to it.

"I'm going to grab a sweatshirt quick," I tell him, tossing my plate into the fire before unzipping the tent. Pulling on an olive-green hoodie, I zip the tent back up and settle back in my chair.

"Can I get you anything else?" Graham asks, meeting my eyes with an intent stare.

I shake my head, but my eyes catch on something out of the corner of my eye. "Actually, after all this work today...I think I've earned a guitar serenade."

The way his eyes light up sends a rush through me. I watch every move he makes as he skirts around the fire and opens his case.

"Now, remember, I never said I was any good. And don't even think about asking me to sing." He sits back down in his chair, lazily laying the guitar over his thigh.

"Scout's honor." I sink back into my own chair as he starts strumming a few strings, pausing to tune a few times. He settles into a quiet, smooth melody, just loud enough for me to hear faintly over the crackling of the fire.

As he plays, I relax and become entranced by the slow-burning fire, watching the embers as they float into the now completely dark sky. A subtle warmth runs through my veins all at once, stemming from a place in the very center of my chest. Its absence in my life makes it easy to recognize, as it feels foreign and unnatural.

Happiness.

Somehow, out here on this dark, quiet night in the middle of the woods, I'm feeling happy. The realization alone has a sharp pang of anxiety hitting me with the next breath. I feel it deep in my bones, and the intensity of the panic is jarring. All of a sudden, my heart is racing, uncomfortable and unsure of how I feel about the stark difference and the wide range of these new feelings.

Is this what normal is supposed to feel like? A life of constant ups and downs? Nothing that ever lasts? Because it doesn't exactly seem very appealing to me—in fact, it sounds downright exhausting.

I slump back in my chair and zone out, watching the fire. Maybe I've got it all wrong in trying to feel better. Maybe it would be better to stay comfortably numb. Lately, it's been feeling a little bit like I'm starting to break the surface of the water, coming up for air after being underneath for so long. Being on Takini has awoken my senses in a way that I wasn't expecting—and I'm not entirely convinced that it's a good thing. I don't fully know what awaits above the surface.

I stare at the orange-red flames, zeroing in on the way they crackle and fully envelop the logs that lay underneath.

"Hey," Graham says gently, interrupting my thoughts. I blink and look up, realizing that he's stopped playing. His fingers hover over the strings, and his eyes burn into mine.

"Where'd you just go?" He treads lightly, his voice coming out small.

My cheeks instantly heat in embarrassment, ready to shake my head and shrug it off. But then I remember how it felt when I opened up to him in the first place. How comforting and freeing it felt to let him see a small part of me.

"I'm just wondering how people do it," I answer, equally as soft. "Go through life just letting circumstances and events happen to them, constantly pulling their emotions in different directions. Is it all worth it, if it always ebbs and flows? Does happiness ever really last? Does the sadness come on stronger the next time because now you've had farther to fall from?"

I cut myself off from rambling further when I meet his gaze. My heart is racing, yet I feel surprisingly comfortable with my honesty.

You're safe here.

I watch as his eyes soften by the second, raking over every inch of my face.

"That's called being alive, Blair." His words reach a part of me that I didn't know was desperately needing to hear them. He pushes his lips together in a way that says he doesn't exactly like it either.

"Look, I'm probably going to say the wrong thing here. What do I know? I'm just a simple guy out here, living a simple life...but yeah, life is shitty a lot of the time. I don't know anyone who's been able to figure out how to avoid that part. But there are also some really incredible moments too, if you can hold out long enough. Those heart-soaring, feel-like-you're-about-to-burst kinds of times." He tilts his head in a shrug. "And to me, life is all about grasping onto the high moments and hoping like hell that they'll carry you through the low ones."

Emotion tingles my eyes as I breathe in his words, allowing them to settle as deep as I can get them to go.

"You just gotta find what lights up your soul, Blair—and cling to it for dear life. 'Cause those moments are worth everything else—in my opinion, anyway." He offers a crooked, humble smile.

"Thanks, Graham," I whisper, holding his gaze. The intensity of the conversation hangs heavy in the air as he resumes playing, and I can feel his gaze locked on me as I go back to watching the fire.

I'm not entirely convinced that I will ever truly feel a high moment like the way he described, but I do think the potential of it is worth fighting for. I'm not going to give up now.

I deserve more.

I look up at the star-filled sky and count the stars, feeling a myriad of emotions. Trepidation at the thought of experiencing such varying emotions, having already experienced the very bottom. But more so anticipation for a life that is full of ups and downs—one that's fully felt and experienced. I can feel it within reach now, closer to it than I've ever been before.

With a sigh, I lower my head to find Graham calmly staring at me, patiently giving me time to process our conversation.

"You know what I do sometimes when I'm having a particularly bad day?" he gently probes, quieting his chords.

I shake my head slowly.

"I think of one good thing that happened that day." He shifts forward slightly. "Even if it's small. No matter what, I can always find something good."

One of the wooden logs pops with a crackle, sending a puff of gray smoke into the air between us.

"I'll give you an example. One of the baseboards behind the bar sticks out just a little bit too far, and I always run into it when I'm not paying attention and rushing back into my office."

I stare at him blankly, not following. I wonder how I misunderstood where he was going with that.

"I didn't stub my toe today." His shoulders lift in a shrug. "That's a good thing."

A smirk plays on my lips. His head dips, and he resumes picking at his guitar, respectfully not asking me to offer a good thing of my own.

After a quiet moment, I do anyway.

"I guess I didn't get mauled by a wolf today." My voice is barely above a whisper.

"There ya go." He nods his head enthusiastically, aiming his finger at me. "You get the concept."

Despite the exhaustion that weighs on my chest, I let the smirk grow into a soft smile. "Alright, I think I'm going to call it a night."

We stand at the same time, and when I move toward the tent, I'm hit with the sudden realization that we never discussed sleeping arrangements. There's only one tent. How did I not think about this before? I pause in my tracks, taking note of my options at this point.

Graham walks past me and unzips the tent. He pulls out one of the rolled-up sleeping bags, then takes it with him to return to the fire.

"You're sleeping out here?" I ask in surprise.

"Yeah." He doesn't look up as he rolls it out onto the ground. "Somebody's gotta protect you from bears, remember? And the wolves? Gotta keep your good day ending on a high note now."

Relief and appreciation hit me all at once.

"Thank you," I say quietly, convinced that he doesn't understand the depth or cause of my gratitude toward him at this moment—for this night and everything that encompassed it.

He twists to meet my stare over his shoulder.

"Goodnight, Blair."

TWENTY-THREE
Graham

"Graham, are you coming out with us? I hear the walleye are hot up near Wiley's," Mack, a local fishing guide from Angle Inlet, says from behind the bar.

"Nah, too much to do today." I wipe the counter down, feeling his eyes follow my every move.

"You know, there's talk in town that the lodge is in trouble. Financial trouble. Everything going alright out here?" he asks.

"We're just fine, Mack. You know how the town talks." I brush him off as nicely as I can. I'm not in the business of airing out my dirty laundry, especially when I know, nine times out of ten, it makes it back and spreads all the way through the surrounding cities. I'm just thankful nobody has figured it out and that my dad is too preoccupied to get caught up in any of it.

"Did they book a half or full-day guide today?" I turn the subject back to the guests staying in cabin eight who hired Mack as their guide.

"Full-day."

"Looks like great weather for fishing." I tap the counter and turn to address the large pile of mail that I've been avoiding, having let it stack up on the back shelf. Fully aware that there are prying eyes out here, I take the mail back into my office. One by one, I sift through bill after bill, some of them with a last-notice stamp on them. Every single one of them causes a ball of dread to build in my stomach.

There's just no way that I can prioritize the small amount of money we have coming in to get these all paid off, especially if I'll end up needing to pay a fine for the lawsuit. I can't see a clear way out of this one. I don't even want to think about what will happen if we have to shutter our doors, but I'm having a hard time not seeing that that's most likely where we're heading. An ache in my chest tightens as I think of how much this place meant to Mom. To Gram and Gramps. To our whole family.

Abandoning the pile on my desk, I head back out just in time to see Mack and the four guests heading out of the harbor in his own Lund Alaskan fishing boat. The lodge is now quiet, aside from Nita and Shirley, bustling in the kitchen, and Blair, sitting at the far corner of the bar.

"So I just got off the phone with the plaintiff's lawyer," she says in between bites of French toast casserole.

"Oh yeah? How'd that go?" I grab a freshly cleaned tumbler glass and dry it with a towel before placing it back in the glass display case, feeling uneasy about hearing her answer.

"I don't know, honestly. It almost seems kind of like he's stalling. I'm hoping it's because they're having trouble creating a solid case...but he didn't give me any real updates. He said they'll be in touch soon."

"Does it usually take this long?" A nervous energy swirls in my stomach.

"It's not uncommon." She shrugs, the ends of her long, curled hair lifting up when her shoulders do. "Just depends on the case."

I nod, taking her empty plate when she slides it to the side.

"Thank you," she says with a small smile, and my chest starts to warm. I like seeing her smile, especially knowing how hard she fights for a genuine one.

"It's kind of quiet around here. What are you up to today?" she asks, leaning closer over the counter.

"Yeah, everyone's gone fishing for the day. I kept Nita on the schedule, though, to handle any stray island hoppers so I can paint cabin twelve. She's in desperate need of a fresh coat."

"You're painting?" Her eyes light up, which sends a whisper of anticipation through me. I've come to expect that she'll tag along with whatever projects I'm working on. I've gotten used to her company and have been enjoying it immensely—admittedly, maybe more than I should.

I chuckle. "Let me guess, you want to help me paint?"

"I am a pretty good painter." She looks at me somewhat convincingly.

"Do you have painting experience?"

"Absolutely none." She points a finger in the air. "But I'm a quick learner."

"If you're up for it, you know I won't turn down the company."

"I'm up for it." She nods vigorously.

"Let's get to work, then." I hang the drying towel on the side of the sink.

"After you." She extends her hand as a gesture to let me pass, and then follows me out of the lodge.

"What color are we painting it? I didn't even know the cabins were painted. They all look like brown wooden logs to me," she says as we approach the shed.

"It's more of a stain—basically the same color as the natural wood itself," I say, grabbing two paint cans from the corner and swinging them onto the back of the ATV. "But we do it to protect the wood."

"Like a barrier? Against the elements?"

"Exactly." I grin at her. "Look at you, city girl. I might just make an outdoorswoman out of you yet."

"That's been your plan all along, hasn't it?" she teases.

"I don't divulge my secrets." I wink at her playfully. Once the tub of paint supplies is loaded onto the back and we climb onto the ATV, I head slowly for cabin twelve.

We pass the row of quiet cabins and then park next to a tree along the shoreline. I help her hop off, and then we start going through the supplies.

"So, which one of these is a paintbrush?" she asks, digging into the tub.

I stare at her blankly, processing how to respond to a question like that, before the corner of her mouth turns up into a barely there smile.

"Kidding." She nonchalantly grabs the two paint cans and brings them to the porch while I keep my gaze held on her, fully enjoying this lighthearted side of her. It's a new side, but one that I desperately hope I'll get to see more of.

"I would have told you to go back to the lodge if you were serious," I say flatly.

With that, her smile grows a touch wider. She helps me get set up, pouring the stain into paint trays and unwrapping new paint brushes that I found in the back of the shed.

"Alright, teacher. Tell me what to do." She stands with hands on her hips, her gaze sliding over the small cabin.

"So you're going to take one of these brushes and dip it in the stain like this." I demonstrate what to do and bring the brush over to the wall.

"Then run the brush through the crevices and spaces between the logs like this. After that, we'll run through the rest of the logs with a roller brush. Easy, huh?" I hand her the wet brush, which she takes out of my hand.

"Easy," she repeats. "Like this?"

I watch as she makes small passes at the very top of a log, stopping short before she makes a full stroke.

"Almost." I come behind her, careful to not get close enough to make her uncomfortable, then grab the handle above where her hand is. Then I guide the brush in a deep stroke in the middle of the crevice, her arm following mine as her hand stays connected to the brush. I breathe in the almond-vanilla scent of her hair that's only inches from my face, and I foolishly allow my heart to pick up its pace. The energy between us sparks, creating a soft buzzing in the air that feels almost palpable.

Her shoulders rise in front of mine as she takes a slow breath in. She flicks her gaze sideways, back at me, ever so slightly turning her head. When our eyes connect, she quickly brings her attention right back in front of her, but I swear I caught a glimpse of something in her eyes. Anticipation maybe? Did she feel what I just felt?

Clearing my throat, I release the handle and step back.

"Got it," she says quietly.

"I'll start over here." I grab a brush of my own and start on the logs next to the front door, twisting my wrist in an attempt to shake off the effects of being close to her.

"So how worried do I need to be about these lawyers dragging their feet?" I ask, running my brush along the entire length of the wall.

"I mean, these things take time. But like I said, their vibe is off. I'll check in with them again in a couple days just to be sure."

"Have I mentioned lately how much I appreciate you working on my case?"

From the corner of the cabin, I can see her smile as she focuses on the painting.

"You have. And you don't need to thank me. It's what friends do, right? Help each other out."

"That's right," I confirm. Although, I'm quickly realizing that I would like to be anything but her friend. We spend a little while painting quietly, moving from the front of the porch to the other side of the cabin.

"You don't really talk about your family much," I say the random observation aloud as it crosses my mind. "I take it you're not close with them?"

I keep my attention on my own paintbrush, not entirely convinced that she'll even give me an answer. She hasn't talked about her personal life much, which I completely respect.

"My parents and I aren't close," she admits. To my surprise, she continues on. "We haven't spoken since my graduation from law school. That was three years ago."

"You're kidding." I look over at where she's intently working.

"Nope. Having children wasn't really part of their life plan. I don't think they knew what to do with me. I spent most of my time growing up with my nanny or with my best friend, Annie."

"I'm sorry," I say genuinely. I can't help but wonder if the lack of solid parenting has anything to do with her grim outlook on life. I can only assume that it does.

"Don't be." She offers a smile across the cabin, her expression telling me that it's something she accepted long ago.

Once again, we fall into a quiet rhythm of painting and chatting effortlessly. We end up finishing the entirety of the log cabin in just a few short hours, which is way less time than it would have taken me on my own.

"What do you think?" I ask her when we step back to inspect our finished job.

She places her hands on her hips beside me and starts to nod her head slowly.

"By far my best painting job," she says.

TWENTY-FOUR
Blair

My breath comes out in soft pants, out of breath from the hike, as I come out of the trail and back onto the resort grounds. My thighs burn, my shoulders ache, and my ankles are sore, yet I relish the way my blood pumps through my veins.

I can do hard things.

The mental reminder to myself acts as a salve to my screaming muscles, and I push myself forward, one step at a time.

I've settled into a nice little daily routine—helping Shirley or Graham in the mornings with whatever needs to be done around the lodge, spending the afternoon in the library, getting sucked into my latest book, and then I've been ending my day with an evening hike around dusk, just before nightfall.

The subtle shift in my mood and overall state of mind has been a pleasant surprise the last few days. Simply existing—just being—has felt easier in a way and less burdensome. I'm cautiously hopeful that this slow, peaceful routine has been slowly bringing me back to life.

"Hey, Blair," Travis, one of the guests from cabin eight, who I had a conversation with this morning at breakfast, calls out as I round the back corner of the main lodge. The group of guys that he's with are settled around the campfire on the beach, Graham included, who's dressed casually in jeans and a gray T-shirt that lightly hugs his frame. My eyes catch on him and the way he looks in front of the fire. He looks like he belongs on the cover of one of those sporting goods magazines with his sun-kissed skin and rugged good looks.

"Hey," I reply to the group as I walk onto the sand toward them. There's a flock of pelicans in the bay to the right of me, gathering near the fish-cleaning hut in search of any scraps that might be thrown their way.

"We convinced Graham to let loose and hang out with us tonight since we're the only people here. You should join us," Nate says, offering me a Coors Light.

"I can stay for a bit." I take the beer and slide into the only empty chair that sits next to him. I look across the fire to find Graham slowly watching me, slouched back in his chair with a drink of his own in his hand. The corner of his mouth tilts up in a slow smile, and something about the way his eyes stare at me sends goosebumps running across my skin.

I've made a conscious decision to not overanalyze or second-guess anything when it comes to Graham. And just like yesterday, when we were painting, I remind myself to not question it and just let it be.

Whatever it is.

He's seen the most vulnerable part of me, and if that hasn't scared him away, then I'm sure as hell not going to push him away. Besides, I would be lying if I said that I haven't been enjoying this tension that has been slowly building between us.

"How was your hike?" Travis asks me while the others chat amongst themselves.

"It was great. I went a little bit farther than I normally do. How about fishing? Did you catch a lot?" I open the beer and take a sip, enjoying the earthy sweet taste.

"We caught quite a few. A ton of crappies."

"Is Shirley going to fry them for you? It's actually not as disgusting as it sounds," I say.

He chuckles. "Yeah, I love fish. I think she's going to make some tomorrow. You'll have to try it." He smiles at me out of the corner of his mouth.

"I might have to." When my eyes glance up, they snag on the intensity of Graham's stare. He's full-on brooding across the fire from me, pushing his lips together with obvious tension. Is that jealousy? Directed at Travis? I can't help a small rush that swoops low in my belly under his surly gaze.

"Do you have plans for the rest of the evening?" Travis asks me, completely oblivious to the man across the fire that's now gripping the armrest so hard I'm surprised it hasn't cracked in two.

"Just a quiet evening," I say politely, feeling Graham's eyes raking over me. "In fact, I'm in desperate need of a shower after my hike, so I'll see you gentlemen later." Before I even come to a full stand, Graham cuts in.

"I'll walk you," he blurts out, already rounding the circle of chairs. My brows lift, and a smile tugs at the corner of my mouth.

"You know...because it's getting dark."

"Okay." I say a quick goodnight to the guests and then fall into place next to Graham as we find the path. The twinkle lights above our heads cast a gentle glow in the rapidly disappearing daylight, and all the while I'm starkly aware of how close he is to my side. I don't mind the closeness one bit.

"I'm heading into town tomorrow," he says, sliding his hands into the pockets of his jeans. "I want to stop by the nursing home, and then there are a couple things I need to pick up at the hardware store. You're welcome to come with? If you feel like getting off the island at all?"

"I would love to," I say eagerly. I've only just passed through Baudette on the way to Takini Island, so the thought of exploring more of it sounds nice.

"Not that there's a whole lot to do, but it's something different anyway." He shrugs.

"For sure. I'm excited to see a little more of it. It's such a sweet little town."

"I've never referred to it as *sweet*, but sure, that's one way to describe it." He huffs a small laugh.

Cabin four comes into view, and it might just be me, but it feels like we both have slowed down a bit, as if to stretch out this time alone for as long as we can.

"You know, I've never seen you walk anyone else to their cabins," I point out as I climb the first step.

"Travis will be next," he says flatly, and I laugh, turning on the step to find him lingering close.

"Is that right?" I hold his stare, daring myself to not look away.

"Nah. I only walk the ones I care about," he says the words quietly, his deep voice melting a place deep inside of me.

"You care about me?" I whisper, continuing to hold his gaze, a part of me silently challenging him to come closer. I savor the feeling of a rush that runs through me. He inches slightly toward me but stops short, a hesitation in his eyes.

Instinctively, I know that he doesn't want to make the first move. I can tell from what he's not saying, just by the look in his eyes, that he doesn't want to push me into something I might not be ready for.

"I do," he says simply.

Nerves build up inside my stomach, yet a part of me wants more—yearns for more of a connection with him. I step down and reach my hand out, lightly grabbing the spot on his arm right above his wrist, searching his face for a reaction as I do. I slide my hand down slowly, and he twists his hand up to meet me halfway. He slides his fingers through mine, gripping tightly.

Each movement is slow and cautious. We're treading lightly, tiptoeing the line, testing this new situation.

The pad of his thumb gently grazes the back of my hand, and already, his touch feels a million times different than any way I've ever been touched before. There's a layer of tenderness and affection in the simple way that he holds my hand. I can't remember anyone's touch ever feeling this way. Certainly not from either of my parents. And God knows Barry didn't touch me like this.

I deserve this.

My chest tightens with emotion, and I act on impulse when I tug on his hand, pulling him closer until his legs brush mine, our stomachs lightly grazing each other, our joined hands now hanging between us by our sides. Hoping that was enough of a first move, and ready for him to take over, I tilt my head up to find his lowering slowly toward mine. His eyes flick up at the last moment before his lips touch mine. A shiver runs down my spine instantly as I press my mouth back against his. His kiss is soft and warm, the scruff on his face lightly scratching against my chin.

My heart races wildly, and a warmth starts running slowly through every inch of my body. His free hand raises and cradles the side of my head while the one holding my hand tightens around my fingers, making me feel cared for and delicate. Like I'm something valuable to be gentle and cautious with.

The kiss is small and slow. Tentative and gentle. Yet the way it feels to me on the inside is almost earth-shattering. My heart is pounding, adrenaline running through me, awakening a deep, long-lost part of me. This surely must be what he meant by being alive. One of the high moments that makes everything else worth it.

I'm alive.

When he pulls away, he rests his forehead on mine, and I spend a moment soaking it all in, feeling the entirety of the high from the kiss we just shared. When I open my eyes, my growing smile matches the one on his face.

"Goodnight, Blair," he whispers, slowly pulling back. Our hands are the last to disconnect. I instinctively bring my fingers up to touch my lips that are left slightly tingling.

"Goodnight, Graham," I say, eventually forcing myself to turn and climb the rest of the stairs. When I get to the door, I peek back to watch him walking away before pushing it open.

TWENTY-FIVE
Blair

I stretch my arms above my head, willing my body to wake up one muscle at a time. My stomach flutters with the butterflies that have not subsided since last night. A shiver of excitement rushes across my skin as the memory of our kiss flashes in my mind. That was a kiss straight out of a movie, the ones I used to watch with envy, convincing myself that those kinds of moments and connections don't happen in real life.

Or at least not to me.

Acting on the surge of excitement that sits deep in my stomach, I roll out of bed and get myself ready for the day. I pull on a pair of light-wash jeans and a black tank top. Before heading down from the loft, I slide my arms through a cream cardigan just to be on the safe side. The mornings have been getting chillier the last few days, and I've learned the hard way that it's better to be prepared with layers. The weather seems to have a mind of its own up here.

In the kitchen, I grab a large mug and fill it with coffee to enjoy by the lake as I do every morning. When I open the door, I almost don't notice the brown paper bag that's sitting in the center of the floor mat. I pick it up, reading the sticky note stuck to the front of it that says *Meet me at the dock at 9? G.*

A new rush of butterflies comes to life as I run my thumb slowly over his words, pausing at the way he curled the G. Even his handwriting is somehow comforting. Inside the bag is a cinnamon-streusel muffin, still warm from the oven. I bite my lip to hold back the smile that wants to grow wide, almost as if my body instinctively isn't used to these new feelings and is trying to thwart too much happiness from arising, like it doesn't know what to do with it or how to be. I try to let myself feel it anyway.

I carry the bag down to the shore and have a seat on the ground, intent on enjoying my coffee and warm muffin while staring out at the lake. It's a beautiful morning. The water is calm, a deep blue, with little waves disrupting it. The sun hangs in the sky with a certain brightness that seems to seep into me. I hold onto the lingering glimmer of happiness, not even letting the pesky mosquitos that swarm my head irritate me. I gulp down my coffee in record time, ready to get the day started and anxious to see him. After bringing the mug back inside, I quickly head down the trail.

I find Graham on the dock, inside one of the fishing boats, securing a fishing rod into the compartment near the bow. When he spots me approaching, he pauses, standing all the way upright as he watches me. His expression is almost unread-able—a mix of trepidation, eagerness, and curiosity.

"Morning," I say as cheerfully as I can in an attempt to put him—and maybe a little bit of myself too—at ease about last night. To reassure him that I'm okay and on board with what happened. More than okay.

"Good morning," he replies, relaxing enough to let his smile spread the entire length of his face. "How did you sleep?"

"Really good." I take his outstretched hand and climb into the boat, lowering into the chair next to him. "You?"

"Best night of sleep in a long time." He tilts his head in my direction and gives a sly wink that causes my chest to warm.

"Thank you for the muffin. It was delicious." Surely he can see the hint of a blush that warms my cheeks.

"Of course. Shirley deserves the credit, though. I just reheated it before I brought it to you," he says as he unties the ropes from the dock, throwing them inside the boat.

"Well, I appreciated it anyway."

He shifts into gear and takes us slowly out of the harbor. We bob slowly along the surface of the soft waves while he busies himself securing a couple bags under the seats.

"What's in the bags?" I ask.

"Stuff for my mom," he says quietly. "I bring her a few things every time I see her. From her life. My childhood. Things that might jog her memory. I've been doing it for a while now."

His expression is solemn. I wonder how many items he's brought to her over the years and what—if any—has actually helped. My heart twists for him, and all I can do is nod.

"Ready?" He perks up and shoves his hat into the glovebox with one hand on the throttle.

"Ready." I smile and then squeal as he shifts into gear and takes us up on plane, soaring across the water. The lake is relatively calm today, so it's a pretty smooth ride. We pass a few islands and another fishing boat as we continue. I close my eyes, letting the crisp wind beat against my face, occasionally wiping away the stray splashes of water that land on my cheek.

Eventually, the shoreline comes into view and we come to the marina, where Graham slows and effortlessly guides us next to the dock. I hang onto the wooden pole of the dock to hold us steady while he grabs the ropes. Once he securely ties us to the dock, I hand him his hat from the glovebox and take his other hand to climb out of the boat.

"My truck should be parked over here in this lot," Graham says as we make our way up the gravel driveway of the marina.

"Wait, you have a truck?" I ask, not hiding the surprise in my voice. I don't know why he wouldn't, but I guess I haven't pictured him driving anything other than his four-wheeler. I shake my head to clear it of my brain lapse. "I mean, of course you do. Why wouldn't you?"

He chuckles. "Yes, I do know how to drive, thank you very much."

"That's not what I meant." I giggle.

"It's nothing special. Same truck I've had since college. My buddy Eric stores it for me at his mechanic shop down the road. He'll take it out of storage and park it here if I tell him I'm coming in."

"That's nice of him."

"Like I said before…" He smiles softly. "We take care of each other around here."

We walk the rest of the way up the gravel slope, past the diner that looks like it also serves as a convenience store, and sure enough, a blue Chevy is parked in the very first parking spot.

"Your chariot, miss." He opens the passenger side door for me to climb in, and then he shuts it gently behind me. After climbing in himself, he shifts into drive, and we head off into town.

"Mom's nursing home is right up here, so I can show you a little more of the town on the way back if you want? Give you a tour of where I grew up?" he asks, gripping the steering wheel with one hand.

"Sure, I'd like that. I'm along for the ride, so I'll go wherever you need to go."

He nods and then runs his free hand along his stubble, hiding a hint of a smile behind it. Clearly he approves of that answer. I like being able to keep him company like this. I like even more that my presence makes him smile like that. He turns right at the bait shop on the corner, taking the gravel road. We continue a few miles down the country road, passing a few farm fields, until we take a left and arrive at the nursing home.

"I can stay in the truck if you want. I don't want to intrude or anything," I say as we come to a stop in the parking lot. I don't want to put any kind of weird pressure on him to introduce me to his family. Not that I wouldn't want to, but I understand if he would be unsure of how to introduce me.

"Are you sure?" he asks, looking over at me. The emotion behind his eyes tells me he would be fine with whatever I'm comfortable with.

"Yeah, you go ahead. I'll be here whenever you're ready," I insist.

"Alright. Sounds good. I won't be long, I promise. These visits are mostly about checking in with Dad and letting Mom hear my voice for a little while."

I nod with a sympathetic smile while he unbuckles and grabs the bag of stuff he brought for his mom.

"No rush, seriously," I say intently when he opens the door and climbs out.

He hits me with one last stare, then he dips his head and smiles, shutting the truck door.

TWENTY-SIX
Graham

Mom's floor is quiet today without too many visitors roaming the hallway. I knock and head into room thirty-three, where I spend the next twenty-five minutes chatting with Dad, convincing him that I've got the lodge under control. All the while, Mom sits in the chair by the window, staring blankly at the farm field next to the building. These visits are always emotionally draining for me, but I do my best to push through and enjoy the time with my parents as much as I can.

"Blair is waiting in the truck, so I should get going," I say to Dad.

"Let me know what I can do for the lodge. I'll plan to come out there in the next couple of days," he tells me with a shaky pat on my shoulder.

"See you then." I give Mom a kiss on the cheek, which she doesn't even flinch from, and then head back outside, a lingering darkness following me as it always does after being with Mom.

Blair is sitting sideways in the passenger seat of my truck, her feet perched on the floor board, the door hanging open. Her eyes soften when they meet mine from across the parking lot, and my legs inadvertently walk faster to reach her.

"How did it go?" she asks.

"It was good," I say simply with a reassuring smile. No point in going into further details. I don't want to dump the heaviest part of my life on her when hers is already heavy enough. "Thanks for waiting."

I climb back in the truck and take us out of the parking lot. All the while, I push down the impulse to take her hand in mine. Now that I know what it's like to hold it, it's all that I want to do—along with kissing her. But I've managed to restrain myself on both fronts, as tempting as it has been. If kissing her last night was any indication of what being with Blair would be like, I'm determined to tread slowly and let her take the lead on this so I don't screw it up somehow. I have no idea what she's ready for, and the last thing I want to do is ruin this. I'm still partially convinced that my brain has made the whole thing up.

"Where to next?" she asks, and I swear there's a hint of excitement in her voice.

"I was thinking of stopping at the hardware store quick to pick up a thing or two...unless you wanted to stop anywhere while we're here?"

"Hardware store sounds great." She says it in a way that makes me think she really doesn't care where we go. I love that she's along for the ride and is interested in my small little town.

I drive us through the city of Baudette, pointing out the establishments and gas stations along the main drag. It's a small and quaint town, filled with family-run businesses and rows of motels nestled along the road. It's the kind of small town where everybody knows everyone else's business whether you want them to or not. Each street corner holds an overwhelming number of childhood memories. It's my home in every sense of the word, with Takini Island being its extension, and I love it with all my heart.

"I just need a little space heater for cabin seven," I say as we pull into the hardware store parking lot. "And then two light bulbs for the main lodge."

We walk through the sliding doors and grab a basket. "Oh, and a dock line to replace the one that's on its last leg."

"Do you want me to go pick one out for you?" she says, a hint of a tease in there.

"Absolutely not," I retort, which earns me a giggle. We find the light bulb section, where I grab the two bulbs I'm looking for. I debate grabbing a flood light to replace the one that I'm expecting might burn out soon, but I decide to not spend the unnecessary money until I absolutely need it. The dock lines are on an end cap as we pass by, so I grab what I need and keep us moving.

"Here we go," I say, leading us into the small appliance section next.

"This one looks cute." She points to something on the bottom shelf.

"It is cute," I agree with a nod. "But it's a generator. Not a space heater."

"So...not what we need?"

"Nope. Nice try, though." I smirk. "I think this one will work." I find the cheapest option in the size I need and carry it to the front while Blair grabs the basket.

"Hey, Ned." I lift our supplies onto the counter in front of the gentleman working the checkout lane, who happens to be my old neighbor.

"Graham, how's your mother doing?" the older man asks as he rings us up.

"She's hanging in there," I say, doing my best to put a positive note in my tone.

"And that lodge of yours?"

"Still running," is all I say. Blair stands next to me, her hands in the pockets of her jeans, seemingly content to be tagging along.

"Looks like a chance of rain this afternoon," Ned says as he finishes the transaction. "Been keeping an eye on the radar."

"I saw that too. Thanks, Ned. Stay dry," I call out with a wave, lifting the space heater and bag before walking out of the store.

"I'm assuming everybody here knows your mom?" Blair asks once we're back in my truck, veering out of the parking lot.

"Every single one."

"Does that bother you?" I can feel her gaze on me out of the corner of my eye as I drive.

"Yes and no," I tell her honestly. "Sometimes I find it comforting, and other times I hate that everywhere I turn is a constant reminder, you know?"

"I get that," she says sadly, placing her hand on top of mine that's resting on the center console. My chest tightens at the way she curls her fingers cautiously in between my knuckles, lightly gripping it the rest of the way through town.

"What's this cute little place?" she asks when I pull into the parking lot of a small strip mall.

"Only home of the world's best ice cream," I say before we climb out of the truck.

"Is that an award-winning tagline or a self-imposed one?" she asks when we reach the sidewalk.

"It's a personal opinion," I admit. "But still well deserved. I thought we could get a scoop to take on our way back."

"That's a big title to live up to." She huffs a small laugh.

The bell dings above our heads as I pull the door open for her. A sweet vanilla scent hangs in the air as we approach the register.

"Mrs. Bishop," I say to the familiar face behind the counter with a dip of my head.

"Hello there, Graham. Who's your friend?" Her eyes scan expectantly back and forth between us.

"This is Blair Williams." I don't dare go into specific details about where she came from or what she's doing here. I like the fact that I can keep those details—keep her—to myself for a bit longer.

"Well, aren't you a pretty little thing," Mrs. Bishop gushes.

"Oh, thank you. It's nice to meet you," Blair replies with a shy smile.

"I've known Graham, here, since he was in diapers." Mischief plays behind her eyes, and I internally cringe at what memories she's conjuring up from my youth.

"Alright, we don't need a trip down memory lane," I chuckle, cutting her short. "I promised Blair two scoops of your best ice cream."

"What do you recommend?" Blair peruses the wide assortment of flavors that are spread out in the display freezer.

"Are you a sweet or a savory kind of gal?" Mrs. Bishop asks. I watch as Blair hesitates, pushing her lips to one side of her mouth while she thinks.

"I'd say sweet," she finally says with confidence.

"Then I would definitely try this cake batter flavor over here. It's one of my favorites." Mrs. Bishop winks.

"Sounds perfect." Blair grins back at her. I decide on the rocky road flavor and pay for our bowls.

"Hope to see you next time!" Mrs. Bishop calls as we wave and head back out to my truck. We both take a big spoonful of ice cream as we walk.

"World's best?" I ask while I hold the door open for her.

"Pretty darn close," she mumbles through a bite.

I take us slowly through town, content to be taking my time, then I park my truck back in the same spot at the mechanic shop. I hide the keys inside the gas tank door before unloading our supplies and tossing our garbage.

"Ready to head back?" I ask her as we walk down to the dock of the marina toward where my boat is bobbing gently in the waves, lightly banging against the dock bumper.

"Aye aye, Captain," she says, stepping into the boat. I untie the ropes and start the engine, letting us putter out of the harbor slowly while I get situated. We bob along the water at a snail's pace while I stow the space heater and bag from the hardware store, slowly inching out toward the deeper water.

"Thanks for showing me around," she says from the chair next to me. When I glance over, ready to give her a quick reply, the look on her face makes me pause. The color of her eyes looks a deep blue, the lake water behind her making them pop. There's a quiet intensity hidden underneath as she stares directly into mine. a hesitation seeping through.

"It was nice seeing where you grew up, more of what your life is like," she says quietly.

"You mean this doesn't scare you away?" I ask gently, half joking, half terrified of her response.

"Not at all." She gives a shake of her head, searching my eyes for something. Every cell in my body is urging me to lean forward and kiss her right here, right now, in the middle of the lake. But again I resist the urge, not sure of where her head is at and what the look on her face means—what it is exactly that she's looking for from me.

I turn in the swivel chair of my captain's seat until the sides of my knees frame her seat, and then I lean in slightly. My heart starts to race, and I act on the urge to give her transparency and tell her what's on my mind.

"Can I be honest with you for a second?" I ask gruffly, becoming affected by our close proximity already.

She nods her head slowly in return, her chest expanding deeply with her inhale. "I don't know exactly where you're at right now or how you're feeling—and I completely respect whatever it is you want to do—but...I mean, I feel like it's obvious, but just in case...in case it isn't clear...You know that I like you, right?"

Anticipation ever so slightly crosses her face, along with the tiniest hint of a smile, but I also don't miss how the crease between her brows deepens slightly.

"Why?" she asks quietly, as if she can't understand why I even would in the first place.

My stomach drops at her question, a tiny surge of sadness hitting me that she doesn't see how I would be an absolute fool not to.

I move even closer, wanting nothing more than to prove to her that she's worthy of being wanted, until my face hovers close to hers. I search her eyes for any sign of uneasiness or trepidation, but all I can see staring back at me is the look of someone desperately searching for honesty. For some truth to hold onto. For confirmation. As if me saying the words out loud wasn't enough.

"Why the hell wouldn't I?" I say mere seconds before I press my lips to hers. She melts into me, and I feel the warmth of her hand lightly on the outside of my thigh. I respond by bringing both of mine up to cradle her face. My mouth moves slowly against hers in a gentle but firm way, wanting to prove to her how I feel.

We rock with the waves of the boat, my thumb lightly grazing her cheek as I get lost in the feeling of being so connected to her in this way. When I pull back, I hover close, watching as she slowly opens her eyes.

"Do you feel this?" I whisper, taking her hand to place it on top of my chest where my heart is beating incredibly fast. I press my hand against the top of hers to ensure that she can feel it.

"This is what you do to me."

Her face flushes with a tint of pink, and she bites the corner of her lip. Her gaze holds mine as she slowly nods, accepting what my racing heart is telling her.

After a few charged heartbeats with our eyes locked, I squeeze her hand and gently release it, returning back to my seat. With a wink and a shared smile, I shift into gear and head in the direction of Takini Island.

TWENTY-SEVEN
Blair

My knuckles rap against the wood as I knock on Graham's apartment door. I can't believe I've been here this long and have yet to be in this particular part of the lodge. Anticipation swirls in my stomach as I wonder what lies on the other side. Is Graham a chaotic slob, with dishes piled high and clothes strewn about the floor? Or is he a neat freak with everything in its place? When he opens the door, I'm pleased to see that he's somewhere in the middle.

"Blair, hey." His brows lift in surprise. "I came up here to change quickly, and I was just coming to get you. The dinner rush finally finished downstairs."

"I know, but I have some news and didn't want to wait. Can I come in?" Excitement surges through me at what I need to tell him.

"Of course." He swings the door open wide, allowing me to pass through. He kisses my forehead as I walk past, and I can feel my cheeks heat. I'm still not entirely used to his nonchalant affection. The apartment smells like him. Like woodsy pine and crisp cedar. I wonder if he has a scented laundry detergent or if this smell just innately comes from living in the middle of nature—something that's become a part of his DNA.

"Glass of wine?" He pulls a bottle of red out from a cabinet in the kitchen.

"Sure." I lean my hip against the counter, eager to explain why I'm here. "So, I just got off the phone with the opposing counsel. You'll never guess what he said."

"I have to appear in court?" He cringes, clinking his glass with mine before taking a sip. "I'm telling you, I don't even own a suit and tie."

"They dropped the case," I blurt out with a grin.

"Wait, what?" His face freezes in shock.

"Yeah!" I say breathily. "I guess they realized that it was never a strong case to begin with. The plaintiff finally admitted that it may have been an accident."

"No kidding," he breathes in awe, running his hands through the scruff along his jaw. The relief emanating from him is almost palpable, and I can't help but move closer, my hand reaching for the spot above his elbow. He pulls me toward him, cocooning me into the crook under his arm. I wrap both my arms around his torso, clasping my hands together and allowing myself to sink into the way his hug makes me feel. Feeling the comfort that comes with this new act of being close to him.

"This is huge, Blair," he murmurs against the top of my head. "I had no idea where I was going to get the money if we lost."

"I'm so relieved," I say against his shirt, so grateful that I can take a tiny bit of his stress away.

"So, really, that's it? The lawsuit is just done now?"

I release my hold on him to reach for my wine glass. "Yup. They asked the court to dismiss the case."

"That's incredible. Nice work, lawyer." He clinks his glass with mine again as a devilish grin spreads on his face. "Does this happen with all your cases?"

"Absolutely not." I laugh. "But you don't need to thank me—I actually didn't do a whole lot."

His gaze meets mine, and I watch as it turns serious.

"You've done more than you know," he says quietly. I allow the compliment to seep in before glancing around the room.

"I like your place."

"It's no city high-rise, but it's cozy enough." He shrugs.

"Hey, should we just stay up here for dinner? Now that we're here? I can run down and grab us something from the kitchen."

The thought of an intimate, quiet evening up here with him sounds so much better than being with the guests downstairs, who inevitably get boisterous and loud after they've had a few beers. I've heard enough exaggerated fish tales to last me a while.

"I'd love that," I say, watching as his eyes flare a bit while they smolder into mine. My stomach swoops as I don't look away.

"Alright. You stay put. I'll be right back. Make yourself comfortable." He strolls out of his apartment, leaving me alone in his personal space, unsure of what to do. I wander out onto his balcony, making quick note of the guitar in the corner and the cozy futon with a thick blanket draped on the back of it. But the thing that makes my mouth drop open is the view from up here. It's facing the back of the lodge, so none of the cabins or shared areas out front are visible. Just a thick sea of green, yellow, and burnt-orange trees that are already starting to change colors. It feels every bit a secluded, private oasis among the trees from here, even though I know there's civilization just a few steps away.

The breeze whips through the screen, brushing against my face. I close my eyes at the sensation, noting how the breeze almost has a feeling to it—or at least it's evoking one in me. A subtle, satisfied pull from deep inside, a nearly palpable feeling of being awake and a part of nature. A part of the world.

I'm safe here.

For the millionth time today, my mind flashes to our kiss yesterday on the boat in the middle of the lake.

Why the hell wouldn't I?

His words send a fresh set of shivers down my spine at the mere memory.

"Shirley saved us some warm pot roast and veggies," Graham calls from the inside of his apartment, breaking me out of my thoughts. I find him inside, placing a plastic to-go bag on the kitchen table.

"Oh my gosh, it smells delicious." I open one of the Styrofoam containers, taking a deep inhale of the savory scent.

"Ladies first," he says, handing me a plate, which I load up before sitting across from him at the small table.

"So is this where your grandparents lived?" I ask, breaking the silence after a few quiet moments of enjoying the food.

"Yup." He nods. "I added a few touches when I moved in, but otherwise it has stayed pretty much the same."

"I'm guessing that 'Live Laugh Love' sign above the sink was your idea, right?"

"That would be my sister's doing." He rolls his eyes playfully.

"There's a lot of history in this place for you, huh?" I muse. "Will Ruby Lodge be okay now that the lawsuit is off the table?"

He slides his empty plate over and takes a deep, heavy breath in. "I don't know...it still doesn't look great, honestly."

"Really?" My stomach drops.

"Yeah. At the very least, we'll need to downsize. Close off a few cabins and minimize how many reservations we take—for the immediate future anyway. We'll most likely need to take more drastic measures down the road."

"I'm so sorry."

"It is what it is. That's life, right?" He shrugs as his gaze meets mine, and he offers a sad smile. My eyes roam over the faint worry line that creases his brow.

"Do you want to sit with me out there?" He jerks his head, motioning toward the balcony. "I'll do the dishes later."

"I would love to." I grab my glass of wine and follow him out the door and settle on the futon, pulling the knit blanket over my legs to get comfortable. There's a low flutter in my belly when Graham reaches for his guitar, perching it on his knee next to me on the couch.

He starts playing a slow melody, his head slanted down over the guitar, intently focused on his fingers as they strum. I sip my wine as darkness starts to fall. Eventually, he stops, leaning his guitar very carefully against the futon.

"It's getting a little chilly." He smirks, and I lift the corner of the blanket for him to climb under. He slides a strong arm over my shoulders and snuggles next to me until I'm pressed all the way against his side.

We watch as the sun completely disappears, and the chorus of bugs and grasshoppers start their own music in the darkness.

"How have you been feeling?" he asks quietly.

"A little better." I nod against the crook of his shoulder. He squeezes me tighter in response, and I let myself melt completely into him, soaking up how I feel when he holds me like this. I let myself just be in the moment.

I'm still not entirely convinced that I'm good enough for him or why he would want to be with me in the first place, but the way he's been looking at me has me—maybe foolishly—believing that he really does. Maybe he does see me and isn't scared by what he sees.

Maybe he's seen me all along.

"Good," he says simply, squeezing his fingers against my arm.

We spend an hour on the balcony, chatting sporadically but mostly just enjoying the quiet evening together.

Eventually, when my eyelids start to feel heavy, he squeezes my knee. "Come on, I'll walk you back."

TWENTY-EIGHT
Graham

"You bet," I say into the phone from behind the welcome desk. "I've got one cabin reservation for two guests for three nights, four days. And I'll go ahead and book a fishing guide for you on the second day. Did you want a half-day or a full-day guide?"

"Just a half-day would be great. We plan to hunt the rest of the time we're there. Thank you," the gentleman says.

"My pleasure. We'll see you on the twenty-ninth."

I hang up and mark the reservation in the booking calendar for next month. As per usual lately, I feel uneasy about booking anything more than a month out, especially as we head into the fall season. We typically have a steady stream of hunters that come to the island that time of year, and I'm nervous about being able to keep the lodge running by then. As the cold weather looms closer, so does the impending need for a working heating system.

But I'm not in a position to make any major decisions about downsizing just yet. I'm naive enough—or maybe just blindly stupid enough—to think I'll still be able to figure something out. I'm holding off on limiting reservations for as long as I possibly can.

"Ruby Lodge," I answer the phone when it rings again almost immediately.

"Hi, is your restaurant open today?" the voice on the other end asks. His voice is muffled from the sound of the wind roaring in the background. "We're out fishing by Oak Island and went to Sunset Lodge yesterday for lunch. We'd like to explore as many islands as we can while we're here, so we'd like to stop at Ruby today to grab a bite. I just wanted to make sure you were open before we head that way."

"Absolutely. Yes, we're open and would love to have you." These kinds of drop-ins are a decent part of our business, and I always appreciate the heads up when they're coming so we can be prepared for their arrival. We can never fully anticipate how many boats will stop by for the lunch rush, so it's nice to have a general idea.

"Great. We'll plan to swing by in a couple hours, then."

"I'll be on the lookout to help you tie up." I hang up the phone and finish scribbling a note in the calendar from the earlier booking.

"Hey, Graham," Nita calls from the dining room. "The register locked up on me again. I need change, and it won't open."

"Be right there," I call out. I close the calendar and slide it back into a drawer of the desk.

"It's giving you trouble again, huh?" I ask Nita when I get to the bar.

"Second time today."

I whack the side of the register a few times until it jostles loose. "You gotta use some force—find some anger to put behind the blow next time." I throw her a smile before stepping back.

"Thanks," she says, quickly reaching for the change needed for the guest at the bar.

"Let me know if it happens again." I tap the countertop and make my way to the laundry room. The towels are still warm when I take them out of the dryer and fold them, creating a stack on top of the ironing board. I happily get the folding done, eager to get my chores done for the day. After swinging the dryer door shut, I hoist the pile of towels under my arm and bring them outside.

On my way to cabin two, my mind drifts to Blair, who I haven't seen yet this morning. I don't want to crowd her, so I haven't checked in yet, but I'm sure I'll find her in the library at some point like I always do. The anticipation of seeing her makes my stomach clench, and I start running through some ideas of ways that I can squeeze in some more time with her in the coming days. Maybe I'll take her back into town. Or we can roast marshmallows over the fire once the guests are all asleep.

Cabin two is vacant and quiet. I brush a few stray leaves off the front porch with my foot before going inside. I bring the towels to the linen closet where I stack them neatly inside, then I make a round to re-inspect everything I cleaned earlier. I go from the back closet, all the way up to the loft area, and then back through the kitchen just to be sure. Once I'm satisfied that she's all ready for guests, I head back outside and take the short walk to the docks.

I step into one of my fishing boats to tinker with the engine. I noticed it was acting up yesterday when I took it out. Thankfully, no guests or Blair were with me. The last thing you want is to be out in the middle of the lake on a boat with a faulty engine, and I refuse to send my guests out on one that I'm not completely confident in, so keeping up the maintenance of the boats is a top priority for me.

After a half hour or so, I manage to get the engine in working shape again. One by one, I pick up the mess I made and put the boat back together. I'm just stepping back onto the dock when the faint hum of a floatplane comes from above. Confused, I watch with a hand shielding my eyes from the sun as Sam lands on the water and slowly taxis into the harbor. I meet him on the end of the dock and wave when he opens the door.

"Hey, Sam. I didn't know you were stopping by today," I say, holding the door open for him.

"Hey, Graham. Yeah, I've got a last-minute pick-up for a ride to town," he says, climbing out of the plane and onto the dock.

"For who?" I ask, confused.

"Graham." I don't recognize Blair's tone when she says my name, but it's foreign and jarring enough that my stomach drops. My reaction is all but confirmed when I twist around and immediately zero in on the bags by Blair's feet. Dread rushes through me, knowing there's only one reason why she would have her luggage with her.

"What's going on?" I ask cautiously, drawing closer to her.

"I have to leave," she says frantically. I know the expression on her face well. It looks exactly like my dad's always does—filled with anxiety, distraction, and a hint of guilt.

I can't stop the panic that grips my core. My mind starts racing with questions, but I can't seem to form the words out loud. Why is she leaving? Did she change her mind about being ready for this? What does this mean for us?

"It's just for a little while," she says in a rush, reaching behind me to pass her backpack to Sam while I stand frozen in a state of confusion. "I promise I'll be back and explain everything, but I have to go back home for a couple days."

Home.

I don't like the way she says it or the taste it leaves in my mouth. The reminder that she belongs somewhere else. That Sam's really here right now, and she's really leaving.

"Why? Is everything okay?" I finally force the words out.

"I got a phone call just a little bit ago from a hospital in Chicago," she says breathily, walking back and forth to hand each item of her luggage off to Sam. "Barry's been in a car accident. He's stable as of now, but he's unconscious, and they say things could go downhill at any moment, and if they do, they could go really fast. They want me there as soon as possible. I guess I'm still listed as his power of attorney, so I need to go sort out that mess."

A pang of jealousy hits, along with a myriad of other emotions. I hate that she's leaving just when I was starting to have hope that whatever this is between us might actually go somewhere. I hate that she still has ties to Barry and that she's rushing off to go see him. But what I hate more than anything is that she has to deal with all of this by herself.

"Okay. What can I do?" I ask.

"Nothing," she dismisses me. "I can handle it."

"But you're coming back?" I ask weakly. She makes one last half-jog toward me, this time to kiss the spot right above my cheek bone.

"I'll be back," she says firmly, but her eyes are distracted and not at all convincing. I'm left scrambling for anything she gave me to hold onto, but I still can't make sense of any of it. She climbs in the plane with one last backward glance. I watch helplessly as the door closes and they take off.

TWENTY-NINE
Blair

The door of my apartment softly clicks shut behind me, and I lean my back against it with a heaving breath. The smell of sterile hospital air lingers on my clothes as I slide my purse off my shoulder and onto the floor. Everything about being in this place feels different than the last time I was here. It feels just as empty and cold as it always has, but this time, it doesn't feel comforting like it used to. It feels foreign and uncomfortable. Stark and bare.

I feel as if I'm a visitor, trespassing in someone else's house. I walk slowly into the apartment, an ache of exhaustion thrumming deep in my bones. Aimlessly, I wander around, unsure of what exactly I should do now. As if on autopilot, I wander down the hallway to the bedroom. My suitcase and travel bags lay in the same position against the wall where I set them earlier when I was in a rush to get to the hospital. The bed is neatly made, and it seems that there isn't a single thing out of place in this entire apartment.

A strange feeling sits in my gut as I stand here scanning the room. A sense that I shouldn't be here, even though my belongings are everywhere. My socks and several sets of pajamas are neatly folded in that dresser across the room. That bathroom has my toothbrush and favorite toothpaste in the drawer, and that closet is filled with my clothes. If you lift the bed skirt on the left side of the bed, you'd find my worn pair of gray slippers.

Yet I feel no connection to any of it.

I don't belong here.

I sit on the side of the bed and get a sudden longing to be by the campfire on Takini Island or on Graham's balcony with my feet stretched out under a blanket with a good book. I miss it.

The island.

The way I feel when I'm there.

The friend who's quickly becoming so much more.

My phone buzzes with a text message, pulling me out of my thoughts.

Annie: Call me when you get a chance. No rush, just want to check in.

With a lazy smile, I click on her name and force myself off the bed and down the hallway as it rings.

"Hey, Annie," I say when she answers, sinking into a chair at the glass kitchen table. I rest my cheek on the palm of my hand, letting my elbow that's resting on the table hold my tired head up. My eyes feel heavy and involuntarily drift shut as I relax.

"How are you?" she asks with concern.

"I'm tired," I reply truthfully.

"Any change with Barry since your text earlier?"

"Yeah, he woke up shortly after that."

"He did? Wow."

"Yeah, the doctor said he's going to be okay. He's got a long road ahead of him, though. We only talked for a little bit. I pretty much just made sure he was comfortable and not in any pain."

"What did he say? I mean, how did that conversation go? That must have been so weird."

"It was a little weird," I admit. "But only because I wasn't sure what to say. Once they checked him out and left us alone, he thanked me for coming. I wouldn't say we're on great terms, but there's no animosity or anything. I waited in the waiting room until his cousin could get there a few hours later. Once we transferred the power of attorney to him and signed the papers, I left."

"Wow," she breathes. "Are you planning to go back tomorrow?"

"No," I say firmly. "He has his people there now. I'm not one of them anymore."

"And that's no one's fault but his own."

"Annie," I warn quietly.

"Sorry," she says, and we both fall quiet. I cross the room to fill a glass from the cupboard with ice water and take a few long sips.

"I'm really proud of you, Blair," she says out of nowhere.

"For what?"

"Everything that you're doing. I know how hard things have been for you. I see you trying to figure life out. The changes you're making. I'm proud of you, is all." I can practically picture the way she's smiling softly at the phone. As much as I hate the attention, it also feels really good to be noticed. To feel seen for my efforts.

"It's weird being back here," I admit, looking around the sad space. "It feels different...like it's changed somehow."

"The apartment changed or you've changed?"

"That's a good question." It's as if my mind, my body—my soul—is changing in some small way that I can't explain. And this version of me doesn't fit with the person I used to be when I was last here. Like one corner of my puzzle piece is bent, preventing me from fully fitting together in this world anymore.

As if my body craves any sort of fresh air it can get, I open the sliding door that leads to the balcony and sit on a cold, metal chair in the dark, not bothering to turn the dimmer light on. Car horns buzz, and a faint police siren rings out into the night, a stark difference to the balcony evening I just shared with Graham. A ghost of a smile touches my lips at the memory.

"What's your plan as far as moving out? Obviously you're not going to stay there, right?"

"No, I'll move out. I don't know where yet, but I know I can't stay here."

I deserve more.

"You know you always have a place here with us. Eric would move his video game collection out of the spare room in the blink of an eye if you wanted to come."

"I know," I say softly, grateful for the offer that I know has always been there. "Thanks, Annie. Maybe I will come there."

With a deep sigh, I watch brake lights flashing below. The noise and the smell of the city starts to make me feel suffocated and overwhelmed. My chest squeezes around my lungs, and the uncertainty of my future makes my next inhale so much harder to take. I don't know what my next steps should be or where I'll end up. I don't know what I'll end up doing with my career that can't stay paused forever. But amidst all the uncertainty, one thing is crystal clear since I've been back—I don't belong here. At least not right now.

"Or do you want to go back to Minnesota?" she asks gently. A hint of a flutter rises in my stomach at the mere thought.

"I told Graham I was coming back," I point out.

"That's not what I asked. Do you want to go back?"

"I do." I nod my head even though she can't see me. I want nothing more than to be with Graham right now. "But is that the most responsible decision right now? What about my apartment? Shouldn't I figure out a plan first? I definitely don't want to be here when Barry gets discharged."

"Listen, why don't you pour yourself a glass of wine—I'll do the same—and we'll talk it out. Do what we did in grade school—make a solid pros-and-cons list. We'll finalize some options for you, huh?"

"That sounds like a good idea. We always fared well with those lists, didn't we?" I'm grateful for her positive attitude and enthusiasm, hoping some of it will rub off on me.

"Yes, we did. Okay, let's break. I'll keep my speaker phone on. Meet back here in two minutes?"

"Deal." I set the phone on the small table next to the chair and head back inside to the kitchen. I grab a wine glass and a bottle of wine out of the chiller that I no longer have a right to and pour myself a glass. Then, with a renewed sense of determination, I head back outside to Annie.

THIRTY
Graham

"Any word from her?" Shirley asks from my office doorway. It's the same question she's asked me every day for the last two days since Blair left. A question that leaves me grumpy and heartsick each time she asks.

"Nothing other than the message she sent yesterday saying she was okay and will be in touch soon," I reply, trying hard to not let my bad mood result in a negative tone toward Shirley. None of this is her fault.

Now that the lawsuit is over, there is technically no reason Blair would need to come back. If she did, it would be under a completely different pretense, and I can't help but wonder if there was enough that we built between us to convince her to come back. With each passing second, I find myself getting more and more anxious and impatient. What if she doesn't come back? Did we miss our chance to be something? Is it over before it even really began? I've been struggling to fight the urge to take my pent-up stress out on everyone around me. Unfortunately, Shirley is the one who's most often in my crosshairs.

"By the way, Sam's flying in this afternoon to drop off my food order and some supplies for the kitchen," she says kindly.

"Alright. Let me know when he gets here, and I'll haul it inside."

"Oh, and something's up with the freezer temperature. Some of the meat is getting freezer burnt in there."

"I'll check it out," I say curtly. I can feel Shirley's presence lingering in the doorway.

"She'll be back, you know," she says firmly. I force a deep inhale to compose myself before responding.

"How do you know?" I ask quietly, barely looking up from my computer.

"Just a hunch," she says before backing away.

Just then, an email drops in my inbox from Scott with the subject line *I need an answer ASAP*. I read through the email that's more or less requesting confirmation of the furnace installation as they need to finalize their upcoming schedule for the busy season.

"Argh." I palm my jaw, scratching roughly where my neck meets my ear. I suppose I've put it off as long as I can. I'm afraid there's not much else I can do.

While in town yesterday, I stopped by the bank to look into getting a loan, but I was only approved for enough to do the main lodge and six of the fifteen cabins, which means we'll need to close the other nine for the winter. It's a massive hit—one

I feel right in the center of my gut every time I think about it—but I don't see any way around it.

After typing out my reply and hitting send, the sinking feeling doesn't dissipate. Guilt creeps in as well, weighing heavily on my chest. I feel like a failure and that I've officially let everyone down. My parents. My grandparents. I wonder what will be next. Will we need to close down all fifteen? Keep the lodge open as a restaurant for island hoppers only? I'm sure that wouldn't last long either, eventually leading to shuttered doors.

With a sigh I feel come from deep within, I close the computer and head out of the office. Without Blair here as a distraction or an excuse to take a break, I pick the next thing on my to-do list and head past the empty bar and out to the shed.

I need to maneuver a few things around to get the Bobcat out, but I'm able to drive it out from the very back of the shed and head toward the north side of the property to where a fallen tree sits. The tree fell right across the start of the hiking path, so I spend the next hour breaking it into pieces and moving it out of the way. I work on autopilot, zoning out and getting lost in the work, trying my damnedest to not think about Blair, my mom, or the lodge.

When the trail is sufficiently passable again, I drive the Bobcat back to the shed, taking note that the windows need to be cleaned in cabin nine. After getting the shed put back together, I head back to the lodge. My phone rings in my pocket just as I reach the front door.

"Hey," I say to Sydney, continuing toward the laundry room. I'm aware that my tone is harsher than normal, but I don't listen to the small voice in my head that tells me to slow down and collect myself. There's too much work that needs to be done, and I'm the only one here to do it.

"Hey, Graham. How are you?" she asks in a tone that is far too chipper for my mood right now.

"Fine." I grab the window cleaning supplies from the bucket and huff back outside with a one-track mind focused on getting as much done as I can today.

"I tried calling Dad to check in on Mom, but he didn't answer. How is she doing?"

"Why don't you come home and see for yourself for once?" I snap, losing my patience.

"Whoa...forget it," she says defensively, clearly hurt at my outburst. "You're obviously not in a good mood. I'll talk to you later—"

"Wait," I stop her before she can hang up. I pause for a second. Then, instead of heading toward cabin nine, I force myself to walk all the way down the dock to the very end and have a seat, dangling my legs off the edge.

"I'm sorry." I blow out a huge breath and pinch the bridge of my nose. "I'm just a little bit stressed. I didn't mean to take it out on you."

"Tell me what's going on," she says, her voice softening. I debate skirting around the lodge's financial issues, but what's the point now that I know we're officially downsizing come winter?

"I should have mentioned something a while ago...but Ruby isn't doing so well right now," I say honestly, then I start rambling, acting on the urge to keep going. "We're in trouble. And aside from that, I'm a little overwhelmed about everything that needs to get done around here and...I've got...girl...problems."

"Okay," she says slowly. "That's a lot to unpack there. What do you mean the lodge isn't doing so well?"

"We're in trouble financially. We have been for a little while, but I've been able to keep things afloat. Now there are too many big-ticket repairs needed and not enough money coming in to cover it all."

"What does that mean exactly?"

"It means we can't afford to run all the cabins through the winter. We'll be limiting our allowed reservation number."

"Dang, that really sucks. Why didn't you say anything sooner?"

"I thought I could handle it. And I didn't want to burden Dad. He has enough on his plate."

"You could have told me." Her tone is laced with a subtle hurt.

"No offense, but you're not exactly around much," I say as gently as I can. "And there isn't anything you could have done anyway."

"I would have come up there if you needed me to. I asked all the time," she points out.

"You're right. You did," I agree. "I still don't want you to worry about it, okay?"

"Just keep me posted, please?"

"I promise." A few moments of silence pass between us.

"Can we talk about the girl problems now?" I can almost see the growing smile on her face.

"No," I say firmly. "I shouldn't have said anything. You and I don't talk about that kind of stuff."

"Only because you never let me." She laughs.

I blow out a breath and reluctantly tell her all about Blair. How she first came to the island and how she came back. How she left abruptly, and I have no idea if she'll actually be back or not. She listens with bated breath as I spill most of the details.

"If she does come back, how would that work? Do you think she would move there? Would you do long distance?"

Another possible scenario crosses my mind: the lodge closes, and I'm no longer bound to Takini Island.

"I have no idea. We'd figure it out as we go, I guess. But I'm willing to take that chance for her—if she ever wants to, anyway."

"Who knows? Maybe she'll surprise you and come back. Then you will have worried for nothing," she points out.

"Maybe," I say, but my mind offers a different reminder.

That nobody ever stays.

"Well, I'll tell you one thing—if she can put up with you, then I like her already."

"Very funny," I say, letting the conversation die down as I watch the waves out in the middle of the lake.

"Mom's good, by the way."

"Thanks," she says quietly. "Anyway, I have to get going. I've got a big architectural presentation due tomorrow. Please keep me posted on everything, okay?"

"I will. Bye, Syd." I hang up and keep the phone in my lap for a second, letting my view calm my nerves one slow, rolling wave at a time. Feeling marginally better after talking to Syd and taking a break, I climb up and head off the dock to get back to work.

THIRTY-ONE
Blair

Fun Fact: Minnesota produces more turkeys each year than there are people in California.

I smirk at the random information at the end of Isaac's Gavel Gang update email and the obvious obsession he's developed over Minnesota. I reply back to the group with an email of my own, explaining that I still don't know when I'll be back, but I promise to do a video call this week, per Cassidy's request.

Popping a French fry in my mouth, I stare out the window at the marina harbor, where a few fishing boats and two float-planes are tied to the dock.

"Hey. Back so soon?" Sam has a seat on the stool next to me. The diner in Baudette has stayed pretty empty since I got here an hour ago, but a few people seem to be trickling in now that it's late afternoon.

"Hey, Sam. How are you?"

"Can't complain. You headed back out to Takini?"

"I am. I reserved a boat ferry, but it doesn't leave for two hours, so I'm just killing time 'til then."

"I'm heading out there right now, actually. I can fly you over if you don't want to wait for the ferry."

"Really? You wouldn't mind?" A newfound surge of excitement runs through me. As much as I dislike the floatplane idea—and purposely booked the ferry instead—the thought of getting to Takini as soon as humanly possible does sound appealing.

After determining a plan of action with Annie the other day, I couldn't book my flight up here fast enough. There's a low hum of adrenaline that's been running under my skin ever since, anticipation about getting to the island—and back to Graham.

"Not at all. I'm heading out there to drop off some groceries for Shirley. There's plenty of room if you want to hop in."

"That would be great, Sam. Thank you." I blurt it out before I've had a chance to think it through. Apparently, my brain is willing to sacrifice my personal comfort to get there faster.

"My pleasure. Plane's leaving in five minutes. I'll meet you at the dock." He leaves a five-dollar bill on the counter for the lemonade he just chugged in record time.

"These yours?" He points to the luggage at my feet.

"They are."

"I'll put them in the plane." He lifts my suitcases and heads out the side door of the diner, leaving me to quickly pay my bill.

"Thank you!" I say to the waitress and then rush down the dock after him.

"Watch your step," he says. I take his outstretched hand and climb into the plane, sliding into a window seat.

"Ready?" Sam asks, climbing into the cockpit. I take a steadying breath, mentally preparing myself for the experience.

All I can do is nod and lay my head against the backrest while he takes us out of the harbor. I keep my eyes closed until we've been in the air for a little while and I'm sufficiently confident that we won't nosedive. This flight feels only slightly less nausea-inducing than the first two times I flew, but this time, at least there's a level of excitement that mixes with the anxiety.

My stomach rolls as the floatplane dips with turbulence, tilting my body toward the center aisle. I look out the small window and watch as Takini Island comes into view. My chest warms as I take in the view below. The small island surrounded by water is calling to me, and the familiarity of what—and who—lies below sends a rush of anticipation across my skin. I take it all in. The towering sea of trees that covers almost every square inch of the island. The curve of the point where I know Ruby Lodge sits just around it.

The plane descends lower in a jolt, and for a moment, I curse myself for not waiting for the boat ferry instead. The water is imminent, quickly approaching. My eyes squeeze shut as the floats hit the water roughly, jolting me forward in my seat. A rush of relief surges through me once we're officially out of the air.

I watch impatiently as the plane brings us around the corner into Ruby Lodge's bay. My breath gets stuck in my throat when I notice Graham and Shirley both standing there, waiting at the end of the dock. His hands are tucked into his pockets, his sturdy frame tight and unassuming as he stares in the general direction of the plane.

A rush of nerves hits me. I never told him I was coming back. Maybe I should have checked in with him, made sure he wanted me to come. Fully aware that it's far too late now, I swallow down the thickness in my throat and grab my backpack.

When Sam opens the door, I slide the supplies from the back of the plane over to him so he can pass it out to Graham. When the last of the items are out, I ignore the sudden spark of anxiety that pierces my stomach and follow behind him. Immediately, I register the shock on Graham's face, followed quickly by a high-pitched squeal out of Shirley.

"Blair?" His eyes are wide and disbelieving.

"Hi," I say, a smile tugging at my lips with nervous energy.

"What the..." He wastes no time pulling me into a hug. I drop my luggage as his arms completely engulf me, my arms squeezing around his neck. He tightens his hold, tilting his head into my neck, and I melt into him.

This.

This is what I want.

When I pull back, I notice Shirley is already halfway off the dock with her arms full of grocery bags and a wide grin on her face.

"See ya next time," Sam calls from behind me.

"Thank you, Sam. I really appreciate the ride," I say with a wave as he shuts the door and takes off, leaving Graham and me alone on the dock.

His gaze coasts over my face. "You're here," he breathes, both a statement and a question.

"I'm here," I whisper back.

He reaches for my hand, gripping mine in his as if he somehow still doesn't believe that it's real. I squeeze once with a smile. I didn't anticipate that I would be needing to give him reassurance.

"I told you I would be back," I say softly.

"I wasn't sure if you would," he admits. Holding his stare, our hands entwined, we both fully understand the underlying message of me being here.

The first time I stayed on this island, I was choosing myself.

This time, I'm choosing him.

"Let me help carry these in," I say, reaching for a handful of bags. He follows behind, carrying my luggage and the rest of the bags.

"I see you packed light," he grunts.

"I think it's more that I underpacked the times before," I say with a guilty shrug.

We carry everything up to the lodge. Graham sets my luggage outside the front door, and I help haul the groceries back into the kitchen.

"Welcome back, sweetie." Shirley welcomes me with a hug.

"It's good to be back," I say into her hair before disconnecting. "It seems a little quiet. I'm assuming there aren't any guests?"

"A few left this morning," Graham says, unloading groceries into the fridge. "More are coming tomorrow."

"I've got this. You two go ahead and run off," Shirley says with a wave of her hand.

"Are you sure?" Graham asks.

"Absolutely. Oh, but here, you'll need to eat." She pulls a container of food out of the fridge.

"Ham-and-cheese sliders that I made earlier."

"Thanks, Shirley." I gratefully take the food and follow Graham back outside.

"I kept cabin four open for you, just in case," he says, lifting my luggage. I swing my backpack over one shoulder and head down the stairs.

We fall into step side by side on the trail, and I feel myself drawing closer to him with each stride. I feel the urge to be as close to him as I possibly can. I've missed him.

"I'm sorry I left in such a hurry," I say quietly while we walk. "I feel like I could have explained things better."

He shrugs, giving me a small smile. "It's okay."

"No, I want you to know why I left." We reach the cabin, and I immediately walk right to the porch swing. He sits next to me and pulls open the food container, setting it in his lap. He hands me a sandwich and holds his own up in a cheers before we both take a bite. The energy between us is buzzing like it always is when we're this close.

"I was listed as Barry's power of attorney, and the hospital needed me there," I explain. "It was kind of a frantic, whirlwind of a day. But once his other family arrived and I wasn't needed anymore, I left."

"Is he gonna be alright?" he asks quietly, looking down at his food.

"He is." I take another bite with a nod. "Then I stayed another day to figure out a plan for moving out of my apartment."

His brows lift slightly. I gaze out at the rippling blue lake, taking in the view that I also missed—though not quite as much as him.

"I arranged to have all my stuff moved into a temporary storage facility until I figure everything out."

"That's a big step."

It is. And there are so many details and topics to discuss, but I don't feel the need to go into all of it. There will be plenty of time for that. For tonight, I just want to soak up this moment here with him.

We finish eating, and when he moves the food container off to the side and lifts his arm in invitation, I slide closer to him until I'm pressed firmly into his solid side. His hand curls around my shoulder, and I lay my head on his, feeling a warm current run through me.

"It's nice to be back," I say quietly. "I missed it here."

"You did?" He smiles, relief and contentment passing across his face.

"Yeah. And I missed you." I tilt my head up to look at him. My eyes connect with his, and he brings his other hand to grip my chin.

He leans in closer and whispers, "I missed you too," right before pressing his lips to mine.

I push against him, our mouths melting together, gently at first, making my heart start beating ever so slightly faster, and then the energy between us sparks with a renewed sense of intensity. His hand moves from my chin to slide through my hair, cradling my head over my ear. My stomach swoops, and a shiver runs across the top of my skin at his touch, like my body is again saying *I'm alive, I'm alive.*

In a sudden act of boldness, fueled by the way he's making me feel, I cautiously twist my body so I can climb onto his lap, all the while staying connected by our kiss. My bent legs fall on either side of him, and he grips my hips to help position me on top of him. Then he runs his hands slowly up the outsides of my arms that are resting gently against his chest.

Eventually, I pull back from his mouth, hovering close to his face to look into his eyes, which are smoldering with intensity. Both of us are lightly panting and out of breath.

"It's getting late," I murmur, very aware of the way his hands are burning my skin as they skate across my hips.

"I should go," he whispers gruffly with a nod. Immediately, my body protests. No part of me wants to be away from him right now. The chemistry between us—the way the air feels like it's literally buzzing—is unlike anything I've ever experienced. How can I crave something I've never felt before tonight? I don't know the answer, but I do know that I desperately want more. I need more.

I lay my hands on top of his shoulder and lean in close for a quick kiss, unable to fight the temptation.

"Do you want to stay?" I ask quietly, knowing full well that I need to be the one to initiate the next step. His dark eyes flick back up to mine, scanning back and forth, searching for reassurance.

"Would that be alright?" he asks, his eyes hooded and his voice low and gravelly.

I simply nod, pressing my lips back to his. His hands eagerly run up my back, sending another shiver down my spine. I've never felt this way before when I've been in another man's arms. Graham makes me feel safe and comfortable yet buzzed and exhilarated at the same time.

I relish in the high of his touch until Graham grips my hips roughly. When I pull back and open my eyes, a silent exchange passes between us. He's asking for permission, and I'm all too ready and eager to say yes. No words are spoken, but there's a quiet understanding. He leans forward to bring his lips back to mine, and he effortlessly lifts me as he stands. Staying connected by our kiss, he opens the door, and he carries me into the dark cabin, swinging the door shut behind him.

THIRTY-TWO
Graham

The soft, repeated puff of Blair's warm breath against my skin pulls me out of sleep the next morning. As I blink my eyes a few times to further wake up, I become more aware of our positioning while we were sleeping. I'm flat on my back with an arm around Blair, who's curled into my side with one leg bent over my knee and an arm splayed across my chest. Her warm, naked body heats mine, and I can feel her heart beating through her chest that's pushed against my side. Her long brown hair cascades over my shoulder, tickling my chin. It feels good holding her like this. It feels right.

I can't help but smile in my still-sleepy haze at the memory of last night and spending the night here. I hadn't been expecting anything, of course, and would have happily waited for as long as she needed to, but there's no denying that the connection we forged last night felt monumental—and only further proved to send me head over heels for this woman.

Blair stirs next to me, a soft humming coming from the back of her throat. I gently squeeze her shoulder with my hand that's slightly numb as her body shifts and stretches to wake up.

"Good morning," I whisper. Her eyes blink open, and she tilts her head toward me, her cheek sliding against my skin.

"Morning," she says with a small smile, her voice thick with sleep. She snuggles in closer, returning to the same way she was curled against me all night, but bringing her arm farther across my chest this time. A whisper of a spark spreads across my skin when she squeezes herself tighter against me.

"I had no idea how comfortable this bed in here was," I say. "Never knew what I was missing."

"You mean you don't make a habit out of sleeping with your guests in their cabins?" she teases.

I smirk but keep my tone serious. "You're not a guest, Blair. Haven't been for a while."

I can feel the way her smile spreads against my skin, bringing a satisfied smile to my own face. We lie there, our breathing becoming in sync, with my finger lightly grazing her shoulder. I think about how uneasy I felt when she was gone and I didn't know if she would be back.

"You know," I say quietly. "When you were gone, I was worried that maybe you were second-guessing everything that was happening with me. With us."

She twists her torso so she can rest her chin against her hand on my chest and look up at me.

"Really?" she asks, her brow creasing.

"I thought that maybe you needed time. I know we moved pretty fast after your breakup."

She shakes her head. "No. I didn't need time. I was out of that relationship a long time before we broke up. I don't know that I was ever really in it, actually. I don't think either of us was."

I nod, taking in her words, seeing the truth in her eyes.

"To be honest, I was just living a life on autopilot back in Chicago. It wasn't until I came up here that I realized that the potential for feeling different—for actually feeling something at all—was within reach. I had never felt like it was attainable before."

I bring my hand up to run my fingers through her hair, my chest tightening. I don't like that she has ever been anything but happy. Or that she's been existing in a world that doesn't adamantly remind her of how incredible she is.

"And now?" I ask cautiously.

"Now, I don't really know," she admits with a smile. "But regardless of what happens between you and me, I know that I don't belong there. And I'm taking the steps to build a better, more fulfilled life for myself."

I smile at her with pride.

"I still need to figure out where exactly I want to be long term. But for right now, that's right here with you."

"Well, I'm glad you came back." I run my fingertip down the length of her bare spine, coasting over the goosebumps that rise on her skin.

"I am too." She shivers under my touch and shifts up until she's lying flat on top of me. I bring my lips to hers in a gentle kiss before wrapping both my arms around her back. She lays her head sideways under my chin, and we lie like that for a while, listening to birds chirping right outside the window.

"I need coffee," she mumbles against the skin of my chest.

"That's my cue to get up." I swiftly roll her onto her back, eliciting a squeal as she lands on her pillow. With one more hasty kiss, I reluctantly climb off the bed and pull on my jeans from yesterday.

"Meet you downstairs," I call behind me as I make my way down to the kitchen, where I make two cups of coffee for us. The smell of it fills the cabin, luring Blair out of bed. I leave her rustling around upstairs and bring the coffee out onto the porch. I have a seat on the swing, the cool morning air brushing against the bare skin of my torso. I admire the particular view from here, having not spent a lot of down time on this porch.

"How did you know I like to have my coffee out here?" Blair asks, following behind me a few moments later. My breath gets caught in my throat at the sight of her bare legs stemming out from underneath my gray T-shirt that hangs loosely over her body. Even with her messy hair and without a trace of makeup on, she's stunningly beautiful. Vulnerable and bare. I feel grateful that I get to see her this way. This raw side of her.

"Wild guess," I say after clearing my throat. I hand her the mug and try not to watch as she lowers onto the swing next to me, curling one leg underneath her and bending one up to rest her coffee on.

"I've never been so grateful to not have any guests around," I say, unable to fight the urge to lean in to kiss the side of her neck.

"Unless Shirley's got her binoculars out," Blair murmurs.

"She's been known to do that," I deadpan and laugh when she bats me away with her hand.

"How were things here while I was gone?" she asks.

I fill her in on the last couple of days and the decision that was made regarding the furnaces and the plan for winter reservations.

"I'm sorry," she says, touching my hand. "I know that's the last thing you wanted to do."

"It is what it is, I guess, right? Not much else I can do."

We watch as two squirrels fight over an acorn as they scurry in front of the cabin, rustling leaves as they go.

"So what's on the agenda today?" she asks before taking a sip of coffee.

"Well, I cleaned the cabins yesterday, but the lodge needs a good once-over before guests arrive around eleven. And a few random things like re-stocking towels and linens in each cabin. You know, just fascinating stuff like that."

"Fascinating it is." The way her eyes light up at the prospect of doing tasks around the lodge has me chuckling, but it also fills me with a deep sense of appreciation. For her. For the universe for bringing her to me. I'm fully aware that this is still new and that she could decide to leave at any time, but I choose to live in the present and appreciate what's right in front of me while it lasts. Life is too short not to.

We finish our coffee in peace, watching two eagles as they soar in the cloudless sky above. All the while, my hand rests on her thigh, enjoying the comfortable, easy way about us now. Allowing myself to hold onto brief pockets of hope that we could maybe make this work somehow. Regardless of the uncertainties in both our lives, I'm certain we could build something amazing together if we tried hard enough.

"Alright." She eagerly slides off the swing. "Let's get to work."

I snicker and shake my head at her being so willing and ready to spend the day cleaning.

"After you." I down the last sip of my own coffee and quickly follow her back inside.

THIRTY-THREE
Blair

The burn in my thighs as I finish my evening hike is a little bit less intense than it was yesterday. Each day, it seems to take a little less effort to walk the trail, and I relish the daily reminder that my body is fully capable of doing hard things. Things that once seemed impossible and out of reach. The slow ache in my muscles that has been building gradually every time I go for a hike has become a welcome discomfort. A physical sign of me getting stronger. Not to mention the endorphins have been a welcome help in fueling my newfound positive energy.

I'm happy.

I've been happy.

Ever since coming back three days ago, it's like I've finally given myself permission to jump in head-first.

Into living.

Into experiencing new things and new emotions.

Each day, I feel like I come awake a tiny bit more. I've settled into a nice routine of enjoying the fresh air, moving my body, and reveling in my new relationship with Graham. It's provided a strong foundation for me to thrive here. I had never let myself fully believe that I could feel this way—or even fully reach for it—until now.

A twig snaps under the weight of my shoe as I continue on the last half-mile leading back to the lodge. I wipe my damp forehead with the back of my hand and push forward, my mind wandering to the last few days. They were days spent behind the welcome desk or back in the kitchen with Shirley. Cleaning cabins and late-night bonfires with guests. But my favorite evening was the one I spent with Graham, when we waited for all the guests to retire to their cabins and then snuck up to his balcony for a glass of wine and a game of Shut the Box that we stole from the game cabinet downstairs. I'm quickly realizing that it doesn't matter what I do with that man—I just want to be near him all the time.

I come out of the trail and onto the clearing of the lodge's property, immediately noticing Graham raking the beach in front of where the pelicans are gathered in the bay.

"Hey," I call out, my chest heaving from being out of breath.

"Hi." He smiles broadly when he sees me, and my stomach flutters at the way his eyes unabashedly roam over my workout clothes that are clinging to my body with sweat.

"How was your hike?" he asks when I get closer.

"It was good. I'm all sweaty. I need a shower," I pant. A devilish grin spreads across his face.

"I have a better idea." He gestures toward the lake with a wiggle of his brows. "The water's nice and warm today."

"Oh no," I refuse, instinctively backing away from him. "What about the guests?"

"Just left. Shirley left too." He drops the rake and stalks toward me, sending a thrill down my spine. He lifts his polo over his head effortlessly as he walks, putting his chiseled frame on display.

"Graham," I warn, my tone becoming increasingly less firm. "No, no, no."

I squeal as he lunges, grabbing my legs and swinging me over his back in one fell swoop. My stomach rests against his shoulder, my head hanging down, and I claw at his bare lower back, attempting to maneuver my way out of his hold.

"Graham!" I yell, but this time it comes out in a laugh. His grip tightens on my legs as he starts jogging down the length of the creaky dock.

"Don't you dare!" The last word out of my mouth is a full-on scream that comes out after he jumps off the end and seconds before we plunge into the lake. Submerged under the water, I let myself swirl for a moment. The tips of my toes touch the silky weeds of the lake bottom, causing me to frantically kick my legs faster. When I surface, I gasp, opening my eyes to find Graham popping up a moment later.

"Oh, you're so dead," I hurl at him, treading water to stay afloat.

"It's not so bad, huh?" He chuckles deeply, swimming closer to me. As much as I want to be mad at him, I can't help the smile that tugs at the corner of my mouth. I move my hand to splash him with water and bite back a laugh when it hits him in the face.

"Hey," he growls, gripping my waist to pull me against him. I wrap my legs around his waist and bring my arms around his neck, lightly resting my fingers against the hair at the base of his neck. He grips under my thighs, using one hand to swim us a little farther in until he can touch the bottom. He pauses there, settling both hands beneath me, our shoulders still under the water.

"That was not nice," I tell him pointedly with a smirk.

"I know," is all he says, a flash of mischief in his eyes. "Hey, you wanted to rinse off anyway, right?"

"Yeah, but not in the lake." I tilt my head, letting my gaze settle on his. The lake water splashes against us as the waves softly roll to shore, threatening to take us along with them. The sun is just barely peeking a reddish-yellow glare through the trees.

There's something about being alone, having this whole island to ourselves, that sends a flutter across my skin. He must feel it too. The permission to be free. To not have to worry about being professional or who might be watching.

I sigh when his lips find the base of my neck, his fingers deepening their grip on my legs.

"Hmm," I hum involuntarily, my eyes fluttering closed, feeling the effects of his kiss. I don't know how this would ever get old. The way my body comes alive under his touch. The way it begs for more within mere seconds of him doing whatever it is he's doing with his mouth. I lightly run my fingertips down the base of his neck, then feel his shoulder muscle twitch. He leaves my neck and looks up at me.

"Should we go inside?" he asks gruffly, his eyes piercing into mine. I nod, biting at the corner of my mouth. His eyes drop to my mouth and then flare, slowly raking them back up to meet my gaze. Without another word, he hoists me up and walks out of the water, through the sandy beach, and sets me down on the grass.

"Here, let's get you dry," he says, taking my hand and leading me up the deck stairs. The cold evening air feels chilly against my heavy, wet clothes, putting a slight damper on the energy we were building in the lake. Water drips as we walk through the main area of the lodge, creating a trail of water behind us.

"I'll get that later," he says, glancing down at the mess we're making. By the time we reach his apartment and get dried off, the air between us has cooled.

I head for the primary closet, in a hurry not to drip any more water. I still haven't brought a change of clothes over here, so I grab a pair of his gray sweatpants and a loose T-shirt.

"Red or white?" he asks once he's in comfortable clothing himself, pulling two wine glasses out of the cabinet.

"White, please." I watch as he pours us both a glass.

"I'll be right back," he says, handing it to me. "I'll meet you on the balcony?"

With a nod, I take the wine and get settled on the futon under the blanket and listen to the bugs making their nightly serenade while I wait patiently.

"Here you go," Graham eventually says from the doorway. "I stopped at the library after cleaning up the floor. This is the one you're reading, right?"

He hands me the book from the library that I just started yesterday, and I give him a grateful smile. I'm still getting used to his thoughtful nature, but I'm trying to just accept it and the small ways he shows he cares.

"Yes. And you'll be happy to hear that it's a historical romance. Not a thriller."

"I'm very happy for you. I'm sure your dreams have been more pleasant." He laughs, then proceeds to pick up his guitar, strumming a few strings while I open the book.

Every so often, I can feel his gaze roaming over me, causing a shiver to spread, as if it were his fingers actually running over my skin and not his eyes. With each note that he strums, I find myself being lulled deeper into a lazy exhaustion—one that's tinged with a hint of anticipation. When I start to yawn, he ever so slowly puts the guitar away. He simply holds out a hand, and I gladly follow him inside to his bed, where he finishes what he started in the lake.

THIRTY-FOUR
Graham

"Okay," I say in lieu of a greeting to Blair, who's leaning against the bar top, talking with Nita. "You didn't eat, did you?"

"I did not eat lunch, per your request," she confirms, straightening to stand. "But you have some explaining to do with Shirley. She's not very happy that I refused her food."

"I'll handle Shirley." I smirk. "The lunch rush is officially over, and I've been busting my butt all morning to get my chores done. We officially have three hours until we need to be back to prep for dinner service."

"Where are we going?" Her eyes perk up in anticipation.

"It's a surprise." I tilt my head in the direction of the front door. "Go change into some hiking shoes and meet me back here, okay?"

"Oh, okay," she drawls, scurrying out the door.

"Thanks for covering the bar, Nita. Call me if you need anything, okay?"

"You got it," she says, waving me off as I head back into the kitchen.

"I hear you're mad at me," I tell Shirley as I grab the picnic basket that's settled on a shelf.

"Is there a reason that I can't feed your woman?" she demands.

"I'm taking her on a picnic," I say pointedly, then watch as her expression softens.

"Oh." She crosses her arms in contemplation. "I guess that's okay, then."

"If you'd like, you can help me pack the basket," I offer, knowing that would make her happy.

"What did you have in mind?" she asks, already gathering napkins and utensils. "Oh! I have plenty of pasta salad left over."

"I was just going to make us some sandwiches, but that sounds much better." I take the container out of the fridge and set it in the basket along with an ice pack. I can feel her watching me as I slip a couple key lime sparkling water cans inside.

"What's on your mind, Shirley?" I ask when her gaze lingers.

"It's good to finally see you taking time for yourself," she says softly. "You work too damn hard."

"It's nice to have a reason to take a break." I push my lips together in a slight smile and wink before adding the finishing touches on the basket. "Alright. We'll be back in a couple hours."

"Have fun!" she calls at my back as I make my way out of the lodge.

"Is that a picnic basket?" Blair asks, clapping her hands together in excitement as she comes down the trail from her cabin.

"Sure is. Are you ready?"

With a nod, she slips her hand smoothly into mine, and we head to the shed to find the ATV. She helps me secure the basket onto the back, and we take off down the trail. Once we're on our way, she slides as close to me as possible, wrapping her arms around my torso instead of using the handles by her sides this time. Her touch sends a wave of warmth through my body. I free one hand from the handle to lay it across her arm and give it a squeeze, tilting my head back slightly to smile at her. We head into the rougher part of the trail, and each dip and curve of the four-wheeler has her legs squeezing mine tighter. I make a mental note to find more places on this island to take her by ATV just so I can feel her clamped to my back more often.

Eventually, I park next to a tree, and we hike up the rest of the way with the picnic basket in one of my hands, Blair's hand in my other. Finally, we reach the same clearing on top of the hill where we tented a few weeks ago.

"A picnic lunch at the top of the island," I announce with an outstretched arm, feeling proud of my efforts.

"It's perfect." She beams, bringing her arms around me in a hug. I kiss the top of her head and pause there for a moment. Then I reach for the blanket I placed inside the basket.

"It's so pretty up here," she breathes, taking two corners and helping me lay it out on the grass next to the ashy fire pit.

"I'm glad you like it up here as much as I do."

One by one, we unload the picnic basket. She sits with her legs swung off to the side, and I lower next to her, stretching all the way out onto my side.

"So, have you thought any more about what your plan is for work?" I ask, braving the glare of the sun to look at her, and then immediately brace myself. I've been hesitant to ask her questions that involve her future plans out of fear of her answers. Even though I know it's still a possibility, I'm definitely not ready to say goodbye to her anytime soon. As much as I've been trying to keep a realistic mindset about us, I can feel myself falling a little bit more for her every single day. It's something that's wildly and desperately out of my control at this point.

"No, I haven't." She cringes after taking a bite of the pasta salad. "I need to soon, though. I can't keep them hanging forever. I can only take a leave of absence for so long, you know?"

I nod my head. "I get it. What are you leaning toward?"

"Right now, I'm trying to do some soul searching and figure out if practicing law is really what I want to do. I understand now that I went to law school for my parents, so now I need to decide if practicing law really makes me happy."

"I know you'll figure it out," I say confidently.

"Have you talked to your dad yet? About shutting down the cabins?" she asks, taking a bite of a carrot stick.

"No, I plan to call him tomorrow, though. He should know about the plans for the lodge, and I'd like him to hear it from me and not someone else."

"I'm sure he would appreciate that," she says.

"I think so too." I hand her a bunch of grapes and take one for myself, lazily picking each one off the stem to pop in my mouth. I get caught on the content look on her face as she looks down at her food. Her cheeks are lightly flushed, and a few strands of her ponytail are a little messy from the hike. She looks slightly weathered—a little rough around the edges out here in the elements. But in the same breath, she seems at ease. Comfortable and confident in her surroundings. A far cry from the woman who grumbled her way through forced outdoor activities on her retreat. It's hard to believe that the woman from a few short months ago and the one in front of me are the same.

"What's one good thing that happened today?" I ask gently, curious to hear what she'll say. I can't help but hope that she'll have a hard time choosing one—not because she doesn't have any that come to mind, but that she has too many to choose from. I want that for her. A life where the good things outweigh the bad. Whether I'm factored into the good or not.

"Hmm." She smiles around the grape that she pops in her mouth, her eyes meeting mine. "I talked to Annie this morning. That's always a bright spot in my day."

"Yeah? She sounds like a good friend."

"The best. What about you? What's your one good thing?"

I spend a second thinking of an answer. "I found a fifty in my pocket this morning that I didn't know was there. Judging by how crisp it is, I think it's made it through the wash a few times now."

She lets out a breathy laugh. "That's a fun surprise."

"It was." I place the grape stem back in the basket.

"Well, should we head back?" she asks, pushing herself up to stand.

"Are you trying to rush our picnic lunch?" I feign insult.

"No." The skin around her eyes creases together when her whole face lifts with a smile. "This was lovely. I just don't want to leave Shirley and Nita by themselves for too long if something comes up."

"Alright." Giving in, I finish packing up the basket. I hate to end our time alone together, but I also thoroughly love how much she loves the lodge.

"It's gotta be back here somewhere." I grunt, lifting a large banker's box off the stack to move it out of the way. The back corner of my office is dark and quiet at this late hour. The bar is closed, and Shirley is in her cabin for the night.

"You're sure it would be in with these files?" Blair asks. "Not in a family photo album or anything?"

"I've looked everywhere in our albums. And I think I remember, years ago, Mom mentioned that Gram kept a few pictures inside the folder with the initial bank papers. The problem is, those papers have been moved around so many times over the years that I'm not sure which box they ended up in."

I grab the next box and slide it to where Blair sits cross-legged on the floor, and then I pull one down for me, dropping it with a heavy thud.

"We'll find it," she says reassuringly, lifting the lid off the top of her box. "We've got a few days before we go see your mom. That's plenty of time."

"With my luck, it'll probably be in the last box we check." I skim my fingers through the manila folders unsuccessfully and move on to the next one.

"Oh, this might be it!" I pull a file labeled 'Ruby Lodge' out of the second-to-last box. Tucked behind some mortgage statements and the title certificate are four loose photos.

"Let me see," Blair says, scooting closer to sit next to me. She leans in and rests her cheek against the outside of my shoulder.

"This is Syd and me." I tilt it so she can see. My chest warms at the nostalgia. We were about five and three playing on an old tire swing on the east side of the property. Mom and Dad had a hard time dragging us home from that spot most evenings. "We loved that old swing. Wasn't safe at all, but that never stopped us."

"How sweet. And look at you—so fashionable."

I chuckle at younger me in a gray Minnesota Gophers T-shirt and red-and-white striped Zubaz pants.

"It's all about comfort, baby." I flip to the next picture, relief rushing through me. "Yes! This is the one I'm looking for. That's me, Syd, Mom, and Dad on the front steps of the lodge. This was after Gram and Gramps passed away, and we were officially part owners."

"The lodge looks so different. So new."

"Yeah." I ruminate on the photo and the statuesque, sturdy building in the background. "This place has seen a lot of years. And the weather's often not very kind to us."

I set the photo off to the side next to my leg. "Perfect. I'll add this to the stuff we're bringing to Mom."

As I'm flipping the file shut, my eyes catch on a document that looks out of place and different from the rest.

"What's this?" I mumble to myself. At the very back of the file is an envelope from the bank in town. The date is handwritten on the front of it—looks to be a week or so after the lodge was first opened.

"What is it?" Blair asks as I pull out the papers inside the envelope.

"It looks like old paperwork for a trust savings fund for Ruby Lodge." I run my finger down the lines of the document. "Grandma and Grandpa opened it almost sixty years ago."

"How much was in there?" She peers over my shoulder.

"They opened it with five thousand dollars."

"And you didn't know about it?" she asks.

"No." I shrug. "I handle all the finances now, and Dad never mentioned it when I took over. I'm assuming it was drained years ago."

"Interesting. It's cool to see the old paperwork." She closes the lid on the box she was going through, and I slide the papers back in the envelope, closing my box. After getting them stacked up in the corner of the office, I grab the photo in one hand and Blair's hand in the other to head upstairs to bed.

THIRTY-FIVE
Blair

"Hi, Blair. Tell me about what's been happening with you," Rachel says during our therapy video call. "How have you been feeling?"

"I've been feeling..." I take a second to take stock of my current emotions and can't help the smile that lifts the corner of my mouth. "Good, actually. I've been feeling good. Better."

"Well, that smile certainly says so. Tell me more," she probes gently.

I blow out a breath, trying to form the right words that would portray how I feel. "I honestly don't think I've felt this way since I was way younger, but I just feel...alive. Awake, if that makes sense."

"That definitely sounds positive." She nods encouragingly.

"I think so. And it's not that I feel happy all the time—I don't. I've been feeling a wide range of emotions, but even the negative ones feel different than they did before."

"Can you share an example of that?"

"Like, if I'm exhausted and tired from a long day, I still feel the heaviness and weight of that...but there's also an underlying...buzz. That's the only word I can think of to explain it. A humming circulating inside me that just makes me feel like I'm not drowning in the rest of it. Does that make sense?"

"It does," she says with a smile. "And how are things with Graham?"

My stomach squeezes at the mention of him, and I can feel heat spread across my cheeks. "Really good. I like him a lot. It feels different with him."

"How so?"

"Different in a good way. He's supportive, and gentle, and kind. I've never been with someone who looks at me the way he does. He makes me feel special, and the little things he does remind me that I matter."

She gives an approving nod, jotting something down on her notepad.

"But it's not just him that's making me happy. Being here on this island, surrounded by the lake and the trees...helping out with tasks around the lodge...it's just been really good for me." Saying it out loud confirms what I haven't fully admitted to myself yet. That I like it here. And I really don't like the idea of leaving.

I feel like myself here.

"I'm very happy for you, Blair. And how are things with work? Are you still on your leave of absence?"

"I am. That's one thing that is causing me some stress. I don't know what to do about it. I'm still trying to figure out my next step as far as that goes. I think I'd like to keep practicing law, but I'm uneasy about going back to the firm in Chicago. The idea just doesn't feel good, you know?"

"Would it be a possibility to work for a different firm?"

"Yeah, I could always move to another firm. That's definitely an option. I just don't want to make a rash move and then regret it later, you know?"

"That's understandable. But you know it's okay to not have it all figured out. Most of us don't. And it's more than okay to take baby steps while you get there."

"I keep reminding myself of that." I nod.

"I think you're doing a great job, Blair."

We spend the rest of the session talking about my options for the future and things to do or tell myself when the negative feelings outweigh the good, as they inevitably will. We're just scheduling the next call when I hear a soft knock on the door.

"Come in," I call to the door and then wave at the screen. "I'll see you in a few weeks, then. Thanks, Rachel."

"Bye, Blair. Take care of yourself."

The door creaks open as I disconnect the video chat and close the laptop.

"How did it go?" Graham asks quietly from where he stands on the rug.

"Good." I smile at him, instantly feeling butterflies wake up in my stomach at the sight of his tall, green-flannel-clad frame in the small entryway.

"Good to hear," he replies sincerely before taking a seat at the table next to me.

"How was the rest of the morning? They sure are a rowdy bunch of fishermen." I chuckle at the guests who've been staying in cabins two and five. Breakfast service was loud and chaotic in the dining room earlier, with several of them inviting me to join them on their afternoon fish.

"Yeah." A sly smile spreads on his face. "I might have to hide you away from now on. You're too pretty. They can't help themselves."

A blush heats my cheeks, and I roll my eyes.

"Anyway, are you still good with coming into town with me tomorrow?" he asks. "To meet my parents? You definitely don't have to if it's too much..."

"I'd be honored," I interrupt him, feeling grateful that he finds me worthy enough to meet his parents.

I am worthy. Of it all.

"Awesome." He beams at me. "Then let's go right now."

"Go where?" I ask in confusion.

"Into town. We'll stay overnight. I have a surprise."

"You and your surprises." I shake my head, staring at him in wonder as he rises off the chair.

"Go pack a backpack quick." He motions up the stairs with a boyish grin. "Let's go."

"Are you going to tell me what's in the mystery bag you packed?" I ask Graham as we walk the last couple of steps toward his truck.

"Nope." He shuts the door behind me before I have a chance to say anything else. He's been secretive and distant the whole boat ride over, and my curiosity is definitely piqued. I wonder what he has up his sleeve.

I stare him down when he opens the driver's side door, and he laughs when his gaze connects with mine.

"It's nothing bad, I promise you." He jumps in and starts up the truck, taking us out of the auto repair parking lot.

"You should know those words do nothing to ease my nerves."

"I wasn't trying to." He winks, taking my hand in his to place on the center console. We drive down the main drag, passing a coffee shop and a line of vacant businesses with 'For Lease' signs in the windows.

"Do you think Shirley can handle the guests until tomorrow?"

"This was her idea," he admits. "Not what we're doing exactly, but having the night off was all her. Plus, they'll be gone fishing until after dark, so I think she'll be okay."

We take a right turn and travel down a quiet country road, passing by cattle pastures, farmland, and the occasional house off the side of the road. Eventually, he slows down, taking a right onto a dirt driveway.

"Is trespassing part of your plan?" I ask as we drive past the house and into the pasture off to the right.

"Nah, this is my buddy's place." He grins, driving the truck in a wide circle until coming to a stop. I unbuckle my seat belt, thoroughly confused. I must be missing something. There's nothing but weeds and farm fields around here.

"Stay here and don't turn around," he says, getting out of the truck.

"Wait, what?"

"Just for a little bit. I'll come get you when I'm ready. If you turn around, you're in trouble." He slams the door before I can protest.

I shake my head in amusement and turn the radio up. I listen to talk radio and stare at the farmland that stretches for miles in front of me, every so often feeling the dip of Graham's weight as he walks around in the bed of the truck behind me.

"Okay, I'm ready," he says when he opens my door.

"Oh, now I'm allowed to come out?" I stay firmly in place, ignoring his hand in an admittedly childish show of defiance.

"Get out here," he huffs. I squeal as he grabs me around the waist and hauls me out of the truck. My laughter stops short when I round the truck and see what awaits me.

"Graham," I breathe. The truck bed is covered with four different kinds of blankets that are spread out and two sleeping bags settled on top with three large pillows settled against the back. There's a snack tray with crackers, cheese and olives in the center and a small fabric cooler off to the side. Directly across from the truck is a large projector screen that's hanging from a tree.

"You like?" he asks, looking adorably nervous.

For once, no words come to my mind. No one has ever done anything so special for me before, and I sit in shock as I take it all in.

"Come on." He swiftly lifts me up and sets me on the truck bed, where I crawl toward the back.

"This is incredible," I finally breathe out when I sit. "This is too much, Graham."

He hops up and crawls next to me. "It's never too much."

"I don't know what to say. This is so sweet of you."

"Okay, stop. Now you're making it weird," he teases. "Just sit back and relax."

He grabs one of the blankets to curl over my legs and slides the tray within reach.

"I was limited for movie options, so we're stuck with watching an old western movie," he snickers. "But it's the company that counts, right?"

"Absolutely." I snuggle next to his side with a cracker in hand. "And the snacks."

We lazily eat some crackers and chat while he figures out how to start the movie. As the sky gradually gets darker, we stretch out little by little until eventually we're onto the second movie, snuggled together in one sleeping bag. I'm tucked under the crook of his arm with my hand on his chest, and his hand is drawing lazy circles along my hip bone. My eyelids feel heavy, but I try my best to force them to stay open.

"Should we turn it off, baby?" he murmurs, his voice sleepy.

"Not yet." I shake my head against his shoulder, not wanting to fall asleep yet. He pulls me closer to his side. I let my arm reach all the way around his torso, my fingers bunching at the T-shirt he's wearing. I think being in his arms like this might be my absolute favorite place to be.

It's not lost on me that I used to crave going to sleep. I couldn't wait until I could crawl into bed and finally disappear into my empty dreams. But here with him tonight, I'm desperately fighting to stay awake. To spend a few more seconds in his arms and under the stars.

Eventually, I can't fight it anymore, and with a content smile on my face, I drift off to my welcoming dreams.

THIRTY-SIX
Graham

"Do you think I'll make her uncomfortable because I'm not a familiar face?" Blair asks as she helps me roll up the blankets in the truck bed.

"It's hard to say. But please don't be worried. We'll take it easy and see how it goes." I try to reassure her, but the truth is, I have no idea how the visit will go. We never know what kind of mood Mom will be in.

"Well, I'm looking forward to meeting her." She plants a kiss on my cheek on her way to hop off the back of the truck. "Now that I had a great night under the stars."

"Speak for yourself." I follow behind her, landing with a thud. "The one sleeping bag was a good idea in theory, but you've got some bony elbows."

"You could have pushed me away or sent me back to my own bag," she points out, and I pull her into my arms.

"Not a chance—not even in my sleep." I kiss her softly, cupping her face with my hands while she rests hers softly at my waist. My heart starts pounding heavily in my chest in an almost overwhelming way. I know what it is, this tightening in my chest. The way my stomach feels unsteady—exhilarated and scared at the same time. The words sit at the tip of my tongue, but I choke them back.

"Thank you again for last night," she whispers. "It was incredible."

"Thanks for keeping me company. It would have been a lonely night out here by myself."

The sound of her laugh makes my stomach swoop.

"Shall we?" I open her door, letting her climb in.

The drive to the nursing home is quiet, with music softly playing. I'm starkly aware of her presence in the seat next to me, and I contemplate how I'll be able to hang onto this feeling for as long as I possibly can. I don't wish for the lodge to shut down by any means, but if that inevitably happens one day, I know without a doubt that I'll follow her anywhere.

When we arrive, I shift into park and round the truck to meet Blair, who's waiting with an outstretched hand. I take a firm grip, and we walk, hand in hand, to Mom's floor.

"Knock, knock," I say, slowly pushing her door open. Inside the room, Mom is sitting by the window, looking out with a blank stare. Dad comes to stand by her side when he sees us.

"Dad." I shake his hand in greeting before kissing Mom on the head, keeping a firm grip on Blair's hand. "Mom. This is Blair."

Dad beams and nods in an anxious smile while Mom glances over at us in complete indifference. A pang of grief hits me in the gut at the loss of the person I knew and the shell of her that exists now. A mother who doesn't recognize her own son. It's in these moments when I understand why Sydney stays away.

"It's really nice to meet you both," Blair says to them.

"Likewise. Come on in. Have a seat." Dad gestures to the table.

"I hear you've been a huge help out at the lodge," he says to Blair. "We sure appreciate your efforts."

"It's my pleasure, truly." She waves him off. "You've got a special place out there."

"Have you been up this way before?" he asks.

"Not before our retreat, no." She slides her eyes to me. "But I'm sure glad I did."

For the next half hour, we chat about Lake of the Woods, random stories from my childhood, and then Dad quizzes Blair on her Chicago Bears knowledge, all while Mom sits quietly, watching us, sweeping her distant gaze over all three of us.

"Oh, Dad," I say after pulling out some playing cards. "I meant to ask...do you know anything about a trust fund that Gram and Gramps opened for the lodge?"

"Yeah." His brow furrows as he tilts his head, his interest piqued. "Why?"

"I came across some forms for it, but I'm assuming it's closed now, right?"

"No, it was never closed out. Why are you asking about it?"

My stomach clenches, shock hitting me in the gut.

"Wait, it's still open? Are there funds in it?" There can't be. There's no way that there's actual money that's been readily available this whole time. The thought alone makes me nauseated.

"Well, yeah." He shrugs, eyeing me warily.

"How much is in there?" I can hear how loud my voice is escalating, but I don't seem to have control over it.

"I have no idea. I honestly haven't looked into it in a few years." He squints, his eyes flashing with anger that I'm raising my voice around Mom. I know well enough that we need to keep our voices calm and steady around her.

"Are you kidding me?" I say just as loud, despite my efforts to lower my volume.

"Let's take this outside." He gestures to the door. I hastily glance at Blair, who gives me a nod in approval, and I scratch my jaw in frustration as I follow him out.

"Want to tell me what's going on?" He demands once we get to the hallway.

I blow out a steadying breath, attempting to control my emotions before I go down this road. "I haven't said anything yet, but...we've been in financial trouble for a while now."

"The lodge?" His brows fly up.

"Yeah. That's why I needed to make those staffing cuts. We need a whole new heating system before winter, and I just told Scott that we can only do six of the fifteen cabins. We'll be majorly downsizing our bookings for winter."

"Geez." He looks bewildered and frustrated all at once, sending a pang of guilt into my already mixed emotions.

"The money that's coming in hasn't been profitable for a while now," I say quietly, quelling some of the anger that's ruminating beneath the surface of my skin.

"Why didn't you tell me?" he demands, his voice sharper.

"Why didn't you tell me about an account that has money for the lodge?" My volume matches his. "Isn't that something you should have told me when I started—oh, I don't know—running the damn place?"

"Don't speak to me like that," he hisses, his eyes skirting to the nurses' station where heads are starting to turn our way.

I take a deep breath and shake out my fingers, tapering the adrenaline that still rushes through me.

"I need a minute," I mutter, then turn to walk down the hallway of Mom's floor. I run my hands down my face and focus on breathing in and out while I process what just transpired. Logic helps the anger to dissipate with each step.

It's not his fault that he didn't tell me about it—that accusation goes both ways. I need to focus on moving forward and figuring out where we stand today. I slowly head back to where Dad is leaning against the wall right where I left him.

"I'm sorry," I say, coming to lean on the spot next to him.

He takes a breath in. "I'm sorry too. I never told you about it because I didn't think we needed the money. I've been so focused on your mother that the lodge's finances weren't front and center in my mind. It seemed like you had everything under control."

"That's why I didn't tell you." I dip my head, dropping my gaze to the floor. "I didn't want to add any stressors to your plate."

He nods solemnly. "No secrets anymore, okay? We'll figure this out together."

"Deal. So you're telling me that no money was ever taken out?"

"Nope. There was still a sizeable amount when your grandparents passed away, and the only people who know about it are me, your mother, and your aunt and uncle. But they haven't been involved for years now."

"We need to find out how much is in that account—as soon as possible."

He nods. "Parker at the bank was my point person. I'll call him and set up a meeting for tomorrow."

"Great," I say, pushing off the wall. "Again, I'm sorry for not telling you—and for yelling at you."

He claps his hand on my shoulder. "I'm sorry for not telling you too. Let's get back in there, huh?"

We walk back into the room and find Blair and Mom playing a quiet game of cards at the table. My heart warms, watching her with Mom, and a fresh wave of gratitude for her washes over me. As I go to join them, a voice in the back of my head dares to wonder if the future of the lodge has just been wildly altered.

THIRTY-SEVEN
Blair

"How much do you think is in there?" I ask quietly against Graham's arm that's tucked in the crook of my neck. He's curled behind me, every inch of his body pressed against the back of mine. His long arm drapes over the top of me, his hand is clasped in mine against my chest, and one of his legs is pushed between mine. My own personal cocoon, warming me from the inside out.

"I have no idea." I can feel his warm breath on the back of my neck. "I guess it depends on what the interest rate was locked in at. I'm hoping it's accrued a decent amount of money over the years. Man, that would really help us out."

"That's so exciting, Graham. Can you imagine how much stress this would take off your shoulders?"

"I'm cautiously optimistic. I'm a facts kind of guy, so I don't want to get ahead of myself until I know for sure."

The morning sunlight sweeps across the wall of Graham's apartment, and the birds continue their wake-up call outside his window. The wind softly whistles as it roars and pushes against the cabin walls.

He squeezes me tighter and groans into my hair. "I don't want to get up," he grumbles.

My eyes flutter closed, and a lazy smile grows on my face.

This right here. This is happiness.

"You're not sick of me yet?" I murmur.

I can feel the shake of his head against the back of my neck.

"No," he whispers, getting closer to my ear. "The opposite...I think I'm falling in love with you, Blair."

My heart races, and a swarm of goosebumps spread down my arms at his words. I blink a few times, letting them hang in the air. When he doesn't take them back, I twist my body, turning completely until I'm facing him. His chest swells with a deep inhale as his still-sleepy gaze roams intently over my face.

"You mean it?" I whisper, holding his stare.

Please say yes.

He rolls his lips and nods slowly, his hand lightly touching my lower back.

He loves me.

"I think I've been falling for you from the second I laid eyes on you at your retreat." He tucks a strand of hair behind my ear. "Even when I had no business to. I don't want you to say anything back—not yet. I just can't hold it in any longer."

I quickly press my mouth to his in a flurry. His hand splays out against my lower back, pressing me to him. When I pull back and lock eyes with him, I search them for a moment. If

I ever felt love in this world, the way I feel for him would be the closest thing, right behind the way I feel about Annie and our friendship. But something stops me from saying it back. I'm not even positive I know how to identify what love really is. I'm grateful that he didn't put any pressure on me to say it back, but I do act on the urge to give him a truth of my own in return.

"I've been thinking …would it be crazy if I just didn't leave?" I whisper, glancing down before flicking my eyes back up again. "If I stayed here?"

"With no looming exit date?" he asks, a smile growing on his face. I nod, biting the corner of my lip.

"I like the sound of crazy." His kiss sends a swarm of butterflies flittering deep in my stomach, and he pulls away all too soon.

"What about your job?" he asks quietly.

"I'm not sure yet. Maybe I can work remotely somehow?"

"We'll figure it out." He smiles confidently. With one last squeeze, he reluctantly untangles himself from me.

"I have to get down to get things going for the day. You sure you don't want to come with me to the meeting at the bank?"

I watch unabashedly as he pulls his pants over his hips.

"No, you go ahead with your dad. I promised Shirley I'd help her in the kitchen this morning. I'll be here when you get back, though. I can't wait to hear how it goes."

"Sounds good. The wind's supposed to be really ripping this morning anyway, so it'll be a choppy ride across the lake." He walks through the living area to the bathroom, and I stretch out under the covers as his toothbrush buzzes behind the bathroom door.

My eyes trail him as he makes two cups of coffee across the room at the kitchen counter. When he saunters my way, a mug in hand, I push myself up to sit, pulling the covers up around me.

"Thank you," I say, folding my hands around the warm mug.

"I'll let you know when I'm on my way back. Should be just after lunch." He tilts my chin up with a finger. I close my eyes as he plants a quick kiss against my mouth, leaving them closed for a moment after he pulls back. A smile spreads slowly before my eyes open.

"Good luck," I call out.

"Thanks." With a wink, he shuts the door behind him.

I pull a sweatshirt over my head and saunter out to the balcony, finishing the rest of my coffee in the midst of the crisp morning air and the fog-covered trees.

After taking a long, warm shower in his bathroom, I get dressed and head downstairs. The dining room is quietly buzzing with the conversation of guests while Shirley's voice rings out from behind the bar.

"Don't fool yourself. I know you came all the way out here to sneak my cinnamon rolls," she teases Mack. "Make sure you're not blaming your blood sugar levels on me. I don't need the wrath of your wife."

"She'll never know," he promises with a wide grin.

"Morning, Blair," Shirley says as she passes by me on her way into the kitchen. I smile at her, coming behind the bar.

"Mack, can I get you some orange juice?" I ask. "I think we have a low sugar option back there somewhere."

"Very funny," he says dryly. "Where's Graham heading? Into town?" He jerks a finger toward the window. Graham is just pulling out of the harbor in one of the boats.

"Yup." I leave it at that, placing a glass of ice water in front of him.

"When are you coming fishing with me?" he asks. "I promise it's a good time. I'll even bait your hook for you."

"One of these days, Mack. I promise." With that, I move down the bar to the next guest and spend the morning seeing fishermen off on their excursions and helping Shirley in the kitchen.

After the lunch rush, I pick a new book from the library and sit down by the beach to wait for Graham. My heart gives an anxious flutter every time I hear a boat motor, and after several false alarms, I finally see him come into view. I rush down the dock before he finishes tying up the boat.

"How did it go?" I ask eagerly. His grin makes me overwhelmed with anticipation.

"You'll never believe it," he says with a shake of his head.

"Tell me everything. Is there money in the account?"

"There is." He nods. "Four hundred ninety-two thousand and two hundred dollars, to be exact."

"What?" I gasp. "Oh my gosh, Graham." I cover my mouth with my hand in shock as he looks at me in disbelief, like he's still processing it himself.

"I know." He runs his hand through his hair under his ball cap. "And it's readily available to use for the lodge."

"That will more than cover the heating updates," I point out, feeling the lingering buzz of excitement.

"And then some. Dad and I are going to meet next week to go over plans for the rest of the money, but yeah, getting the cabins updated and fully functioning for winter is priority number one. I already talked to Scott and had him add the rest of the cabins to his list."

"This is incredible," I squeal as he wraps me up in a bear hug. I feel completely exhilarated as he squeezes me tight. My heart feels like it wants to burst just from the simple fact that his life was just made a thousand times better.

Maybe this IS love.

"Well, we absolutely need to celebrate," I say as he releases me.

"What do you have in mind?" There's a twinkle in his eye when he asks.

"Shirley and I made brownies this morning." I offer. "Should we bring some out to the beach? It's such a beautiful day."

He smiles contently as he grabs my hand, threading his fingers through mine. We start making our way off the dock.

"That sounds perfect."

THIRTY-EIGHT
Graham

"Canoeing? Really?" she asks. I bite back a grin at her less-than-enthusiastic tone. The borrowed rain boots that we found in the shed are definitely one size too big, as evidenced by the way her feet are audibly clunking behind me as we walk to the beach.

"What's wrong with canoeing? I thought you would like this surprise." She looks at me warily.

"It's cold. And windy." She cringes, looking out at the lake.

"Aw, come on. Your inner city girl is coming out again? I thought you were adapted already." I grab a canoe off the top of the rack and carry it to the water.

"I am. But apparently, I'm a nature-loving girl that doesn't like to be cold and wet," she says flatly, trailing behind me. I look at her incredulously, trying not to laugh directly in her face.

"You do understand where exactly you just agreed to live, right? This is northern Minnesota. Good luck in the winter, honey," I tease with a snicker.

"I was planning on not leaving the warm lodge all winter long." She shrugs nonchalantly. I huff out a laugh at her serious expression and move in for a kiss.

"That's just fine," I say gruffly against her mouth. "If that's what it takes to have you here. You can be my little hermit."

She flashes me a satisfied smile.

"Come on, we won't go very far. Just a quick little ride around the island?"

She blows out a breath as her gaze pans the lake.

"I suppose. Wouldn't hurt to live a little, right?" She throws my words back at me with an unconvincing wink.

"Atta girl. It'll be fun." I squeeze her shoulder and walk onto the dock where I throw two life jackets in the center of the canoe.

"Watch your step getting in." I crouch to hold the canoe with one hand and offer the other for her to grab while stepping in.

"I hate this already," she says unnervingly as the canoe wobbles back and forth under her weight. I bite back a laugh and climb in as steadily as I can to sit behind her.

"Alright, here's your paddle. You just focus on taking alternating strokes, okay? I'll steer from back here."

She grumbles under her breath as I push us away from the dock, sliding my paddle into the water.

We venture out of the harbor and skirt around the coastline of the island. The towering trees sprouting from the island are hidden behind thick threads of fog on this gloomy, overcast day. The air feels admittedly colder than I anticipated as it gusts between us.

"See, this isn't so bad, huh?" I shout into the wind.

"Define bad," she yells back, attempting to turn her body toward me but quickly facing forward again when the canoe wobbles.

I smile to myself in amusement. Although, I am second-guessing taking her out here if I'd ideally like her to stay. Maybe I should be going easy on her. I push the paddle in roughly, steering us to round the jutted outline of the coast.

"Oh, look!" I point to the top of the hill where a large moose is walking between the trees. The leaves that sway around him are a bright orange-ish red, their colors popping against the light-blue sky behind it.

"Oooh!" she squeals, bringing a hand to cover her mouth. "It's so cute!"

We stop paddling and bob with the waves to watch the moose as it takes a few slow steps along the rocky edge before disappearing back into the woods.

"Cool, huh?"

"Really cool." I can barely hear her over the whistling wind, but I hear enough to pick up that her tone has lost any trace of the fleeting excitement she had just moments before.

"Should we go around this corner and then head back?"

"Yes, please," she says curtly.

With a smile, I force the paddle into the water, continuing on before turning to head back home.

"So, I take it canoeing wasn't your favorite activity?" I come up behind Blair as she stands over the stove in my apartment. Moving her hair back with my chin, I lightly rest my head in the crook of her neck, placing a hand against the outside of her hip.

"That's probably a fair assumption." She stirs the pot with her left hand while her right one grabs mine, sliding it from her hip all the way across her stomach. I gladly envelop her in a tight hold.

"We can try again mid-summer," I mumble against her skin as I place a kiss on the top of her bare shoulder that keeps peeking through when her cardigan slips down.

"Here. Try this." She twists in my arms until she's facing me, holding a spoon with a cupped hand braced underneath. I take it into my mouth, savoring the hot soup.

"I think that's the best chili I've ever had," I say. "Don't tell Shirley."

"Actually, you can." She smiles proudly. "It's her recipe."

"Really?"

"Mmhmm." She reaches for two bowls off the floating shelves and hands them to me. "She gave me the recipe yesterday and walked me through her top-secret tips."

"Well, it's amazing. Thanks for making it tonight. This is much better than the ultimate salad bar we served the guests."

"We need some cheese and sour cream too." She reaches in the fridge while I ladle some chili into each bowl. I bring them over to the table, where photos are still spread out from earlier. Gently pushing a few off to the side, I sit down across from Blair.

"Mmm. So good." She closes her eyes, fully enjoying the bite. I can't help but hold my gaze on her, stopping in my tracks at just the sight of her looking like that and the way that it just about knocks the breath out of me. How does she make something as mundane as eating soup look so incredibly sexy?

When she opens her eyes and catches me staring, I unfreeze and give her a wink before focusing down on the soup. A picture off to the side of my bowl catches my eye.

"Look at this one." I chuckle and pass the picture of me in my hockey uniform to Blair. "That's when I was playing in the peewee league."

"So cute. Do you ever play anymore?"

"Not really. A couple years ago, I made a rink out on the ice. It was more for the guests, though." I think back to last year and quietly marvel at how different the state of my mind was. I was stressed out, burnt out, and carrying the weight of the lodge on my back.

Blair came into my life like a slow and steady tidal wave, giving me an excuse to make time for myself. And now that the future of the lodge isn't in question anymore, it's like a huge weight has been lifted. In almost every aspect, my life is lighter and more fulfilled than it has been in a really long time.

"We'll definitely add that to the scrapbook," I say, placing the picture on top of the photo album that we've been slowly making for Mom.

"Did I tell you that I'm fishing with Mack tomorrow?" she asks, taking a bite of the chili.

I choke on my bite of food. "You're what?" I manage to squeak out.

She giggles, watching me as I try to contain my coughing fit.

"I'm meeting him at the dock at six o'clock. Have any pointers for me?"

"Well, if you thought our canoeing trip was cold, then I'd definitely wear extra layers. Do you want my long underwear?"

"Maybe," she laughs. "Do you want to come with us?"

"Nah, I need to replace a part on the Bobcat and set some mouse traps around Shirley's cabin."

"I can stay if you want help?" Guilt plays on her face.

"No, I want you to go. I can't wait to hear how much fun you have." I grin at the thought of her gripping a fish's mouth, but I secretly love the fact that she's making a life for herself here and doing things that don't always include me. I want her to be happy here—and not just with me.

"What do you think?" I ask as I take our empty bowls to the sink. "Balcony or bonfire tonight?"

"A bonfire sounds nice."

We clean up our dinner and then head to the bonfire pit, which is deserted with no trace of guests in sight. After I get the fire roaring for us, I motion with a crook of my finger for Blair to move out of the chair she's currently sitting in. When I take her place, I grab her hip to guide her onto my lap. She leans all the way back so she's flat against my torso, her head resting just above my heart. I fold my arms around her, curling my fingers around her forearms. My arms rise with the movement of her body as she takes a deep, contemplative breath in.

"I can't believe I didn't even know this place existed a year ago," she whispers as she gazes up at the stars. "That feels so wrong."

I nod, my cheek sliding against the side of her head as I stare at the rippling fire, overcome with emotion.

"I'm so glad that you fought for yourself, Blair." My voice is low as I mutter into her ear the truth that I feel deep in my bones. "That you didn't let yourself drown. You searched for your own slice of happiness in this world, and I'm sure as hell glad that I get to be a small part of it."

The outline of her face is lit up from the orange-red hue of the fire, and I watch as the apples of her cheeks raise when her smile grows.

"You're not a small part of it, Graham," she whispers. "You're a big part."

THIRTY-NINE
Blair

My phone buzzes in my pocket as I attempt to zip up my suitcase. Temporarily giving up on fitting all my clothes back in the same luggage it came in, I pull the phone out to see Annie's name lighting up the screen. With a smile, I hurry down the loft steps of my cabin and answer.

"Hi, Annie," I say.

"Oh, look, it's my long-lost best friend. What happened? I thought you weren't going to forget me?"

I laugh, having a seat on the porch swing. "Hey, you're the one with a job right now. I've been around. You could have called at any time."

"I know, I'm just kidding. Life has been busy lately. But how are you?"

"I'm great!" I love that I can actually say that and mean it now. It feels really good.

"And your hunky mountain man?"

"Great there, too." I take a deep breath, looking out at the lake, feeling a wave of sadness wash over me. As soon as it hits, I mentally brush it off just as quickly. There's no reason for it. It's not like I'm leaving this place for good. I'm just moving to the main lodge with Graham. But I think that cabin four will always hold a special place in my heart.

This is where I found myself again.

"Eric and I were thinking of coming up there over fall break from school," she says. "Would that be okay? To visit?"

"Are you kidding?" A surge of excitement expands in my chest. "Of course that would be okay!"

"Yay!"

"I know just the cabin to set you up in too."

"Awesome, I'm so excited!" Her tone turns serious. "I just saw an ad for a mosquito net hat that wraps all the way around your face. Maybe I should get that, huh?"

I stifle a laugh. "Please do. And then please, please, let me be around when Graham sees you in it."

Talking to Annie like this further proves how far I've come with my depression. I don't feel myself desperately trying to reach a different version of myself anymore. I'm already there and more than enough just as I am.

We finish our conversation just as Graham comes walking down the trail with a handful of cookies in his hand, and my heart skips a beat at the sight of him.

"Hi there," I say to him after hanging up with Annie.

"How's packing going?" he asks, having a seat next to me on the swing.

"Good, there are just a few things that I can't fit back in my suitcase. I'll have to carry those over."

"I'm here to help with that. Here." He hands me a cookie. "Shirley asked me to give this to you."

He lifts his arm, and I slide into his side, inhaling the crisp pine smell that lingers on his clothes. We eat our cookies quietly while watching an eagle dip down into the lake water in hunt of a fish.

"I'm going to miss this view every morning," I say quietly.

His hand tightens on my shoulder with a squeeze before slowly sliding down my arm. "Good news is we know the owner of this cabin. We can visit anytime we want to."

I smile with the last bite of my cookie. "I'd like that."

"Alright, shall we?" he asks, holding his palm out for me to slide my hand into.

"Let's do it." We head inside to grab all my luggage and close the door shut behind us.

I run my fingers over the number four, just like I did when I first left the island, feeling sentimental about the life I've lived here in such a relatively short amount of time. Feeling grateful for the comfort and security that this little cabin has given me.

Then I turn and catch up to the person who gave me even more.

Once we make it to the lodge and up the stairs, I push the apartment door open and haul my bags over to the small closet.

"Welcome home," he says, his lips brushing against my temple as he passes by. A tingle of adrenaline rushes through me. Of excitement. Anticipation. Of happiness.

He drops my suitcase with a huff next to the bags and goes to sit at the edge of the bed to take his socks off. I'm turning toward the bags when I see it.

A bookshelf.

Nestled against the wall between the bathroom and the closet is a small, wooden, four-shelf bookcase. On the second shelf sits a lone book—the one I've been reading from the library this week.

"Um, Graham...what is that?" I point and look over at him with bewilderment.

"I built you a bookshelf," he says nonchalantly with a shrug, as if it's no big deal. As if it was an obvious, effortless thing to do.

"You what?" The corners of my eyes starts to tingle with emotion. My hand covers my heart, and my mouth drops open.

"I made you your own bookshelf. I thought you might want to start making your own collection that you don't have to share with guests."

I blink a few times, letting his words sink in. Then I feel an all-encompassing sense of gratitude that spreads thickly in my chest. I let the overwhelming feeling surge me forward and over to him, where I lower myself directly onto his lap.

He holds my gaze, gripping my hips as I settle with a bent knee on either side of him. Emotion runs through me as I bring my hands to the very top of his neck, cradling the outline of his jaw.

I love him.

I stare into his soft-blue eyes, letting the truth of those words run through my veins.

"I love you," I whisper, finally ready to say it back. Because I know what I deserve now. What I'm worth. Because in order to love him, I needed to love myself wholly first. I needed to put my heart back together before ever being able to give it to him. Now that I'm at this place, I can finally recognize that what's between us is, in fact, love. A sweet, steady, consuming kind of love.

His brows lift in surprise at my sudden admission, his eyes piercing intensely into mine. The corner of his mouth tugs up in a crooked smile, and he brings his forehead to rest against mine.

"I love you too, Blair." His voice is thick with emotion. I squeeze my eyes shut at the sound of his voice and the way he says those words. His strong hand runs up the length of my spine, sending a shiver across my skin.

"I'm so glad I came here," I whisper. "And I can't thank you enough for everything that you've done for me."

"I haven't done anything." He starts to shrug his shoulders, dismissing my comment, but I need him to hear me. To know how I really feel.

"No. Don't do that. Don't downplay the role you've played in my life, Graham. Because I promise you, it's monumental.

You. This place. It's like you breathed life back into me." My voice cracks as this feeling overwhelms me.

His throat bobs with a thick swallow before shaking his head. "I think you just needed the space to finally see your worth for yourself."

His words hit the center of my chest in full force. I watch as his eyes trail the lone tear that slides down my cheek before covering it with his mouth. Then he moves to my jaw, planting a kiss there. My eyes flutter closed at his touch.

I drop my head to the side, allowing him to move slowly down the entire length of my neck, sparking a shiver along each spot. All at once, I'm consumed with wanting more. I desperately need more. So, I lift his head up and press my mouth firmly against his. My fingers slide around his neck and into his hair as his hands firmly run along the outsides of my thighs.

I roll my hips against him slowly, eliciting a groan from the back of his throat, and the next thing I know, he has swiftly picked me up and turned us around. His knee is pushed into the bed while his arms hold me up, my legs squeezing around his waist. He pulls back, his dark hooded eyes pinning mine. I give him a slight nod, and he throws me firmly—yet gently—onto the bed.

FORTY
Blair

"This is the last of the bags," Graham says, tossing luggage into the front of the boat. "You're all set." The three men shake Graham's hand and then get situated in their seats between the sea of bags and coolers full of fresh fish.

"Thanks for staying with us. We'll see you next time!" I wave as the ferry boat pulls away from the dock. When the vessel rounds the corner out of the harbor, Graham slides an arm around my shoulder. I tuck my hand into his back pocket, hooking my thumb in his belt loop, pressing myself against his strong side.

"That was the last of them," I say to him as we look out at the tiny ripples that move across the top of the calm lake. "The next batch of guests arrive in the morning, right?"

"Yup, they should be here around nine." He pulls me into a hug, wrapping both arms around my shoulders. He rests his chin on top of my head. "What do you want to do for the rest of the evening? It's not supposed to rain."

"Hm, I'm not sure."

"We could go into town? Find a new spot to pitch a tent for the night? I could take you on another surprise date if that's what you want? The world is your oyster. Just tell me what I can do for you."

I smile and shake my head against his arms. "I don't need a big romantic gesture tonight." While I always appreciate his surprises, I've come to find that the only two necessities I need are Graham and this island.

"Let's just have a quiet night in," I suggest, suddenly craving a relaxing evening. "How does that sound?"

"Sounds perfect, babe." He kisses the top of my head, and we walk with our arms around each other off the dock. The wind rustles the trees that line the lodge, and several leaves float onto the grass as we pass by. Even in the cooler weather, my heart feels content here.

It seems like a lifetime ago—not just a few months ago—that I thought about disappearing up here. I wanted to fade away from the rest of the world and live a quiet, insignificant life away, alone. Instead, I wound up finding the only place I've ever felt like I belonged.

My home.

"After you," he says, holding the front door open for me.

"Thank you." I take two steps past him just as Shirley comes around the corner from the dining room.

"Oh, good. I'm glad I caught you," she says with a wide smile. "I'm heading to my cabin for the night, but I wanted to make sure I got you some leftover apple pie first. We can't possibly let it go to waste."

She shoves the pie in my hands forcefully, as if I would refuse her offer. I don't think I've turned her down once.

"Oooh," I purr. The warm cinnamon scent is already making my mouth water, and the bottom of the pan perfectly heats my chilled hands.

"Thanks, Shirley. Wow, does that smell delicious," Graham says.

"You bet. I'll see you in the morning. Have a great night!" she says before disappearing out the door. Graham peers out the window, watching after her, until he sees that she made it to her cabin.

I carry the pie in my hands down the hall to flick off the foyer lights while Graham locks the front door. We make the rounds, turning off the lights by the bar and making sure everything in the library is in order. Then we retreat up to our apartment.

"Fork or spoon?" Graham asks once we get inside.

"Fork, please." I stop at the kitchen table and pick up the scrapbook with my free hand before following him out onto the balcony. I set the book down on the coffee table, and we sit together on the futon with the pie in between us.

"Should we go through what needs to be done in the morning?" I ask.

"Sure." He nods, shoveling a bite of pie into his mouth. We enjoy the rest of the dessert while making a mental list of the chores we'll need to get done when we wake up. Mundane things that have quickly become a welcome part of my daily routine. Taking care of this place and the guests that visit it has given me a wonderful new purpose—one that I look forward to fulfilling.

"Here, have the last bite." He smiles, offering me the tray.

I take it without objection and then set the empty tray off to the side. Graham picks up his guitar, and I grab the scrapbook to pick up where I left off yesterday. I'm just about to pick up the top picture off the stack to tape on the page when Graham's words stop me.

"Did you see the last couple pages in there?" He dips his head, pointing it at the scrapbook.

"No. Why?"

"Just look," he says with a sly smile. I turn the book all the way to the back and gasp when I see that the last three pages are filled with pictures of me and Graham.

Taped to the top of the page, there's one of us that he took last week at our favorite picnic spot. Another one is angled below it—a selfie of us on a hike together. And one of us on his boat from the morning we caught over twenty-five walleye together.

"Why?" I ask in disbelief, my eyes roaming over the many pictures.

He shrugs. "I know they won't spark any memories for Mom from the past. But you're a big part of my life now, and it just felt right to include you. It's another way for her to see our life together now, I guess. We can show her what we've been up to."

My chest warms, and I lay my head against his shoulder, reaching my hand over to squeeze his arm. I can't seem to put together the words to correctly appreciate what he did. He starts strumming, not needing any more of a response from me.

I slowly get to work, a half-smile sitting lazily on my lips as I listen to Graham's music fill the air. When my phone dings with an email notification, I set the scrapbook down and grin, already knowing who it's from. I only receive emails from one person through my old work email anymore.

I skim the email from Isaac, smiling at his update on things happening at the firm—the usual inter-office squabbles and lunchroom gossip. Then my mouth drops open in shock when I read the fun fact at the bottom. *Fun Fact: Takini is a Lakota word meaning 'survivor or one who has been brought back to life.'*

Goosebumps spread across the surface of my skin as I read it over and over at least three times, letting it sink in. Eventually, I put my phone down and curl the blanket around me, thinking how nothing could be truer.

My time on Takini Island brought me back to life.

I snuggle next to Graham and lay my head against his shoulder.

This moment right here. This feeling. This is what I fought for.

I fought for me.

EPILOGUE
Blair-10 months later

"Welcome back to the second annual Gibson Law Retreat," I say with a wide smile to my old coworkers who fill the dining room of Ruby Lodge. "Everything you need should be located in your cabins, but please let us know how we can be of service to you during your stay."

I'm about to turn the attention over to Paul so he can give his opening speech when Cassidy shoots her hand up in the air from where she sits at a table in the corner next to Isaac.

"Um, Cassidy? Do you have a question for me?" I ask, an expectant smirk playing at my mouth.

Yes." She jumps up with a beaming smile on her face. "Are you able to be a part of The Gavel Gang? We need Blair-Bear on our team again."

"I don't think that's allowed, unfortunately," I say with a low giggle.

"But you're technically still a lawyer," she points out with a hand on her hip.

"I'll leave the rules up to Paul on that one." I give him a quick nod of my head as I walk past to let him speak.

As he starts his boisterous speech, I walk back behind the bar, where I spend most of my time these days—when I'm not at my law office in town, that is.

I leased one of the vacant buildings in Baudette a few months ago to open my own law firm. I'm only there three days a week to see local clients in person, but otherwise, I'm able to work remotely from here, which means I have plenty of time to do the other thing I love to do—help run the lodge.

"Darn register," Shirley grumbles next to me.

"Here, let me." I thwack the base of the register with one swift movement, the drawer sliding open with a ding.

Aside from replacing the heating system to get us through winter—which was a necessity—we've been holding off on making any of the other updates needed around here. Sydney is drawing up a proposal to use the trust money to renovate and add on to Ruby Lodge. In the meantime, we've been doing our best with what we have.

"Thanks, dear," she says, squeezing my arm in gratitude.

I watch as the Gibson Law staff heads down to the docks for their fishing excursion, taking pride in being able to host them this way. Graham sends the guests off with Mack and another guide, waving as they head out of the marina.

"I'll be back in a little bit," I tell Shirley, rounding the corner of the bar to head outside.

"I'm told I need to convince you to join the scavenger hunt this afternoon," Graham snickers as he walks toward me on the dock.

"I might just have to, for old time's sake." My grin is wild on my face, matching the way my chest feels as I wrap my arms around his waist in a lazy hug. He brings his arms around my upper back and holds me there while I take a deep breath, enjoying the warm summer air.

"Sit with me a while?" he asks, pointing to the bonfire pit. I tilt my head up, resting my chin on his chest.

"Sure," I say against his lips as they brush mine. We walk off the dock, past the pelicans waiting patiently in the bay. When he sits down, I slide effortlessly onto his lap.

"Annie and Eric are still coming next week, right?" he asks, resting a hand on my thigh.

"Yes. They're excited to come in the summertime finally." They've come to visit us twice now, once in the fall and then again in the spring. I've loved having them here, one of the only reminders of my previous life—aside from the occasional email from Isaac.

I did work up the courage to reach out to my parents a few days ago, but truthfully, it doesn't matter if they respond. My worth isn't tied to them—or to anyone else, for that matter.

Not even Graham, as much as he means to me.

"Tell me one good thing," he murmurs against my ear, asking me the daily question we've been asking each other for a while now. He rests his chin on my shoulder and squeezes my hip.

I push my lips together, pondering which good thing to choose from today.

"Someone let me sleep in this morning," I finally say quietly. "You?"

"This moment right now. You in my lap," he says, his breath hot just under my ear. A tingle shoots slowly down my spine, and I burrow myself deeper in his arms.

We sit like that for a little while under the beaming sun, with his fingers lazily roaming against my skin, until eventually we get up and get to work on our never-ending to-do list.

ALSO BY MEGAN REINKING

The Hawaiian Getaway Series

The Ohana Cottage
The Summer Break
The Perfect Tide
The Holiday Prize

ACKNOWLEDGMENTS

Right off the bat I'd like to thank YOU, reader, for choosing to read Say You Mean It! Out of all the books in the world to choose from, I'm truly honored that you would give my book a chance and spend your time with my fictional characters who I've grown to love so much!

To Nick, thank you endlessly for your love and support of this crazy author dream of mine! Thank you for saying 'go for it!' to all of my new ideas and story concepts, as wild and larger-than-life as they may seem. Thank you for answering all my questions and sharing your own experiences of Lake of the Woods. Also for helping us to create memories of our own as a family this past summer on Oak Island! Thank you for being such a solid backbone of support and for giving me a kind of love that is greater than any love story I could ever write.

To Jamie, Lindsey, Erin, Brooke, Jessee, Shelby, Hannah, and Lexie for reading Say You Mean It in various stages and providing such amazing feedback! I am so beyond grateful for each and every one of you! You are all an asset to me professionally, but more importantly, trusted friends. Also, thank you to Darci for reading it on short notice and helping me after a minor panic incident! Your reassurance eased my fears and gave me encouragement to move forward!

To all of the book bloggers, bookstagrammers, booktokers, and book reviewers, I don't have enough words to portray my gratitude to you! Thank you so much for sharing your excitement for Say You Mean It on your platforms and for creating buzz about it! Your support is absolutely vital to my success and I do not for one second take that for granted!

To my editor, Jenn, thank you for squeezing me into your schedule, and for providing your expertise!

Sarah, thank you for fine-tuning and polishing the manuscript as my proofreader! I appreciate you!!

A HUGE thank you to Lorissa for designing the cover of my dreams! I'm still in shock that you were somehow able to jump inside my brain and create the most perfect and beautiful work of art that I get to stare at forever!

Say You Mean It is a heartwarming, healing, romance story at its core, but it's also a love letter to my home state, Minnesota. I hope you all enjoyed spending time (mentally) in the beauty that is northern MN. I wish I could take you all to Lake of the Woods! Again, thank you so much for reading Blair and Graham's story.

About the Author

Megan Reinking is a wife and mother who lives in Minnesota, where she spends her days reading, writing, or chauffeuring her three children around town. She's a homebody who loves quiet, lazy days and connecting with family and friends.

www.ingramcontent.com/pod-product-compliance
Lightning Source LLC
Chambersburg PA
CBHW022102310726
48972CB00007B/1847